File Under Dead

BY MARK RICHARD ZUBRO

The Tom & Scott Mysteries

A Simple Suburban Murder

Why Isn't Becky Twitchell Dead?

The Only Good Priest

The Principal Cause of Death

An Echo of Death

Rust on the Razor

Are You Nuts?

One Dead Drag Queen

Here Comes the Corpse

The Paul Turner Mysteries

Sorry Now?

Political Poison

Another Dead Teenager

The Truth Can Get You Killed

Drop Dead

Sex and Murder.com

Dead Egotistical Morons

File Under Dead

MARK RICHARD ZUBRO

ST. MARTIN'S MINOTAUR NEW YORK

www.minotaurbooks.com

Library of Congress Cataloging-in-Publication Data

Zubro, Mark Richard.
File under dead / Mark Richard Zubro.—1st St. Martin's ed.
p. cm.
ISBN 0-312-28097-1
EAN 978-0312-28097-0
1. Mason, Tom (Fictitious character)—Fiction. 2. Carpenter, Scott (Fictitious character)—Fiction. 3. Gay youth—Services for—Fiction. 4. High school teachers—Fiction. 5. Chicago (Ill.)—Fiction. 6. Gay men—Fiction. I. Title.

PS3576.U225F55 2004
813'.54—dc22
2004042828

First Edition: August 2004

10 9 8 7 6 5 4 3 2 1

With special thanks to
Barb D'Amaro, Jeanne Dams,
Rick Paul, and Kathy Pakieser-Reed

File Under Dead

1

I always arrived early at the Oscar Wilde Gay Youth Services Clinic. The faux-pine door at the alley entrance to the tatty old building looked like the next puff of a breeze off Lake Michigan could blast it into oblivion. If Bette Davis were looking for a dump, she would have to look no further than the overgrown Victorian mausoleum that served as the main building of the complex. I'd been the sponsor of the Eponymous Gay Teen Club at my high school, Grover Cleveland. A couple of the kids in the program had begged me to volunteer at the clinic as well. They insisted that I was the only adult they knew who was realistic about their problems. When I told them that I was sure the adults at the clinic were highly qualified, good people, they responded that their elders were mostly concerned with infighting and one-upmanship. Infighting in a gay organization? How could the kids be wrong?

Over time the clinic had expanded from one building with services only for gay teens to half the block on the west side of Monclair near Addison. It was as close to a real gay community center as Chicago had but its main focus was still helping gay teenagers. It was another do-good organization with not enough money.

Two years ago a former student of mine, Lee Weaver, had accepted a job at the clinic. His position at the clinic was his first since he'd gotten his master's degree in social work. I'd helped Lee come out when he was a senior in high school. He'd been shunned by his parents and picked on unmercifully by the kids in school. I'd intervened as often as he'd permitted.

Between unpatrolled washrooms, bus stop torment, hallway hell, and other random unsupervised moments, bullying teens are able to inflict incalculable amounts of mental and physical damage on their peers. These unpoliced venues incubate teenage misery. Even the adults in the supervised places aren't always all a gay teen could wish for.

Lee had vowed to spend his life helping gay kids. He had run into tons of problems finding the job he wanted. There weren't that many openings for helping gay kids exclusively and he had competed against a flood of applicants for every job. He had known that the clinic didn't have a great reputation as a positive work environment, but it was doing exactly the kind of work he wished to be involved in. After being employed there several months, Lee explained that working at the clinic was like swimming in a vat of molten lava on the way to a living hell. He'd added his voice to those of the kids pleading with me to pitch in.

I was heartily sick of the incessant infighting inside gay groups and Lee had graduated from student to good friend. I thought gay kids needed a break and Lee needed help, so I had volunteered. But I'd refused to go to any staff meetings or to participate in the bureaucracy. By coming in early in the mornings I was most likely to avoid Charley Fitch, the notoriously nasty boss of the clinic. He was known for working late into the night. An amazing number of people volunteered for morning duty. I didn't know if anyone noticed this or not and I'm not sure I cared.

Whether volunteering or being paid, arriving at a job at seven in the morning every other Saturday was not my idea of a good time. But I'd promised to sub for a couple months for one of the volunteers who had been in a near-fatal car accident. It was the first warm day of spring in early April and I'd rather have been out enjoying the pleasant day. At least I could get a lot done in the quiet hours before the clinic began to fill.

The clutter in the office I used looked worse than normal as I tried to find a spot for my coffee. The space had originally been a storage closet and still partially served that function. Despite being so cramped, it was used almost continuously by people like myself—occasional volunteers and low-level staffers. I'm certainly not a neatnik, but the people I shared the office with were total slobs. I prefer to keep my lack-of-cleaning peccadilloes confined to private spaces in my home. These people had no problem leaving their papers and paraphernalia spewed everywhere.

Someone had stacked a ton of files on the desk I used. I found a spot for my coffee on top of the filing cabinet and transferred enough crap from the top of the desk to the few remaining feet of space on the floor. When done, I had enough room to place an elbow and a pad of paper on the desk.

The buzzer rang for the front door. Usually on Saturdays, no one else arrived until after 9:00 A.M. I thought about ignoring it, but whoever was ringing the bell wasn't letting up. I turned on lights as I maneuvered through the mess and then hustled through the litter in the hallway to the door. When whoever it was saw the lights go on, the buzzer stopped.

I opened the door.

Max Bakstein, a junior at Grover Cleveland High School, and another kid I didn't recognize stood in the doorway.

Max said, “We gotta talk to you, Mr. Mason.”

I held open the door. Max was a tall, scrawny kid with jet black hair. He was on the track team at school. He’d come to one or two Eponymous Gay Teen Club meetings with Felicia Lucinzki, the head of the group. Felicia was a cheerleader and aggressively heterosexual. She was part of a trend I’d noticed in the past few years—straight teens, mostly girls, taking up for gay and lesbian kids. At the time, Max had been introduced in such a way that I’d assumed Felicia was his girlfriend—very possibly a deliberate obfuscation on his part.

We stood in the main room. Outdated machines—answering and fax, computers and printers—poked their heads above the sea of clutter. The plastic desk chairs were any of three unpleasant colors: maroon, pink, or fuchsia. The couch in the waiting area was cracked green vinyl. Someone had painted the tin ceiling with swirls of brown. The place was always unpleasant to look at and noisy to distraction during the work day. The computers had been donated by a company that didn’t want them, which meant the damn things got ornery, froze, or crashed frequently and all the programs on them were outdated. The frustration of downloading more modern items onto them was monumental.

Max indicated his companion. “This is Abdel Hakur.” He was shorter and scrawnier than Max with skin slightly duskier than Max’s olive complexion. “He goes to Grover Cleveland. He’s a junior, too.”

“What can I do for you guys?”

“Is there someplace we can go to talk?” Max asked.

“No one else is here.”

“But someone could come in.”

That was more paranoia than I cared to deal with, but teenagers had their needs. I led them to the back.

“How’d you know anyone was here?” I asked.

“Felicia talks about the work you do, says you can be

trusted. We tried a couple times before. Then I heard Felicia say you're here early on some Saturday mornings."

"You could've come talk to me at school."

"No. Here's safer," Max said. More paranoia.

"Or talked to one of the counselors who was on duty."

"No," Max said. "We wanted you."

I guess it's good to feel needed, even if it is by teenagers you barely know.

I pulled two folding chairs in from other offices and placed some of the clutter from the floor onto the piles in the hall. This opened up a few square inches on the floor on which to rest the tips of their chair legs. I sat in the creaking swivel chair behind my desk. On good days the chair had been known to swivel for up to an inch and a half. It creaked more effectively than it swiveled. The two boys leaned toward each other, their knees touching. Max was nearest the door while Abdel was crammed between him and the filing cabinet. Max wore jeans and a letterman's jacket, which hung open over a white T-shirt. Hakur wore black jeans and a gray sweatshirt with a picture of Grover Cleveland on it.

Max sniffed the air. "Kind of stinks back here."

"The whole place always stinks," I said. "The floors have been musty since they built this place sometime after the invention of dirt. In the summer the basement really reeks. What can I do for you guys?"

"We're in trouble," Max said. He spoke in a breathy rush.

"How can I help?"

They exchanged looks. Max said, "You've got to promise not to tell. You can't tell anybody you even saw us together."

Teenage drama queens or the harbingers of teen tragedy? I was sure I would find out soon.

Max said, "We're lovers." They clasped hands.

I nodded. I hoped they weren't expecting gasps of astonishment.

"We're not sure what to do."

"About what?"

"Well, we're gay."

I figured I'd hear the litany of the usual problems with being gay in high school.

Max said, "It's a real problem."

"Are the kids harassing you at school?"

"Nobody at school knows. You can't tell. Nobody knows about us."

"What about Felicia?"

"I guess she suspects, but I haven't told her for sure."

She knew. A common delusion of gay kids, and many gay adults for that matter, is that the rest of the world doesn't know. The world has usually figured it out a long time ago and except for some loud, angry exceptions, doesn't care as much as many think.

"What can I help you with?"

"Can't you tell?"

"Sorry."

"I'm Jewish. Abdel is Muslim."

I've never been really good at doing ethnic. I have enough trouble listening carefully to people without worrying about the proper label. These two just looked like worried kids to me.

Max said, "Our parents are strict. Really strict. As nutty as the craziest Baptists about religion. If they knew, they'd kill us."

Good to know being prone to violence wasn't limited to the fringe elements of only one denomination.

Abdel said, "I'd be thrown out of the house. My relatives wouldn't take me in." He had a soft velvety voice.

Max said, "My dad's a strict Orthodox rabbi. He lives and breathes Kosher, and obeys all the Torah regulations, rules, and laws. He's memorized huge chunks of the Talmud."

Abdel said, "Strict interpretation of the Koran is paramount in my house."

Max said, "We want to tell everyone. We're not ashamed." Abdel nodded agreement. Max continued, "But we need help. We want to plan ahead. Abdel can't stay at my house. After I tell, I'll probably get thrown out."

"What about your mothers?" I asked.

"Mine would freak," Max said.

Abdel said, "My mom is not the one I have to worry about."

"Why have you decided that it's important to tell now?"

Max said, "You're out. You should understand. We want to be able to live openly and honestly."

I said, "You know there will be pressures from the kids at school as well as your parents. Grover Cleveland is in a very conservative area."

Max said, "Yeah. We don't care about the other kids. We can handle that. It's our parents."

"How old are you?" I asked.

"I was seventeen a couple of weeks ago," Max said.

Abdel said, "I'll be seventeen next month."

"Where would you go?" I asked.

"Maybe we could get a place together," Max said.

Ah, the dreams of teenagers. I didn't laugh. As a teenager, I'd always assumed I was terribly realistic and pretty smart. Looking back on it, I'd rather not make a list of all the times I was embarrassingly stupid or even worse, out-and-out dreadfully wrong.

"You guys have jobs, savings?"

"We've both got college funds," Max said. "Other than that, not much."

"And if your parents throw you out, do the college funds go away?"

They looked at each other.

"I hadn't thought about it," Max said.

Abdel said, "I just figured it was mine, but I don't have any idea how to access it."

"Jobs?"

Head shakes.

"How long have you guys been dating?"

"Since last summer," Max said.

Nine or ten months, a decent amount of time for a teen relationship, but not near enough to happily-ever-after for comfort. Whether or not the relationship would be permanent, the key was that these two certainly seemed to think it would be. This concept was undoubtedly backed up by as much teenage passion as they could summon. Being teenagers, that could be a great deal of passion indeed.

Abdel said, "We met at one of those youth camps where they bring over Palestinian and Israeli kids to try and get them to talk to one another, so they can learn to get along."

Max said, "Abdel and I never met or talked to each other at Grover Cleveland. At the youth camp Abdel and I got along better than they thought."

I asked, "If your parents are so strict, how come they sent you to such a place?"

Max said, "I was president of my youth group. My dad got a lot of pressure from all the other Jewish groups to send a delegate. If he heard about the two of us, he'd never send another representative. He'd probably try to wreck the program. I'm sure he'd think somebody tried to recruit me or molest me. Of course, nobody did."

Abdel said, "I thought going to the camp would be a way to get my dad to unbend and it definitely gave me a chance to get out of the house. Some of the kids I know thought I was nuts, but I think fighting and wars are crazy. I put a lot of pressure on my dad so he finally let me go."

Max said, "We've been sneaking around ever since. It's really tough and getting kind of absurd. Funny sometimes. We make out in any place we can. At Grover Cleveland the last stall in the third floor west boys' john in the late afternoons has been our most frequent spot. But we're tired of lying and hiding." He took a deep breath. "And we want to go to the prom."

"The one the youth group here is having?"

"No," Max said, "the one at school." They looked at each other and smiled.

Some gay youth groups have "safe" proms for kids in their areas who don't feel comfortable going as a same-sex couple to the one at their own high school.

"I'm a little confused," I said. "You want to tell everyone, but you don't even want to be seen here. If you go to the prom as a couple, you might as well hang a neon sign around your necks. Shooting off fireworks would draw less attention. Are you ready for that kind of spotlight?"

"Absolutely," Abdel said. "Can we take a guy to the prom at Grover Cleveland?"

"I'm not sure what the reaction would be, but I can help you there."

"We want to be in control," Max said. "We want people to know when we want them to know. Going to the prom at the youth group here wouldn't be much of a statement."

I said, "You want to take a great risk, but one that has minimal consequences?" What they wanted was for the world to be a perfect place, a safe place. I wished I could assure them that it would always be so.

Abdel said, "I understand about consequences. I'm ready to take some risks, but I don't want to end up living in a box under the El tracks."

Max said, "All I heard about the prom here was that the adults were fighting about it. I don't want to be part of some adult hassle."

The Prom Committee at the Clinic had indeed fought over everything, with the bureaucratic rule applying: The more minor the issue, the greater the fight.

"Reactions to you coming out aren't in your control," I said. "From what you say, at the least, you'll have parental problems when you announce you're going to the prom. Once people know, events can get out of hand."

"No," Max said. "We want to be the ones to do what we want."

I tried the gentlest lecture I could on the ways of the world but it didn't make any difference. They were sure they could control the whole thing.

Finally I said, "You need to keep in mind what all the consequences might be and plan your reaction."

"Are you telling us not to tell?" Max's tone began to get a hint of teenage hostility.

I added a bit of a tone of adult sternness in my reply. "No. I'm saying that the things we do don't happen in a vacuum. Do you think they do?"

"No."

"I'm giving the best advice I can. In general I think living a life of secrets is a bad policy. I think there are circumstances in this situation which militate against that being a blind policy. You've got to think about where you would live. You should talk to the legal people here about that. You know if your parents throw you out, you are not old enough to live on your own."

"We could manage," Max said.

"The state may not allow you to manage. In Illinois you are considered underage."

"What would happen to us?"

"The courts are unlikely to do anything that would remotely resemble looking positively on a young gay teen couple. You would most likely be sent to different foster homes, where they might or might not be amenable to you seeing each other."

"We won't put up with that."

"Which part, the fact that you're underage, being involved in the court system, or the possible hostility from foster home personnel?"

Max glowered.

Abdel said, “Aren’t there gay couples who have foster kids?”

“On television. I’m not sure about around here.”

Abdel said, “Maybe we’ll have to run away. I’ve got enough money to start us out.”

“How much?”

“Four hundred bucks.”

I said, “I’m afraid that wouldn’t last long.”

“Are you going to help us or not?” Max asked.

“You came to me. I’m not going to say things simply to please you. I cannot change the reality you’re going to have to deal with. There are a multitude of things to consider and not just for today and next week. You’ve got to think about college and beyond.”

Max looked at Abdel. “I don’t care what happens to me as long as I’m with Abdel.” Their arms went around each other and they hugged.

Abdel said, “I’ll never leave you.”

Max murmured, “I love you.”

No question in my mind, they were in love in that teenage way that is so passionately intense. I’d been there. Heady stuff when not a little nauseating. I doubted if they were ready to listen to anything but their own passion. Emma Bovary, move over.

At least neither of them indicated any thoughts of suicide, a problem endemic to gay teens. A problem we saw too often at the clinic.

We talked for nearly an hour. At the end they decided to do some more thinking, and after several more pleas for my complete silence, I walked them to the door. In the clinic they had their arms around each other. At the door they unclinched, thanked me, and left.

I thought their fears of their families’ reactions were likely very well founded. Both sets of parents could look at their age, combine that with fears for their future, add fundamentalist blindness about gay people, and come up with a lot of pain and agony for their kids and themselves.

Those considerations left aside the normal strains in any teen relationship. Straight or gay, how often did such bonds last beyond high school? I didn't have a lot of hope for their future as a couple. Still, I would help them as best I could.

I returned to my office. Max was right. The reek was stronger than usual today. The window had enough coats of paint around the edge to keep it from opening with anything less than a nuclear device. I propped open the back door to get the warm breeze in the hall and left the office door ajar to catch any chance whiffs of freshness from the corridor.

I decided to try wading through the blizzard of papers and do some filing. I reached for a stack. Shuffling through them, I realized they were case histories from several years ago. I thought I had put these away myself the last time I was in. I fumed about people who used files but didn't put them back while I carried them back over to the file cabinet.

I opened the top drawer. A severed head grinned horribly up at me.

2

I slammed the drawer shut and backed away. I stumbled over several heaps of useless junk as I staggered into the hall. I'd been in the Marines and seen a lot of grim things. But a decapitated head where you don't expect one, no matter how hardened you are, would give anyone pause. I paused.

I spent some time breathing deeply. For a few seconds I thought maybe it was just a mask and some special effects, a sick joke done by somebody who knew I came in early. There were several theater majors who volunteered in the office.

The picture of the head flashed in my mind. It was no fake. I sat on a stack of papers and put my head between my knees. I waited for the feeling of nausea to pass.

I realized that I recognized the face. It was Charley Fitch, the clinic's executive director. His nickname was Snarly Bitch. He was a jerk of the first order, first place in the Rude Olympics for years. The nickname was almost inevitable, but nobody had ever called him that to his face that I knew of. Now nobody would have to worry about him being rude to them again.

Snarly had founded the clinic, donated the majority of its

money, and was the major mover and shaker in fundraising for the rest. The board of directors never went against his wishes. Snarly was notoriously friendly to possible donors and almost pathologically cruel to anyone else—all the meanness of *Boys in the Band* and not a smidgen of redeeming humor. It was almost impossible for him to keep volunteers. His verbal abuse made George and Martha in *Who's Afraid of Virginia Woolf?* look like saints. Asking him the simplest question could set him off on vast tirades. His management style included heavy doses of status consciousness and nasty bitchiness. Why being snotty and rude isn't a class A felony, I have no idea. The slightest break in his routine could cause explosions of volcanic proportion. But get rid of him and the money would go too and so would the clinic.

While working there, I thought about him barely at all. Avoiding him was reasonably simple. If he was rude to me, I wasn't much interested. He made little difference to my happiness.

I had some fame connected with my lover, Scott Carpenter, the openly gay baseball player. Nobody said it out loud, but I'm sure people at the clinic hoped that large donations might gush in around me. I often thought they'd rather have our money and not have me hanging around. Sometimes I got the notion that many of the paid staffers were jealous about my connection to fame, or worried somehow that my being Scott's lover might diminish them somehow.

I got along better with the kids than many staffers, but not as well as some. Snarly Bitch wasn't the only problem. I learned firsthand what Lee and the kids had told me about the clinic. Many of the people on the staff were dedicated to infighting, territoriality, creating bureaucracy, undercutting each other, and hating the boss.

Snarly Bitch might not have thought it would be politically or financially expedient to keep me out completely. He certainly did think it was politically safe to keep me in the back.

Mostly what I did was help file, stuff envelopes, talk to a few kids, and listen to the staff complain. They were masters at this. As a union rep at my high school, I'd heard people complain ad nauseam, but these people had turned bitching into a high art. No problem was too small or too petty that it couldn't be magnified out of all proportion. And Snarly Bitch was always in the background, willing to throw gasoline on smoldering embers.

After the nausea passed, I stood up and took several more deep breaths. Before dialing 911, I called my lawyer, Todd Bristol.

His first reaction to my news was, "A what?"

"A head. In a filing cabinet drawer."

"Where's the rest of the body?"

"I didn't look."

"Maybe it was just misfiled."

"You can joke at a time like this?"

"Only you, Tom. You're my only client who has corpses plopping into his path."

"This one didn't plop, and I don't have the whole corpse. Just the head."

"It's around. You're a corpse magnet. I'm not sure I want to be in the same time zone as you."

"A social critic is not what I need at this moment."

"I suppose not. Don't touch anything else. Call the police. Wait for me. Don't find any more body parts."

"I'll do my best to refrain."

I'd been told an old cop story once. I'm not sure I believed it when I was told it. A young detective was working his first homicide. He, an older detective, and a number of other cops were looking for a corpse in an alley in Chicago. The older detective lifted up a garbage can lid, pulled out a head, held it up, and called to his lieutenant, "Is this the guy?" The lieutenant replied, "No, he was shorter." Sitting in the reception area of the clinic at that moment, I doubted the story more than ever, but I smiled for a second. Didn't mean it wasn't a funny story. Finding my first severed head wasn't turning out to be a knee-slapping laugh riot. With any luck it would be the last severed head I would ever find, tall or short.

I decided not to call Scott. He was on a road trip to the West Coast with the team and would still be asleep. I waited for the police in the bright sunshine outside the front door on Monclair Avenue. I found myself pacing and trying to get the image of what I'd seen out of my mind. Nothing seemed to do much good.

I didn't bother to call any other members of the clinic staff. To do so, I would have had to touch more things to find their numbers. When Todd told me not to touch anything else, I fully intended to comply with that directive. Not for me the madness of picking up the weapon and leaving my fingerprints behind, or being caught holding it in my hand. Or, more likely, screwing up any residual evidence of the identity of the killer.

I thought about Max and Abdel's presence. The police would ask if I'd seen anyone else around. The two teenagers qualified. If I told, they would be questioned. If they were questioned, their parents would find out they'd been to the clinic. Full parental interrogations would follow. They'd lose the control they so desperately wanted. They had no reason to know the executive director of the clinic. They had no motive I could think of to kill him. Dismembering someone and then stopping in for a chat with me didn't make sense, even for teenagers. They were tense and nervous, but they were concerned with love and truth and beauty, not killing.

I wondered if someone had put the head in my room as a message to me. It could also have been a message for one of the others who used that room. I thought of several possible messages: never file anything again, never give in to the impulse to clean again. Certainly it wouldn't take a severed head to get me to listen to either one of those messages. For a much less violent threat, I'd be willing to give up cleaning forever. Now, if they wanted to take away my access to chocolate, I might put up a fight.

It took only a few minutes for a couple of beat cops to show up. One stayed with me while the other followed my directions to the back. A crime lab van pulled up, followed five minutes later by two detectives, Lynn Stafford and Jason Abernathy.

They found a left foot in a cabinet in my office. Throughout the clinic's main building they discovered body parts stashed in trash cans, file drawers, and other seemingly random receptacles. They found the site of the decapitation and dismemberment in the basement.

Todd showed up while the detectives were still examining the interior of the building. "Are you all right?" he asked.

"I've been better."

"Can I get you something?"

I shook my head.

The detectives brought Todd and me to the executive director's office. Geographically the clinic stretched along the west side of the street for five city lots. The first three buildings in from the corner were formerly substantial homes, now all interconnected. The last two lots had been covered by a two-story office building long since past its prime. The entrance I had used in the back was in the oldest building nearest the cross street, Addison. This part of the building was nearest the stairs to the basement. They had found body parts in this first building. The director's office was in this same first building.

There was no crap crammed compulsively in Snarly's office, the surfaces were clear of debris and dust other than a small stack of papers on one corner of the big desk. Snarly Bitch's computer was state of the art, including a half-inch-thick flat monitor. He had pictures of exotic dog breeds on his walls, and photos of the dogs he owned on his desk. His favorite object was a foot-high, black cast-iron poodle, about as warm and fuzzy as he was. He'd caress it when he was nervous. His swivel chair swiveled a hundred eighty degrees with nary a squeak.

Detective Stafford sat in the swiveling swivel chair. We went over the basics. I didn't say anything about Abdel and Max. Not yet anyway.

"You called your lawyer first instead of calling us."

"Yes."

"Why is that?"

"While I figured it might make you more suspicious during initial questioning, I wanted to make sure I didn't screw something up. I wanted to make sure I was treated correctly."

"Did you think there would be cause for you to be treated incorrectly?"

"I don't like to take chances." I wasn't about to get into a pissing match with them about the ability of Chicago cops to treat suspects properly.

"How well did you know the victim?"

"He was the boss. In the past couple months I worked here once every two weeks on Saturday mornings. Before that maybe one or two nights a month. I also filled in at random times when they needed someone and my schedule permitted. I didn't see him very often."

"How'd you get along?"

"He was usually reasonably nice to me."

"How was he when he was unreasonable?"

"He had a trick of seeming to be busy in order to avoid normal human interactions. I got that a lot. Not a big deal, but disconcerting."

"How did the others get along with him?" Stafford asked.

I began, "Snarly Bitch . . ."

Stafford raised an eyebrow and interrupted, "Snarly Bitch?"

"That was his nickname among the staff."

"He wasn't well liked?"

"An understatement. He had turned being rude to people into a high art. I'd heard about his nasty reputation before I even got here. He wasn't just snarly and rude. He felt he was above everyone else. It was as if he didn't care enough to even bother being effectively contemptuous."

"How did he do that?" Stafford asked.

"It was an attitude. A way of treating you as if you weren't quite clean enough."

Why would I bother to hide this information? Certainly, others would tell them this as well. I had no reason to lie about his attitude toward the hired help.

"But you worked here anyway?"

"Helping gay kids is valuable work. I kept out of his way. From what I saw he was snarly and rude to everyone except huge donors."

"Did his being unreasonable piss you off?" Stafford asked.

I knew she was pushing. I could feel Todd stirring. "We didn't have any big or small fights. Several months ago, I led the group in the office that went to talk to him to try to get him to change his way of dealing with people."

"How come you were the leader?"

"I had the least to lose. I'm a volunteer. If I was the spokesperson, the people on salary didn't have to take as much of a risk. I've been on negotiations teams in the district where I teach. I'm used to dealing with recalcitrant management."

"Was he recalcitrant?"

"Among the worst."

"In what way?"

"He wouldn't give in to any of their demands. In fact, he wouldn't admit there were any problems."

"How come he was still in charge?"

I told them about Snarly and his money.

"But he didn't fire you after you led the opposition?"

I told them about Snarly's presumed desire for loads of donations from Scott.

Stafford nodded. "A lot of people quit or get fired?"

"They went through a lot of volunteers, but the regular staff has been pretty much the same in the time I've been here."

"Who, besides you, had keys to this place?"

"All the full-time staff do, and some of the volunteers have keys to that back door. They took normal precautions about security, but no self-respecting crook is going to rob this place. It's a fairly big complex, but it's pretty run-down. I offered to come in early on Saturdays, and they gave me a key. That back door isn't enough to keep out a determined chipmunk, much less someone who wanted to break in."

"He have any fights with other people?"

"He fought with everybody."

"Major fights that stick out in your mind?"

"On the days I was here, I heard his voice raised at least once each time, toward one of the volunteers or one of the staff."

"Why didn't these people all just quit?" Abernathy asked. "There's got to be plenty of places for folks to do good."

"Actually, not that many that can afford to pay you a decent wage. There are the big charities that have huge budgets such as the Red Cross. Most of these small outfits are on a pretty slim budget. Snarly Bitch wasn't the only one who fought. There were a lot of egos in a fairly tiny organization. Infighting seems to be endemic to any gay organization."

"Why is that?" Abernathy asked.

"Don't know. All I know is the reports I read in the paper. An outfit starts out with these fabulous ideals and within a very short time, it falls apart from infighting and lack of funds."

Abernathy asked, "Is this the group with the bicycling scandal I read about in the paper?" A number of gay fundraising groups had gone through scandals in the past few years. One of the bicycle marathons had been among the most prominent.

"One of them," I said. "Snarly Bitch accused the organizers of holding back on the money they owed to the clinic. One of the planners said Snarly Bitch drove as many people away as he helped recruit."

"Who was that?"

"Ken Wells. I'm not mentioning his name here because I have reason to single him out. He and Snarly did have a big fight and a fundraiser fell through. You hear a lot of rumors and I learned right away to discount most of them. The rumor on this one was that Snarly had sabotaged it."

"Why would he do that?"

"I have no idea. I mention Ken because this was a recent dust-up. I have no reason to suspect him or anyone else."

"Any other fights?"

"A lot of people in the office seemed to take turns sniping at each other. Snarly Bitch's leadership style encouraged that."

"How so?"

"He didn't follow up on phone calls or much of anything else unless they were rich donors. He'd put off decisions to the last minute. He'd deign to tell everyone about some vital project or the paperwork for some grant the day it was due. Then there would be a mad scramble to get it done. Later on the people who did the work in that mad, slap-dash way would be blamed if there was something wrong with their work or his presentations. If a grant didn't come in, the blame game would start. Snarly Bitch would claim it was someone else's fault, everyone else's fault. Besides the hassles with the boss, there was the usual wrangling you get in any organization. People would fight about responsibility and territoriality."

It was a mystery to me why Snarly Bitch didn't tell people weeks or months before a deadline instead of the day something was due. What was the hold up? Laziness or meanness or ineptitude? A combination of all three? Certainly the money meant more to their jobs than to his. He had money.

"Didn't he want the clinic to succeed?" Stafford asked.

"I assume he did."

"Where were you last night?"

"Home, alone, reading a book."

"What else did you touch in that room?"

"About everything. I use the office. I wasn't being particularly careful."

"We'll be taking everybody's fingerprints so we can eliminate the ones who belong and establish the ones that don't."

Obviously my fingerprints would be on the filing cabinet. If mine were the only ones, I would be very depressed.

The door to the office swung open. Jan Aiello swept into the room. Jan was Grover Cleveland's and the clinic's budding teen drag queen. A red-faced beat cop followed him into the room and tried to clamp a hand on the kid's arm.

"Oh, sorry." Jan held up his hand to his face and tittered. "Are you the police?"

Jan knew they were. He wasn't stupid and his entrance wasn't accidental. He was ushered out of the room. The police asked me to hang around. I acquiesced.

In the hall several members of the clinic's board of directors asked to talk to Todd.

Lee found me. "I'm in trouble," he said.

3

Police personnel swarmed over the scene. People milled about in the three body-part-free buildings on the south end of the complex.

After I was fingerprinted, Lee took me into an office the police hadn't cordoned off. It was a cubbyhole slightly larger than mine but with about half the clutter. It was in the third of four buildings from the north end. A poster of two soccer players exchanging shirts at the end of a game covered part of a wall.

Lee looked pale and his hands trembled. He had weighed over three hundred pounds as a freshman in high school. He'd gone out for football. By senior year he'd lost all the weight and felt better about himself, but the coaches hated him because he was no good to them as a skinny faggot. Fat faggots were okay, I guess. Nowadays he kept his red hair brush cut and wore mostly khaki pants, blue shirts, and pale yellow and blue ties. He worked out at a health club two hours every other day and ran several miles along the lake-front on the off days. His hands usually trembled slightly from caffeine overload. He'd never smiled much as a kid. He was one of the first ones to come to the Eponymous Gay Teen Club at my school and his dedication to the kids at the clinic was total. He was determined to do everything he could to prevent gay kids from having to go through what he had.

Lee asked, “Mr. Mason, are you okay?”

“Been better.” I’d told him once that it was okay to call me by my first name. I was no longer his teacher and he’d graduated from college and had an MSW. But he rarely used my first name. I didn’t harp about it. Whatever made him comfortable was fine with me.

“Jesus, that must have been awful. You just opened the . . .”

“I’d rather not go into great detail.”

“Yeah, right, sorry.” He hesitated a moment, then asked, “How much does your lawyer cost?”

“What’s wrong?”

“Snarly Bitch fired me last night. I think I may have been the last one to see him alive.”

“What happened?”

“The goddamn prom committee met last night. They meet every fucking night. How hard can it be to plan a fucking dance? We had fights every night. Could kids come in drag? Should there be any dress restrictions at all? Should there be a separate prom for transgender kids?”

“Were there a lot of transgender kids?”

“Probably none, but at least two people on the committee were concerned that the needs of these possibly nonexistent kids were met. I graduated from college in three years and lost tons of sleep in grad school to put up with this petty shit? I got fed up.”

“But you get fed up a lot. Remember the committee for the Pride float last year?” The stories I’d heard about those legendary meetings were harrowing. What kinds of flowers to use and what colors they should be had taken fifteen hours to decide! And that was one of the quicker decisions.

"I know," Lee said, "but this time I said something. I know I shouldn't have, but I couldn't help it. I'd been at the hospital yesterday with a gay kid who tried to commit suicide. I'd dealt with his parents, who were in stunned shock, and his younger brother who found him. It was even more sad because the parents claimed they didn't care he was gay. All the boy's anxiety about their reaction had been in his own head."

Lee had a tremendous reputation at the clinic for dealing with suicidal teens. He'd brought many back from the brink and was also fantastic with those who had made the attempt.

"What happened when you got back here?"

"Snarly Bitch insists the full-time staff has to be at all committee meetings, no matter how trivial, or how easy it would be for only a few people to make the plans and come to the others with their decisions and get review or more input. Nope. We all had to be here. So I came back. I'm used to working ten-, twelve-hour days. We all are, but I was exhausted. I thought every issue they discussed at the stupid meeting was crap. Just total, mind-numbing crap. People bickered endlessly. I just wanted the damn meeting to end. I kept my mouth shut. That's never good enough for Snarly Bitch. He insisted I give my opinion about the color scheme of the decorations. I give a rat's ass about the goddamn color scheme. But he pushed and he pushed. I snapped. I told him to back off. We went at it hammer and tongs. I said everything I'd been holding back since the day I started. It felt great. At the end I told him to fuck himself. He fired me on the spot."

"Lots of people had fights with him. Why fire you?"

"It's not so much that we had fights with him. It was more he bullied and ranted after we tried to explain. We usually didn't fight back. Certainly not in front of everybody. Of those who did fight, nobody had been fired. I'm the first he just out and out canned in front of everybody."

"There must have been others."

"According to what I've been told, I'm it. After what you found this morning, they called in everybody. I asked around. I'm the only one."

"But I led the protest committee."

"But you're a volunteer. Your lover's rich. And you didn't fight. You were so calm in the face of his sarcasm. I don't know how you did it. He held back with you, but he was pissed."

"If you'd already been fired, what do the police think would be the point in you killing him?"

"I'm not sure what they think. Revenge? They're sure to find out about the fight. Then again, half the people in that room despised each other."

"They'd also have reason to kill him. Most of them would have longer histories with him."

"Yeah, I guess, but I was the last one to leave. I stayed to clean out my desk. I didn't see anyone else inside or out. My office has one of the doors you can get out of, but you've got to go around to a different entrance to get back in."

"You didn't want to wait for the morning to clean out your desk? Maybe he'd reconsider after he cooled off."

"He told me specifically that he would not reconsider, that I was to clean out my desk right then. I went out and came back in three or four times with stacks of stuff. I had a lot of personal things, a lot of files of my own, for clients of my own. I used this office to see private clients as well. Between trips to the car, I smoked a cigarette in the alley for a few minutes. The light was on in his office the last time I walked out. I didn't notice anybody else. They're going to think I did it."

"Everybody fought with him," I reminded him.

"My fingerprints will be in his office."

"So will everybody's probably."

A uniformed cop knocked at the door. “The detectives are ready for Mr. Weaver.”

I got my lawyer, put him together with Lee, and returned to the office to wait.

Daisy Tajeda poked her head in. “I’m in trouble,” she said.

4

Daisy was a slender woman in her early forties. She'd been with the clinic for years. She, along with Lee, had begged me to be the spokesperson who went to Snarly Bitch to try and get him to change his management style. She was one of the few people in the clinic who'd been pleasantly friendly to me every time we met. She was less territorial than many of the others.

She threw herself into a chair. I sat on the edge of the desk.

She said, "This is awful. You really found his head?"

"Yep."

"How could someone do that, cut off . . . And they'd have to carry it around? And the other parts? I can't imagine it. One leg was in the bottom drawer of my filing cabinet. Thank god I wasn't the one who found it. I'd have panicked. At least you're calm. You can handle things."

I wasn't about to volunteer to be the designated body-part finder. To her comment I said, "I think I was more numb and shocked than calm."

"Don't underestimate yourself. What I don't like is that the police have been through everything in the clinic. They'll probably go through all the kids' files. Those kids need their privacy."

"Why would they read all the private files? I'm not sure they can, legally. I'm not sure there's a purpose—some of these files go back years."

"Most of the old files are in the basement. They're probably covered in blood." She shuddered.

I wondered what the killer had used to cart the parts around to avoid leaving remnants of blood and gore on the surfaces he passed. Then again, I wondered why the killer would care if he left drops of blood and bits of flesh and bone. What difference would it make if he made a bloody mess? Why bother taking the time to distribute body parts? Did he want more than one person to experience the shock effect as had I? Did the killer think after the first was discovered that the police wouldn't be called? Or that the police would allow the staff to hunt for cut-up bits of their former boss? Now that I knew the killer had scattered body parts around, I assumed he wasn't sending a message to one person. The image I didn't relish conjuring up was someone grasping bleeding bits of flesh and walking the same corridors I had.

I tuned back in to Tajeda. She was saying, "You heard they found a mess down in the basement? I presume it was horrible. Are you okay?"

"Not as good as I was yesterday at this time."

"What did the police say to you?"

"Usual questions. Did I know him? What was he like? Where was I last night?"

She looked worried. She asked, "Is your lawyer expensive?"

If this kept up, maybe Todd could retire from the referrals from today alone.

"What's up?" I asked.

"I think I may have been the last one to see him alive."

"How's that?"

"After that horrible meeting about the prom, I went to talk to him in his office. He stays late every night. He does most of his business then, personal interviews, phone calls—probably waking up people on both coasts and across the ocean. I needed to make my point. I was glad he was still here. I can't believe people don't understand how important it is to do everything right for the kids at that dance. I want it to be perfect for them. I don't understand Lee's unconcern. He's got to understand why this is so important. But still, he shouldn't have been fired over it. And the decision to fire him should have been discussed at all levels."

"What exactly happened at the meeting?"

"Lee sat there pretty quiet. I knew he'd had a rough day. We had a huge number of items to get through on the agenda. Actually it's not bad when somebody's quiet. When one fewer person talks, there's that many fewer fights. Snarly Bitch insisted Lee give his opinion about the color scheme. Lee just blew up. He really let him have it. Said that Snarly Bitch was a petty dictator who cared more about himself than he did the kids. That he cared more about insignificant details and petty interpersonal victories than he did about helping kids. Lee ended up saying that Snarly Bitch could take his money and fuck himself."

"He actually said 'fuck himself'?"

"Yep. I cheered inside as he hurled each insult. Everything he said was true. Snarly Bitch is evil, but still I went to talk to him after the meeting. I wanted to appeal to him not to fire Lee. We need Lee. Among the full-time staffers, he's the best. He's better at paperwork than I am. I relate to the girls better, but I've got to admit he's better than I am with the boys. He's intervened in some pretty rough cases since he's been here. Kids who haven't opened up in years trusted him. We can't afford to lose him."

"What did Snarly Bitch say?"

"He told me that if it was necessary, I'd be next. I got angry at that. I raised my voice."

"But he didn't fire you?"

"No, but I got that damn smirk of his. I'd like to slap that smirk off his face."

One of the major complaints the staff had about Charley Fitch was that while he said rude, mean, or demeaning things, he kept this nasty smirk on his face. This outraged them almost as much as what he said. They interpreted the smirk to mean Fitch was saying, "I've got power over you and fuck you." A lot to read into a smirk, but I agreed. Added to that, when someone was trying to have an ordinary, nonhostile conversation with him, Fitch often kept a fatuous smile on his face, as if he were the older, wiser adult, just waiting for the silly child to finish prattling on. The workers at the clinic had learned that the fatuous smile usually immediately preceded the smirk, which would be followed by the next mean, stupid, or rude comment.

"Are you sure you were the last one out?"

"I thought I was. I didn't see any other lights, but I didn't check the whole clinic. I made sure the door was locked behind me when I left. We always do. This might not be prime real estate, but we're all pretty careful."

"Did anybody else defend Lee?"

"Nobody spoke up at the meeting. Even I didn't have the nerve to do that. We're all cowards. Look how we had to get you to lead that meeting."

"I'm sure I didn't make that much of a difference."

"You did. You stood up for yourself and us, and you didn't get fired. It exposed the hypocrisy around here."

"I'm a volunteer. I doubt it had anything to do with any ability I may or may not have to communicate or be brave. I suspect he thought I might be a source of big donations. Were there any other fights with other people at the meeting?"

"No. You know Snarly Bitch's style. He fixed on one person for no very good reason. He snaps and snarls at them. It's like he's egging them on and hoping for a fight. When was the last time you heard a question asked at a meeting? It doesn't happen. He'd leap down the throat of anyone who had the nerve to make the simplest inquiry. He takes everything as a challenge to his authority."

"Did he have any fights during the day yesterday?"

"Not that I remember."

Jan put his head in the door. "We're talking," Tajeda snapped.

"I need to talk to Mr. Mason," Jan said.

I said, "In a few minutes."

I told her I'd put her together with my lawyer.

As Tajeda left, Jan swept into the room.

5

Jan never just entered a room. He turned the act of arriving into a grand performance. He flounced. He twirled. Wrists limped. Hips swished. Outside a Broadway show, why anyone would want to waste energy on such an act, I couldn't imagine. At sixteen he wore black silk capes draped over flowered shirts and always carried a battered paperback copy of an Ayn Rand opus in one hand. Among a few select young gays, she had become quite the rage. Many of his classmates enjoyed his ability to entertain. Keeping them entertained didn't mean you were accepted or liked. On the other hand, many of them did their best to make him miserable. I doubt if Jan dared to enter a washroom at school. Conscientious teachers spent their time getting kids to stop picking on him. His parents spent their time in denial. Jan spent his time craving attention. I'd heard one severely closeted teacher say he wished he could be a free spirit like Jan, someone who didn't care what others thought. Jan wasn't a free spirit. He cared very much what impression he made on others. He dressed to get reactions. Being gay isn't learned, but being an outrageous, attention-craving, effeminate queen is. But then without drag queens, there would have been no Stonewall. And without drag queens the media would only have hundreds of thousands of other gay people to take pictures of at Pride parades.

For Jan the clinic was a welcome respite. He was immensely popular among the other members of the youth group at the clinic. At the same time the members of the staff mostly tolerated him. His one-man drag-queen symphony annoyed all of the adults some of the time and some of the adults all the time, but while he hadn't annoyed everybody all the time, he was well on his way to completing the trifecta.

Today, Jan wore a flaming pink feather boa over a muscle T-shirt, which had to be a little cool even for the pleasant temperatures. If the world ever needed another Dennis Rodman, Jan was ready to take his place. His skimpy shorts strained to cover the beginnings of an unattractive bulge around his middle. Jan often talked about wearing 'tighty-whitey' underwear as if talking about underwear was a great breakthrough in the war between adults and teenagers. Said war mostly existed in Jan's head. At least that way he could win. He had his Ayn Rand book. Jan had seldom met an impulse that wasn't worth giving in to. He rarely controlled himself. Worse, his parents were certifiable wackos. I wouldn't have been surprised if he began confessing to the murder. I would have been far more surprised if he had actually done it.

Jan said, "I know they're going to accuse me." He flipped his feather boa back over his shoulder. He always did that stupid flip with his right hand when he wore the damn things. I thought if he did that too much more often, I'd strangle him with it myself.

"Why would they do that?" I asked.

"The police are talking to everyone. I was at the clinic last night. I wasn't supposed to be. I told my parents I was going to a friend's. Which I did. I just didn't stay long. I need for my parents to trust me."

"Then maybe you shouldn't have done something that would cause them to lose trust in you."

"They can't be fascist and bully me around."

"You're underage. They can make all kinds of decisions about your life. What is it you want?"

I got the same litany of being on his own I'd heard the first time and almost every other time I'd met him.

I said, "Why are the police going to accuse you?"

"I hid in the basement last night until after everyone was gone. I was the last one here. Us kids use the basement as a hangout. A few of us sleep overnight down there when we don't have anywhere else to go."

I'd never been in the basement. I asked, "How big is this basement?"

"It's kind of spooky. It stretches under all three of the old houses. When they started that renovation they put a lot of old files and stuff in the one farthest from Addison. You can't even find a place to sit down in there. There's still tools and crap scattered all around down there. The second one is still mostly dirt floors and cold brick and empty. They renovated the one under this building a few years ago. They only half finished. You can hear stuff when you're down there."

"Does anybody know about the teens using it?"

"None of the clinic staff people do. A few years ago somebody tried to turn the space down there into a rec room. They put down somebody's used linoleum. They brought a tatty old couch and a lamp. The bulb burned out months ago. It's pretty dark, but you get light through one of the basement windows."

"Why did you need to hide out?"

"I needed a place to meet a friend."

Jan with a boyfriend? He might be popular, but he'd never shown interest in one person. He was always the loudest one in the middle of a crowd, never quietly holding hands with one boy. His flamboyance and ability to entertain couldn't hide his inability to relate sensibly on a personal level.

"Did your friend stay late with you?"

"No. I stayed awhile after."

"By yourself in the dark?"

"We can't turn any lights on. I had my laptop computer lid up."

I'd dealt with kids long enough as a teacher to at least have some notion when they weren't telling the truth. I didn't believe he was with someone. I'd bet all my teacher's manuals along with the answer keys that he was lying.

"Who was the friend?"

"I can't tell you."

"Can't or won't?"

"Can't. He's closeted."

"So are most of the kids who come to the clinic, but they aren't closeted when they're around here."

"I can't tell you. It's somebody from school. I promised not to tell."

I gave up on pressing for the name. Maybe the police could use his feather boa to torture it out of him or just strangle him and save the rest of us a lot of grief. I asked, "How did everybody get in and out down there without people noticing?"

"It's not hard. This place is such a dump. From the areaway on the north side of the building there's an old entrance. I think maybe they used to bring coal in through a chute. Somebody knocked a few boards loose to widen that entrance."

"Who's somebody?"

"Different kids. The opening got wider over time. We used to go down there to smoke and stuff. It's a refuge. A make-out place."

"You're sure none of the staff knew how you were using it?"

"Yeah."

"What time did you leave?"

"I don't wear a watch. I don't like to feel encumbered."

"Don't computers have the time on them?"

"Mine was always wrong. I shut off that function."

"How long does yours work on battery?"

"I've got a good one. It goes for more than three hours."

Count on Jan to be on the cutting edge of everything. He certainly thought he was the most trendy thing in the Midwest.

"Even if you can't say exactly, can you give me a guess about what time it was?"

"Not really, but I hadn't heard footsteps above for a while. You can hear people moving around."

I asked, "Can you get upstairs from the basement without a key?"

"Sure. With or without. But we keep it a big secret about what goes on down there after hours. Which is why I think they'll suspect me. Anybody could get up from there."

"How would they know you were down there?"

"DNA tests. Fingerprints."

"But you were there more than once. So your print could have come on one of your other visits."

"Yeah."

Unless he told on himself, he might never be found out. Then again, here he was blabbing to me. He was the kind of kid who might as well be wearing a sign saying "Don't Talk to Me, I've Got a Secret." If he was down there, the police needed to question him.

"You're right," I said. "Nobody's going to be able to keep that kind of thing secret. Somebody will blab, although I figure that will be you."

"I can keep secrets."

I asked, "Did you see anyone when you left?"

"Not in the basement. I left through the alley. You know how dark it is back there. I thought I heard some movement. I couldn't tell if it was a rat or a person. I called out and looked around."

"You could have been mugged."

"I didn't think about that. It may have been a person. Maybe it was the killer. I could have been within feet of him. I wasn't scared. I know karate."

"Outside of the movies, how good is karate against somebody with a weapon?"

"I can defend myself."

I went back to the more important point. "But you're not sure it was someone?"

"Not really. I came back here early this morning. I saw Max Bakstein across the street at the Rainbow Café. What was he doing there? If it's a secret, you don't have to tell me. Did you talk to him? I thought he was with somebody from school. I wasn't sure I recognized the other guy. I didn't see them leave. Did they come here?"

I had no intention of confiding in Jan. He was the ultimate school gossip. I had no desire to lie to him either.

I asked, "Where were you?"

"In the coffee shop. I was waiting for the clinic to open. I can't start my morning without coffee. I need caffeine."

Like the Titanic needed an iceberg.

"How come you were here so early on a Saturday?" I asked.

"I had a lot to fix in the library here. There's a new guy from the north suburbs who volunteered to help in the library. He's hot. I wanted to get to know him."

"You should to talk to the police."

"My parents will find out I was here. Can't you tell the police for me?"

"No. This is going to have to be you."

I realized I was setting up a double standard here. I wasn't going to rat out Max and Abdel, but then they hadn't been in the building the night before. They said it was their first time here. They wouldn't have known about the basement.

Jan's words also meant the killer didn't have to have left

through the clinic. He or she could have gotten in or out through the hole the kids had made. I introduced Jan to Todd.

Todd asked Jan to wait outside. When the door closed, Todd said, "Do you know anybody who isn't connected with the murder?"

"I could check my address book." I told him about Max and Abdel.

"Tell the police," was his prompt reply.

"I don't want to if I don't have to."

"You might not have much choice."

I told him about Tajeda and Jan. He said, "You should probably keep a list. One of these folks might have killed him. Maybe the cops could just videotape your life. It might save them a lot of work. Or maybe you could just have every third one who shows up here executed."

"People who work in a gay organization, how could that be a bad thing?"

"Too tempting. Forget I suggested it."

6

After Jan left, the torrent of possible suspects let up. If there were a lot more of these "last people to see him alive," I'd have to start giving out numbers. I eased into the hall. Police personnel stood in the entrances to parts of the clinic that were off limits. Several people stood in the halls and offices nearby.

Lee walked up to me. "How'd it go?" I asked.

"Okay. I told them the truth. I'm not sure that was a great idea, but your lawyer said it was the only idea." He frowned. "A couple of us are getting together across the street at the Rainbow Café. Why don't you join us?"

I wasn't eager to spend a lot of time with more of these people from the clinic. At the same time, I didn't relish being alone with my visions of what I'd seen. Through a pane of glass, I saw Jan gesticulating at two uniformed officers. Todd was with him.

Lee added, "We can compare notes on what the cops said."

I agreed to accompany him.

Outside we walked through a cluster of people, some of

whom I recognized from the clinic. The full-time staff was about twenty people. There were at least a hundred part-time volunteers, more if a major project was on hand.

The Rainbow Café was an institution in the Chicago gay community. Before Unabridged Bookstore opened, the café was one of the few places in the city you could find legitimate gay literature, fiction, and non-fiction. It was now a used bookstore, coffee house, and meeting place for the community. It was a series of storefronts merged into a complex that now took up nearly an entire block. The owner had purchased a corner space and expanded northward numerous times. Each former storefront now had a spacious interior archway connecting it with the others. Every room had tables and couches, and overstuffed chairs clustered in the middle. Tiffany reading lamps, brass fixtures, green plants, and more comfortable seating filled nooks and crannies and quiet corners and cozy alcoves. The interior had a very English pubby feeling, sconces and hanging smoked glass lanterns, everything dark wood: chairs, tables, booths. Upstairs was a variety of meeting rooms, the largest of which, the size of small ballroom, was the proposed venue for the oft-discussed prom. On the sound system, the owner played a mix of classical music and blues. Used books lined the floor-to-ceiling shelves. One room was exclusively devoted to mysteries, another to American literature, a third to science fiction, and so on. With all the wood and books and old-world prints on the ends of bookcases, it was a delight of a place to be. There was even a separate room for those who wanted to tap on their laptop keyboards. Early in the afternoon on a Saturday it was crowded.

Lee and I wound up in the furthest room to the north, the quietest, most removed from the cash register. This room was filled exclusively with theater books: scripts, plays, and numerous editions of complete Shakespeare in hardcover. Several people from the clinic had placed some tables together. I wasn't in the mood to sit with them, but Lee said, "There isn't really another free spot."

Lee, Tajeda, Ken Wells, David Frouge, and myself were on hand.

The general consensus of the people present was, Snarly Bitch was rude but we should try not to speak ill of the dead, with the secondary thought, What's going to happen to our jobs? There was a great deal of discussion about what the police had asked whom. Nobody discussed their whereabouts from when Snarly was last seen to my discovery of the head. I guess everybody just assumed if you were present in the coffee shop, you weren't a killer.

For a group that generally didn't like each other much, at the moment they seemed to be trying to rein in their inherent hostility. No one asked for details about my experience.

A lot of the job discussion revolved around the possibilities of funding in the future. They figured if they could get cash, the clinic and their jobs might survive. Tajeda said, "Snarly Bitch may have been an asshole, but he was our meal ticket. Say all you want, but he was fantastic at fundraising."

Lee Weaver said, "He could suck up to wealthy donors better than anyone I know."

Ken Wells said, "He was sweet to them in direct proportion to how rotten he was to us." Ken was the grievance collector and fairness barometer of the group. He remembered every slight, or possible slight, or what could turn into a slight, or what might be interpreted as a slight if he complained about it to enough people. He was the kind of guy who knew precisely when and exactly who had gotten how many paper clips. He had a degree in accounting and another in social work. His idea of fairness was that everyone should get what was coming to them as it related to Ken Wells. He used fairness as a club and a means to beat up people in an argument, and as a method of getting that which was favorable to him. I could have predicted the words I heard him say: "This just isn't fair."

The second time he repeated it, I asked, "Unfair to whom? You're not dead."

He said, "This clinic could have been something. I was in charge of community outreach. Snarly thought that meant sucking up to donors. What it really means is reaching out to other groups, finding common ground, making common cause. We started that gay, lesbian, bisexual, and transgendered domestic abuse program. It was a huge success, but he wouldn't pursue other programs like it. That was stupid. As it is, we've got other gay organizations meeting in many of our rooms for lots of hours and days a week. They pay fees for that. At least that's something. It gave us an income of sorts. Not much. But Snarly wouldn't listen to my other plans. Nobody appreciated what I was doing for that clinic. This place could have been better than anything San Francisco or Los Angeles has, but people just don't realize what it takes to build a real community organization. In connection with this café, we'd have been really something."

Tajeda said, "We supported everything you did. We wanted you to succeed."

David Frouge, a great bear of a man, said, "Community outreach was not the clinic's mission." Frouge was the 'original intent' person on the staff. Frouge had been one of the first employees hired by Snarly Bitch years ago. An MBA, he had decided the clinic needed a mission statement. They spent months of committee meetings deciding that since they were a gay youth clinic, their mission statement would be that they would help gay kids. He was one MBA who needed to get a grip. When with Snarly Bitch, Frouge was your basic milquetoast suck-up. More than any of the others, he gave meaning to the term *rigid*. Everything had to have been done before, and then had to be done the way it had been done before. Under this system, how the first thing ever got done was a mystery to me. I'm not a change-for-the-hell-of-it kind of guy, but if you looked up *rigid* in the dictionary, you would find a picture of David Frouge. He always wore the same pair of faded blue jeans. In summer he added dark blue T-shirts, in winter dark blue flannel shirts. If he had a redeeming quality, I didn't know about it, unless you count unswerving loyalty to Snarly Bitch as a virtue. Normally, he wouldn't have been having coffee with this crowd, but this was not a normal moment. He said, "I know you all think I was this big suck-up, but I got yelled at a lot by Charley, probably more than most of you. Everybody blew problems out of proportion. There was no need for some delegation to meet with Charley about how to handle staff. Even more, I never did see why Mason had to lead the group to talk to Charley."

Lee asked, "You approved of the way he dealt with us?"

"He was the boss. It was his clinic. For all the complaining, if it was really that bad, people could have left."

Lee said, "The thing I hated most about him was that fatuous smile." Nods around the group. "I used to fantasize that the fat end of a baseball bat up his ass might wipe it off his face."

Wells said, "He was contrary enough to enjoy that."

"You don't have to be contrary to enjoy that," Frouge said. A couple of us raised our eyebrows at this comment, but nobody asked questions. I was glad of that.

Sloan Hastern, Jakalyn Bowman, and Irene Kang, three other employees of the clinic, joined us. Hastern was in charge of volunteers. Bowman was in charge of relations with the press. Kang was the executive assistant. We crowded more closely around the tables.

Hastern announced, "The cops have got hold of the volunteer list. They're calling in everybody. Those poor people who just wanted to do a little good in a quiet way are gonna get blasted."

"It's going to take them a hell of a long time," Wells pointed out. "The volunteers never stayed long."

Lee said, "Most of them were teenagers, a notoriously flighty bunch, or adults who weren't committed to these kids. I was committed to helping them."

Frouge interjected, "Charley was, too."

Wells said, "He stabbed me in the back all the time."

I added, "I'd heard he sabotaged one of your recent fundraisers."

"That asshole went behind my back and convinced several big donors to pull out of a major dinner benefit we were having. Yeah, I wanted to kill him at that moment."

"Why would he wreck a fundraiser?" I asked.

"His own goddamn ego," Wells said. "Everything was his own goddamn ego."

Frouge said, "If you were that pissed off, why didn't you just quit?"

"Maybe I don't confide in you or anyone else around here about my job-hunting plans."

"Are we still going to have the prom?" Tajeda asked. I figured she was attempting to change the subject and head off full-scale war. "A lot of these kids have been looking forward to it. Everything's ordered. We got all the last-minute planning done last night. There's nothing left to do."

Lee said, "As long as there are no debates, no more meetings, no more anything."

Frouge said, "As far as I can see, you would have no say in the matter. You were fired."

Wells said, "No one's sure who's in charge right now. There may be no clinic. There's enough money in the bank to pay the rent, which is due next week. I'm not sure we'll meet payroll the week after that. Snarly's family foundation was due to make its quarterly infusion of cash."

Frouge said, "I wish you wouldn't refer to him as Snarly Bitch while I'm around. He's dead now."

"He earned it," Lee said.

A few of them looked abashed. It was a cruel, if well-deserved, nickname.

"Would you really go broke?" I asked.

Frouge said, "Without his money, the clinic is in deep trouble. It made up half the annual budget."

"Which was what?" I asked.

Frouge said, "About ten million a year. The payments for five lots in this neighborhood are astronomical, much less all we had to do for upkeep on that old office building and the three houses."

I said, "So the fundraising had to take in five million or so a year."

"Yeah," Wells said. "It averaged out to just under fourteen thousand dollars a day, winter or summer, rain or shine. The cash had to flow."

Tajeda said, "I'd hope we could at least still afford some things. I'll talk to some of the members of the board of directors about the prom. I know Charley's sister. She's on the board. She doesn't take an active role in the clinic, but she might have some influence. We can't lose sight of these kids in all this."

Sloan Hastern said, "Maybe he had a will and left all the family's cash to the clinic." Hastern took a sip of coffee. Sloan was the type of guy who would take out a cigarette and a lighter and hold them in his hand and keep talking or listening while holding the things and holding them until you wanted to tell him to light the damn cigarette or stick it up his ass. Or even better, light the damn thing *and* stick the lit end up his ass. I'm sure he thought of it as an action that made him look more thoughtful, perhaps even gave weight to his words. It struck me as an annoying affectation. He was in his early thirties. He was in charge of the volunteers. He was tall and thin with almost no ass.

"Did he even have a will?" Tajeda asked

Lee said, "I'm not sure he had much money of his own. I think it may have been all the family's, not his."

"I have no idea about his personal finances," Frouge said. "As for the clinic, the Board of Directors will have to meet. They'll make some decisions."

Many of them sneered at this pronouncement. The gist of their cracks about the directors was that the members of the board didn't have a brain cell to spare between them. Even Frouge only made a half-hearted defense of the board.

Lee said, "Some of the board members were there before we left. If the situation can be made worse, they'll find a way to do it."

Tajeda pointed at me, "I heard they were going to talk to you about being interim head."

Lee said, "They probably think you can raise lots of money because of your lover."

"No offense," Ken Wells said, "but I think there are a lot of people who have been here a lot longer and deserve to be considered before you are. It takes more than a rich lover to make someone qualified to be the head of a volunteer organization. Do you have fundraising experience?"

I chose to ignore the insult in his words and tone. I said, "I'm not trying to horn in on anybody's territory. I don't want the job. I am not going to apply for the job. If they offer me the job, I will turn it down. If they give me a paycheck for the job, I will not cash it. I was happy to help out in a peripheral way. I am not willing to be any further involved." It would have been delicious to add that there wasn't enough money minted on the planet to pay me to work with this bunch of simpering jerks on a daily basis.

Wells wasn't ready to let it go. "The job requires some basic skills."

Lee said, "As far as I can see the basic skills are be born rich, be rude to underlings, and be able to suck up to fat-cat donors."

Frouge said, "He wasn't always rude."

Wells said, "He'd turned being rude into a way of life." Wells organized most of the big fundraisers at the clinic. He did banquets and bike rides and bake sales—gourmet wedding cakes, not your backyard birthday brownies. Last June he had four thousand people bicycling down old Route 66 from Chicago to St. Louis in a smash-hit of a successful fundraiser. His most recent idea was to set up a bike tour along the entire route of the "mother road," as he incessantly referred to it. He wanted to have different gay groups in cities along the way sharing in the proceeds and helping with the set-up and contributing volunteers. If anyone did, he had the energy to make a two-thousand-mile money maker happen. He could get items for gay auctions that other people marveled at. Of course, how could you prove it was Greg Maddox's jock strap you were bidding on?

Tajeda said, "I've never been involved with a death in this way before. It's awful. I can't imagine trying to work anymore at a place where this kind of thing has happened. What are people going to think? Even if we had nothing to do with it, and I'm sure no one here did, people are going to look at us funny. They'll think we were involved at least until they find out who did it. And we'll always have a taint about us. If we put the clinic down on a résumé as a place of employment, they'll all know we were connected in some way to murder."

Lee said, "The police have lots of suspects. Anybody who ever worked at the clinic is going to be on the list. I hope it doesn't spread to any of the kids. They've got enough hassles."

Frouge said, "They shouldn't be looking at people who worked in the clinic. Charley was our meal ticket. We had no reason to kill him."

"He wasn't my meal ticket anymore," Lee said.

"And killing him wouldn't make him your meal ticket again," Tajeda said.

Jakalyn Bowman said, "This is a public relations disaster. I don't know what I'm going to do. I've gotten calls from all the media. They want statements. The board members don't have a clue about what to say or do. It's just chaos. I wish someone at the clinic had at least a little experience with the press besides myself."

Bowman was a woman in her fifties with a figure that resembled Queen Victoria after her prime. She abused underlings almost as often as Charley Fitch did. Most of the time she put on a huge smiling show for the mainstream press and sucked up to them like a vacuum cleaner gone berserk. She was pretty rude to the gay press in general. She thought it was beneath her dignity to deal with them.

"We've all talked to reporters," Lee said.

Bowman stated, "None of you has the experience I've had. The whole clinic would be better off if people would direct reporters to me. So many of the people who work here think they know how to deal with the media, and they don't. They aren't professionals. I am. I know what to say. All of you and the board should let me talk to the press. I can try and make this not as awful as it seems."

"It is as awful as it seems," Lee said. "How can you possibly minimize it?"

"A good press person can always help a situation."

I wondered if a jury would convict someone who machine-gunned all these people. All the accused would need on the jury is one other person who had ever worked for a gay organization—that jury would never convict him, probably give the killer a medal.

Frouge said, "The police should look at all the right-wing homocons in town. They all hate each other. There's violence there waiting to happen."

Heads nodded sagely. The latest feud in the gay community to get media play was right-wing versus left-wing. Since at least the Sixties, the majority of gay people have been at least vaguely in favor of the left and certainly vote heavily Democratic. The right has been the enemy. Recently, a small minority of gay people had decided that "economics is our friend." Unfortunately, the people who support the economic policies gay right-wingers claim will set us free happen to be homophobic, right-wing, Bible-thumping morons.

Each side in the gay left/right feud seem to be in a contest to see who can be more supercilious than the other. Snarly was good at supercilious and managed to add snide and rude. He had well honed the talk-show virtues of rudeness, interrupting, and talking over the opponent. He was a staple on a local right-wing cable television show. The host, Benton Fredericks, a washed-up PBS host (almost an oxymoron), kept Snarly around as a patsy for right-wing attack dogs. To be fair, Fredericks abused both sides evenly, though his bias was decidedly in favor of stupidity. I'd seen Snarly on the show once. I thought he'd come across as an inarticulate boob, perhaps an appellation that could be appended to anyone who appeared on a right-wing show.

Lee said, "That crowd feeds on outrage."

"Did he meet them outside of a television or radio studio?" Tajeda asked.

Frouge said, "This isn't that big a town. You've seen some of the blind gossip items in the local bar rags. Like that crap in the 'Blithering Bullshit' column in that scandal sheet *Party On*. 'Which two battling activists were in the back room of the Black Pit bar pissing on each other, and we don't mean with their zippers closed.' Charley would talk about trying to sue those publications. The attacks they made were sneaky, underhanded, and unprincipled."

Lee said, "You would have preferred them to be openly unprincipled?"

I didn't admit that I knew the reporter who wrote the column in question. Actually, he was Scott's acquaintance. Scott has always been good with the press, even vermin from the gutter papers. I don't know how he's so patient. I thought it might be a good idea to get this reporter's perspective on all this.

Frouge said, "You people just never understood Charley. Who reads that crap in the bar rags? Who gives a rat's ass? Anybody here ever hear the song 'I Don't Care'?" Head shakes. "It's wonderful. The singers go through a mound of modern gossip moments followed by the singers and audiences chanting 'I don't care.' One of the great moments in radio history."

"But people do care," Tajeda said. "I heard the stories about the fights between Charley and the others were true, but except for the chair incident, I've got no proof. I heard about him throwing drinks at right-wing enemies at cocktail parties, but I never actually met someone who saw him do it."

Wells said, "I doubt if there were any fists thrown. Normally, they wouldn't even be at the same fundraisers. The two sides probably wouldn't have appealed to the same donors."

Tajeda said, "There was violence, that once."

"It never came to anything, though," Lee said.

The last time Charley had been on Benton Fredricks' *News Forum* cable show had been a classic. One of Charley Fitch's archenemies in the gay community was Billy Karek. They had been asked to do a panel discussion together. The topic was supposed to be the public image of homosexuals in society. Fitch and Karek started off angry. Snarly accused Karek of being a "homocon," the name some in the media used to describe gay conservatives.

Karek gave a commentary every week on a gay radio program that ran sometime in the middle of the night on a station whose signal barely reached from Belmont Avenue to Fullerton Avenue and from Halsted to the lake. Karek had used the forum to attack Fitch. Before the cable program fiasco, like most people, I'd never heard of *News Forum*. I doubted if ten people listened to it. But Charley Fitch had gotten hold of transcripts of the radio show attacks. Karek had concentrated on how he saw Fitch as an illogical leftist, with ideas that had been barely sustainable in the Sixties. Karek had all but called Fitch a communist. The diatribe that set Charley off was when Karek said, "Have we changed from defenders of the downtrodden to defenders of all the drag queens and transvestites on the planet? Whatever happened to normal people?" On the cable show, Karek had taken off on him again. They'd moved from sparring to shouting. Benton Fredericks made no move to stop them. He knew a ratings booster when he saw one. The way I heard it, both had been waving their arms, pointing fingers, and pounding on the table. Then Fitch had reached over and grabbed Karek by the tie and tried to slam his face into the table between them. Karek had managed to free himself, but the brawl was on. The highlights that played on all the television stations were Karek swinging a folding chair at Charley Fitch's head, and Charley picking up a microphone and trying to bash in Karek's brains with it. They'd both missed. Too bad. Karek wound up cowering under the broadcaster's console. The incident had made national news. The clip had been repeated on local television stations ad nauseam. The enmity between the two men had gone from pre-fight fierce, to post-fight total war.

I suspected mostly these people were fighting turf wars over a very small piece of turf. Huge egos with no place else to go. And it wasn't just the politically correct trying to lead the politically incorrect. More than once I'd seen right- and left-wing gay people on any number of talk shows doing everything but the physical confrontation that Karek and Charley Fitch had done. I'd pretty much sworn off reading articles in which they vilified each other, and the remote control was always within reach when they got themselves on television. Scott was a bit of a problem about this. He claimed he liked watching these people. Guerrilla theater? The equivalent of watching a train wreck? Morbid curiosity? I never could figure that out.

The quarrels among the people at the clinic were very real and very human, filled with very old-fashioned human enmities. I had talked with many of them one on one. At rest and with someone not perceived as a threat, they seemed okay. I thought these were essentially good people, but the situation was out of control.

Frouge said, "They never saw each other after that fight. Charley never mentioned Karek's name."

"Were there other of these homocons that he had fights with?"

"All of them," Ken Wells said.

"Specifically."

Tajeda said, "Albert Bergland was a crazed right-winger. He has a web site dedicated to his own opinions. He would vilify anybody who didn't agree with him. You know, one of those blog things. It's kind of a shame that those people with pointless, witless, and brainless opinions now have an outlet."

"I know I feel better that they do," Lee said. "Never underestimate the power of stupid people in large numbers."

"Hence the Internet," Ken Wells said.

"Anybody else?" I asked.

Bowman said, "There was Mandy Marlex. She's the lesbian of the moment. You see her on all kinds of ratings-starved cable shows. She doesn't have much television presence, but she manages to say just the correct stupid thing so the host can rant against her."

"Did Charley have any friends?" I asked.

Bowman said, "You've got to understand, the clinic was Charley's life. It's all he thought about. He was obsessed with raising money to keep it going. The family money was never enough. He didn't really have much of a life. He may have been an asshole, as you guys say, but he really was dedicated to making the clinic work."

I said, "He must have had friends."

Hastern said, "And a few lovers over the years."

Wells said, "At least he said they were lovers. I always thought the men he brought around looked like Snarly picked them up from Pool Boys 'R' Us and paid for them. To be fair, Snarly could be a charmer. He could work a crowd at a fundraiser like nobody I've ever seen. He was never rude to big money, never."

Lee said to Frouge, "Do you know if they were call boys?"

Frouge said, "I have no idea. I would never have presumed to ask. The man is dead, for god's sake."

"I'm not going to turn into a hypocrite because he's dead," Lee said.

Tajeda said, "Snarly was the hypocrite. How much effort does it really take to be pleasant to your staff? Takes just as much effort to be pleasant as unpleasant."

"He was a friend," Frouge said. "Friends have flaws. We all do. I won't deny that were times I wished he'd said something different, but he was a good man. Maybe we could change the subject."

We called over a waiter and ordered more cups of coffee and muffins, which were the best in the city. Several people took trips to the unisex washrooms. I leaned back and shut my eyes. I got a flash of the file drawer, blood and gore covering a human head. I opened my eyes. I guess there were worse things than listening to these people.

When everybody had a fresh supply of caffeine and sugar, Lee asked Hastern and Bowman, "Did Jan tell either of you what he said to the police?"

"He was still in there with them when we came over," Hastern said.

Ken Wells snorted. "Who gives a shit about that self-obsessed teen drag queen? I saw him flitting about the clinic all morning. I think one of the detectives was ready to use a pair of handcuffs to attach him by the neck to the highest branch in the nearest tall tree. That kid has got some kind of radar for trying to put himself in the middle of anything. The bigger the thing is, the more he wants to be in the middle of it. I hate that effeminate bullshit. Who teaches them that crap?"

Tajeda said, "Jan's all right. He just has an overactive imagination."

Wells gave her a sour look.

Tajeda continued, "He was frightened about talking to the police. I reassured him. I hope he's okay. Under all that bluster there's a very sensitive and lonely boy."

Wells said, "Snarly kicked him out of the clinic permanently."

"What for?" I asked.

"Being an obnoxious twit?" Wells said. "I didn't ask."

"But he was back today."

Tajeda said, "Maybe Charley took him back. Charley could do that. He'd turn around a hundred eighty degrees on something, sometimes in the same sentence. That's why I thought I could talk to him about Lee's job. Jan was good at sucking up. Maybe he talked to Charley."

I asked, "Did anyone know kids sometimes used the basement after hours for secret trysts?"

Lee watched me closely. Most of the rest of the people at the table shook their heads except Sloan Hastern. Everybody looked at him. He said, "I knew."

"How?" Lee said.

"You're not the only one kids trust."

Well, thank God they were perky enough to snipe at each other and not just me.

I asked, "Did one of the kids tell you, or did you find it out on your own?"

Hastern said, "The volunteers are the ones who do the cleaning and maintenance around the clinic. I supervise. Several times I noticed messes down there in the mornings when there shouldn't have been messes. I accused a couple of the clean-up crews of inefficiency. They all denied it. They couldn't all have been lying. I inspected what was in the messes. It was the usual crap kids might leave behind, fast-food containers, condoms. Once I found a pair of underwear. What really gave it away was a high-school chemistry text-book and paperback Ayn Rand novel. I began making spot checks of the basement the last thing after everyone went home. I tried staying late a few times to catch someone, but I never did. They must have some kind of system of knowing who's there and who's not. I always left it neat and pristine. It only took a couple of weeks to figure out. Wasn't hard. I talked to a few of the kids. A couple even said a few of them had stayed all night. I saw no reason to blab. I told them if they cleaned up after themselves, I wouldn't check up on them."

Frouge said, "We could have been sued."

"Not sued," Hastern said. "Parents might have been pissed and raised a stink, but not sued."

"Why didn't you tell anyone?" Tajeda asked.

"Not in my job description."

Wells said, "You checked the basement after last night's meeting?"

Hastern said, "Yep. I mentioned it to the cops. My under-standing is that, except for the addition of blood and gore, the place was perfectly neat. Did any of you see what it looked like this morning?"

None of them had been permitted in the basement.

"Who cleans up after a murder?" Hastern asked. "I sure as hell am not going to do it. I'm not going to ask any of the kids to do it either."

Tajeda said, "I'm sure the board will try to hire a service. If they can afford it. If the clinic still exists as an entity to do any cleaning."

I asked Hastern, "Today, did you talk to any of the kids specifically about being down there?"

"No, should I have?"

Ken Wells said, "I can't believe you didn't tell anyone about this."

"Or put a stop to it," Jakalyn Bowman added.

"It wasn't my problem."

Tajeda said, "The clinic could lose its license if the authorities found out we had kids staying overnight. They might think we were somehow letting kids get molested."

"Why would they think that?" Hastern asked. "We don't employ any Catholic priests."

"This isn't funny," Wells said. "We've been very scrupulous about not allowing anything that even remotely suggests sex among the kids, but especially sex between any of the staff and the kids."

"More scrupulous than you need to be," Hastern said.

Lee asked, "What does that mean?"

"We aren't recruiting," Hastern said. "That's bogus bullshit. Why do we have to be so scrupulous, when it's just bullshit?"

"You're so fucking naïve," Wells said.

"Do you think these kids aren't having sex with each other?" Hastern asked.

I almost left. No matter how much they hated their boss, you'd think they'd express more than passing grief about it. They were bickering as if nothing had happened. Then again, maybe it was easier to bicker than it was to think about violent death. I couldn't be the only one avoiding unpleasant images.

Irene Kang spoke for the first time. "Maybe it was some kind of anti-gay thing. A bashing gone bad." Kang was in her mid-twenties. Her title as executive assistant hid the fact that she was little more than a glorified secretary. She had blond hair and as far as I could see, she spent as much time buffing her nails and talking on the phone as she did working. The greatest virtue I had observed her to have was the ability to suck up to Charley Fitch whenever he was around. Once he was out of earshot, she was as nasty as he was when large donors weren't around.

Ken Wells gave her a contemptuous look. "Gay bashers don't work that way."

"How do you know?" Kang asked.

"I've been bashed right out on Clark Street," Wells said. "At seven o'clock at night with people all around. Put me in the hospital. I had to have three operations. I've earned my scars. How about you?"

Kang said, "You don't have to get beaten up to have credentials as a gay activist."

Wells said, "They don't come into buildings and hunt people. They find them on the street when they look vulnerable. They're crimes of opportunity. The Neanderthals that do them haven't got the brains to do a lot of planning."

Kang said, "Well, I know Charley Fitch got several phone calls that made him angry yesterday. Maybe somebody was planning to hurt him."

"Who called?" Wells asked.

"There were several. I heard him raise his voice a number of times."

"He was always raising his voice," Lee said.

Kang said, "More than usual with these, I thought."

"You were listening?" Wells asked.

Kang said, "He leaves his office door open. You know he does. My desk is right there. I don't deliberately eavesdrop."

"Anything more specific or different about the most recent ones?" Wells asked.

Kang said, "Not that I noticed."

"Had there been any threatening phone calls prior to this?" Lee asked.

"There's always threatening phone calls," Kang said. "Obscene callers. They don't usually ask for somebody by name.

The loonies usually just call up the clinic and start spouting obscenities or quoting the Bible."

"Somebody asked for me by name," Lee said.

"Happened to me last week," Wells said.

Hastern said, "I got the same thing about a week ago. Asked for me by name."

Tajeda said, "Me too."

They'd all been called. I asked Kang, "Do you remember if the person who asked for them sounded the same?"

"We get millions of calls. I can't be expected to remember the sound of one person's voice."

"When did you get the calls exactly?" I asked.

Lee's had been first, just over two weeks ago. The others had followed on subsequent days. Some came early in the morning, some late in the day.

I said, "You could check the Caller ID and get the numbers."

"Charley Fitch wouldn't pay for Caller ID," Kang said.

Hastern said, "That is so stupid. All you had to do was get the Caller ID, prosecute a few of them, and you'd solve the problem."

Frouge said, "Charley claimed the idea that we might have Caller ID would be as effective as having it. Actually, he was right. We've gotten a lot fewer crank calls since the local phone monopoly added it to their service."

"Doesn't help with people at pay phones or who can block it," Wells said.

"What did the voice sound like?" I asked.

They all agreed it was male, the only thing so far that they didn't disagree or bicker about. After that they returned to form. Several thought the voice was disguised. A few didn't think it was. Some thought he was young, others old. Two found it deep and mellow. Two weren't really paying attention. Several said it upset them too much to be sure.

Tajeda said, "You'd think we'd be used to that kind of verbal attack. I'm not. I don't think anybody ever really is."

"What did he say?" I asked.

Lee said, "Standard anti-gay stuff. Threw the word *faggot* around a few times. Said we were all going to hell. Said we were child molesters."

Wells said, "I have no idea what he said. After the first obscenity, I hung up."

Lee had listened the longest, but the others agreed that the bits that they did hear coincided pretty much with what Lee had heard.

"Does this have any significance connected to the killing?" Lee asked.

"I'm not sure," I said. "It is odd that they came in so regularly right before Snarly's death, but there's lots of possible explanations for that. Doesn't have to be an ax murderer."

Lee said, "We should tell the police about them."

Hastern said, "I'm not going near the cops." Five years ago he'd reported his abusive lover to the police. They'd laughed at him. He'd made a complaint against the reporting officers to the Chicago Police Department's Internal Affairs Division. They'd never returned his calls. He'd gotten in touch with the mayor's liaison to the gay community. She'd given him vague reassurances. The last beating had put Hastern in the hospital. After that Hastern's lover had abandoned him, tired of the activism, blaming the victim.

They spent the next few minutes bickering about reporting things to the police. I'd just about had it. Through the window, I saw Todd cross the street. I met him near a bookcase filled with lesbian mysteries; the most prominently displayed were multiple copies of Ellen Hart's and Katherine Forrest's works. Todd said, "If all gay kids are like that one, I'm going to turn in my ID card."

"You've had the Jan Experience. Maybe we could plant some evidence and have him arrested."

"No prison has enough feather boas to handle him. I have also been talking with several members of the clinic's board of directors. They want to talk to you. They need an interim director, someone to take temporary responsibility. They were thinking of asking you. I'm supposed to feel you out."

"No, thanks. I prefer teaching. Being peripherally involved in a gay organization is a risk to a saint's patience. Being in charge is an invitation to madness."

"You won't talk to them?"

"I'll talk to anybody. The answer is, no."

The detectives, Lynn Stafford and Jason Abernathy, entered the coffee shop. They walked directly back to the group in the theater room. Todd and I followed. They stood on either side of Lee.

"Mr. Weaver," Stafford said, "you're under arrest for the murder of Charley Fitch." Lee turned very pale. I listened to the recitation of the Miranda warning in a fog. Mouths were open around the table. When they put the handcuffs on him and began to lead him away, he turned to me and said, "Help me, Mr. Mason."

The best thing I can say about the next few minutes was that the clinic members present forgot their bickering and carrying on and showed genuine concern. Of course, Wells said, "This isn't fair."

The cops ignored him.

Todd said he would go with Lee to the police station.

I said, "I'll go with."

"It won't do you any good. They might let me talk to him. Certainly not anyone else."

"They can't have any proof."

"They must have something. I intend to find out what."

They left. I had no intention of returning to the other

clinic personnel. I stood indecisively for several moments. Jan walked up. He actually bent close and whispered in my ear. “Can I talk to you, Mr. Mason?”

“Things are a little frantic right now, Jan.”

“It’s important. Some of the kids need to talk to someone.”

7

The Rainbow Café was known as a hangout for gay kids. The owner had strict rules. Gay or straight, kids had to have cash to pay for their stuff. They had to show their money before ordering. The only musical devices allowed to be turned on had to have headphones. If another patron could hear the slightest noise from any electronic device, it had to be turned off. Public displays of affection had to be nearly as chaste as at a Catholic high school dance in the Fifties.

The teens were huddled together in a small alcove in the most obscure corner of the café. The owner could observe anyone in these chairs from behind the counter, but they were hidden from the rest of the customers. Jan put his feather boa, laptop, and Ayn Rand book on the table in front of him. The kids sat in a semicircle around me.

They were a disparate lot. Jan and a girl named Brenda Hersch, whom I knew from the clinic, sat with two guys I didn't know. I was introduced to Cliff Morgan, who was dressed in baggy jeans and an oversized T-shirt. He was scrawny in a freshman-in-high-school way. The other was Larry Mullen, at least six-foot-five with the build of a college linebacker. Both his letterman's jacket and a prominently displayed football pin said Bromfield High. Brenda was fifteen or sixteen. She wore a serious frown, jeans, and a bulky sweater.

I asked Jan how his interview with the police went.

"They kept asking me questions. I think they were pretty pissed. The cops called my parents. They were definitely very pissed."

"Won't you get in trouble for being here now?" I asked.

"My parents left early this morning to go to Bloomington to visit my brother at Illinois State. They won't be back for a couple more hours. I'm supposed to be home. If they find out I'm still here, I'll be grounded until I leave for college."

Pity the college or university that got an untrammeled Jan after he'd been cooped up for several years.

I said to Jan, "I heard Charley Fitch threw you out of the clinic and told you never to come back."

Jan said, "Everything at that clinic was distorted and spooky, except for Mr. Weaver."

"Why'd Mr. Fitch throw you out?"

"I hate to really say much. It can't have anything to do with this murder."

"Everything Charley Fitch did in the past is now open to scrutiny. The truth is going to be important. Some of it might hurt some people, but we've got to get past all these secrets."

He looked at his friends. Brenda said, "Just tell him."

"Okay. Okay. A few days ago, I had some dope with me. It was one joint. Big deal. I was reaching in my pocket for some change for the pop machine. I accidentally dropped the joint. Snarly Bitch went nuts. He carried on as if I'd just torn the heart out of his firstborn child. I was starting to hate the place anyway. I only came back to use the basement."

This was the first time I'd heard one of the kids use Fitch's nickname. While it was familiar with the adults, it sounded odd coming from a kid. I refrained from correcting him. Much as it pained me, I wanted the kid talking.

I said, "You told me earlier you came back today to help with the library."

"Snarly Bitch wasn't going to be in today. I had a deal going with the librarian. Snarly hadn't told everybody else to keep me out. He was so lazy. He'd make these big decrees and then forget to tell anyone about them. Half the time he wouldn't follow through on his threats, or he'd change his mind for the stupidest reasons. He was the most total jerk."

Brenda added, "And Jan thought one of the guys who just started volunteering to help in the library was totally hot."

I asked, "If Charley Fitch was that awful, why did you keep coming back?"

Jan said, "*He* was awful, but it was the only place we had to go. You can't believe how few places there are for gay kids to hang out. We can't get into the bars. The owners or bartenders or doormen get hysterical. If you're cute, older guys try and pick you up on the street. Mostly that's icky. There's no place to be with your friends. Most of us can't hang around the house. Who says, 'Mom, Dad, my boyfriend and I are going to go upstairs and study.' Ha! Nobody's parents are that liberal. The café here is good, but if you want to make out, you've got to find somewhere else. They won't let you sit in here unless you buy something. Most of us can't afford a lot. Two bucks for a cup of coffee? And we only get one free refill." Jan punctuated nearly every comment with a flip of his wrist and a touch or pat on the big guy, Larry's, arm or knee. The teen queen was in full center-of-attention, drag-queen mode. I noted that Larry moved slightly farther away with each physical contact with Jan. Obviously a problem there of some sort.

I turned to the rest of the bunch. I didn't think they'd come just to hear Jan. "How can I help you?"

The big guy, Larry, said, "We've been discussing this for a while. We weren't gonna say anything, but then we saw Mr. Weaver arrested. That is so unfair. We need him. He's the best. Kids who go to the clinic are usually pretty closeted. We don't have a lot of support. I go, but I think most of the guys are way too effeminate. I want to meet normal guys."

"I'm normal," Jan said. He smiled into the light as he said this. For the first time I noticed remnants of what might have been pale pink eye shadow. Jan was normal in the same way drought, famine, and disease are normal.

Larry frowned at him. "I don't know any gay kids who live near me. I can't come out to the team. The guys say some pretty vicious things about gay kids. I'm pretty big so I don't think they'd say something openly, but they might do something sneaky, sabotage my car, steal my gym stuff. I just wish the clinic wasn't so crazy. There's always something going wrong. That Fitch guy was nuts. He'd come into our meetings and lecture endlessly. I don't know how he got to be head of a clinic for helping kids. He didn't have much sense." The other teens nodded agreement.

Brenda said, "And all the adults were fighting all the time. We weren't supposed to notice, but we aren't stupid. Like, we wanted to put out a gay teen newsletter. We wanted to include stuff about what to do if an older person tried to pick you up, about using condoms, about AIDS prevention. You'd think we were trying to write for our high school papers. Every single thing we wrote had to be scrutinized by a committee. After the committee ripped it to shreds, Mr. Fitch managed to screw it up even worse. His decisions about what we could or could not write seemed awfully arbitrary. He'd never set out a clear policy. He wouldn't even let us use a computer at the clinic."

Larry said, "It was like you had to suck up to him for no other reason than he wanted to be sucked up to. Is that the way adults should act?"

"But you all came to the clinic?"

"Jan is right," Brenda confirmed. "It was a place to go, a refuge."

"Did you all use the basement against the rules?"

They all nodded.

Jan said, "It wasn't just us. A lot of kids did. I think it's been going on for years."

Cliff added, "If I wanted to make out with a guy, I couldn't find another place. You don't want to be caught by the cops or anybody else when you're making out in your car with a guy."

Brenda said, "Some of the girls and I got together and smoked pot down there a few times."

"Did Charley Fitch put the make on any of you?" I asked.

"Fuck no," Larry said. Jan laughed. Head shake from Cliff.

Larry said, "There's something we heard that we need to talk about."

Brenda said, "Down in the basement we could hear the adults raising their voices all the time."

I thought I was beginning to get the drift. "You heard something last night?"

Larry said, "Not last night. Before that. We needed to talk to somebody. Brenda knew that Jan had talked to the cops. He called her earlier. We've all got cell phones. We had to do something. Jan said we could trust you."

"I told them you were the best person to talk to." Jan added enough pride and ego to his tone, to suggest that he'd done some miraculous, virtuous thing by suggesting talking to me. And that I should be grateful for his wisdom and insight and faith in me.

Larry said, "We know Mr. Weaver didn't do it. All the kids like Mr. Weaver. You can tell he cares. He's never rude. He's never mean. He doesn't put us down or interrupt us when we talk. He doesn't dump all that older person's advice on us. He listens. He always knows what to say to help you. Or, I guess, if he doesn't know, he tells you that. He doesn't lie to us. If he says he didn't kill the guy, then we know he didn't."

Jan said, "It was that Karek guy. It had to be. I wasn't there when this happened, but it's gotta be true. I've heard people talking about that Karek guy. I saw him on television. He was a crazy person."

Larry said, "Karek came in one time. It was after everybody had left. Brenda, Cliff, and me were down in our space in the basement."

Brenda said, "We were having a prom meeting of our own. The adults have got it into their heads that the prom is a big deal."

"For some of us, it is," Larry said. "I could never go to the prom at my school with a guy. I wish I had someone to take to the prom here. I'd go. I think it's a big deal."

"When was this?" I asked. Because of their disjointed teenage style, I was beginning to get a little confused.

Larry said, "Last Saturday night about nine o'clock."

"How did you know it was Karek?"

"Charley Fitch said it real loud when he was yelling several times. You know like, 'You asshole, Karek,' or 'Fuck you, Karek.' "

I asked, "Did anyone else know about this visit?"

Larry said, "I don't know. Only the three of us were there."

"What did they say?"

"We could hear them," Brenda said. "They were really loud. In some places in the basement you can hear like they were in the next room."

"Can they hear you?" I asked.

Larry said, "Everybody's used to being very quiet down there."

I said, "Explain the geography of this place to me."

Brenda spoke up. "Under the main building, the one closest to Addison, is where we stay. It's the one they renovated. The other parts are still pretty ratty and there's all kinds of junk stored down there. You can hardly get around."

I said, "You're quiet, but you leave messes."

"A few kids do," Larry said. "Most don't."

"It's not right to listen to other people," Cliff said, "although it was hard to miss sometimes. People got loud. My parents do the same thing. Sometimes I think all adults shout to solve their problems." Cliff's voice had that teenage squeak I imagined he desperately wished it didn't.

Jan said, "Some of us liked to listen to them discussing us kids."

"I never did that," Larry said. "But these guys were really loud, you couldn't help but hear them from every room in the basement."

Brenda said, "I never tried to listen to stuff about kids, but Larry's right. You couldn't miss these two guys."

Larry said, "Well, that night the two of them argued. They were threatening to sue each other. They yelled and screamed. Each told the other they didn't understand the gay movement. They got into a screaming match about drag queens at the Pride parade."

"Huh?"

Larry explained, "Karek said that the drag queens dominated the parade. That they were in the majority. That they were an embarrassment. I didn't get it. Who cares about drag queens? I went to the Pride parade last year. There were like three hundred fifty thousand people in the streets and maybe a total of fifty drag queens. That's predominant? Anyway, they both said the other didn't understand the historical forces at work. It was a lot of rhetorical bullshit."

"It sounds like you were taking notes."

Larry said, "That's only the stuff I remember. There was a bunch more."

Brenda said, "I've heard those same arguments before. We all have. One of the seminars you have to attend here if you want to use the services is on gay history. It's all crap."

I said, "I doubt if it was all crap to the people who lived it."

"You know what I mean," she said. "The man and the woman who presented the seminar did nothing but argue. Things don't change."

"How long did the argument between Karek and Charley Fitch last?"

"Maybe half an hour," Larry said.

Cliff added, "We couldn't hear everything they said, but the thing is at the end each one threatened to kill the other."

Brenda said, "I phoned Larry and Cliff as soon as Jan called me this morning." I imagine Jan was on the phone to everyone on his speed dial spreading the news. Getting attention as the bringer of news. The kid had a very different kind of attention deficit disorder.

Jan said, "I called first thing when I found out what was going on. I tried to talk to everybody before the police questioned me." Flip went the boa.

"I told Jan what we heard," Brenda said. "It wasn't like a secret. I remember distinctly Mr. Fitch said he'd be happy to push Karek off any three of the tallest buildings in Chicago. He said Karek deserved to die. Karek said he'd be happy to supply enough arsenic to kill Snarly Bitch. Then he added that Snarly would have to give him time to get a supply together since they'd probably have to manufacture extra tons of it to have enough for a fatal dose for such a big asshole. I thought that was funny. That's pretty close to a direct quote."

Larry said, "What are we gonna do? We want to help Mr. Weaver. Him getting arrested was terrible. He's a terrific guy. I trust him more than I do my dad. No offense to you Mr. Mason, but we really wanted to talk to him, but now he's arrested. We want to do whatever we can to prove he didn't do it."

I said, "He has a very good lawyer." I wanted to help Lee as well. If I got a chance, I wanted to talk to this Karek guy. I'm not sure talk show arguments were a good reason for murder. Most of the time I thought the discussions on those programs were as spontaneous as pro wrestling, with about as much depth of dialogue. Still, I wanted to ask him a few questions.

Cliff said, "Maybe we could see Mr. Weaver or talk to him, kind of cheer him up."

"I'm sure he'd appreciate that," I said, "but right now I doubt if the police would let anyone but his lawyer see him."

Jan said, "We want to investigate the crime. We could put out our own newsletter. We could use the printer at my house and staple it together. We could publish the facts about fights Snarly Bitch had with other people. We can find out stuff." All four of them looked eager enough to run out and be fervent and fixated little Sam Spades.

And then later maybe they could put on a show and buy an iron lung for a kid in a wheelchair. But you don't say that kind of thing. They were kids trying to find a way to do right, to have an effect on their world in a positive way. I said, "There are a lot of legal issues with newsletters, things about slander and libel that are pretty complicated. I think you should avoid that. You could get sued."

"But at least we could talk to people," Cliff said.

I hated to rain on their enthusiasm. I said, "I think the police might get pretty angry if you tried to do any investigating."

Jan said, "I don't care if the police get mad."

"I want to help," Larry said.

"I can keep you informed of developments," I said. "I don't know how much good it would do for you to go around talking to people. They have no reason to trust you. I hate to say this, but they'd probably just dismiss you as kids and tell you to go away. I think the best thing you could do is tell the police what you heard. At the very least, I can use your information as a basis to ask some questions."

Cliff said, "You've got to tell the police this stuff for us. I can't admit I was down there. We were smoking dope."

"Me neither," Larry said. "And if we talk to the cops, won't our parents have to be involved? I can't have that."

"I didn't hear the fight," Jan said, "otherwise I'd tell them myself. If I tell them, it's hearsay, isn't it? I think that's what it is. Frankly, all these legal things just boggle my mind." He had his hand to his throat, in full Scarlett O'Hara mode.

I said, "I don't know if you guys have much choice about talking to the cops. This is a murder investigation. I know you probably all trust each other to keep quiet, but this kind of thing always comes out. You'll never be able to keep it secret. Other kids know about the basement. You've told others about the fight?"

Cliff said, "We did imitations when the adults weren't around at the group discussion meeting last Sunday."

I added, "The police might be questioning some of the kids no matter what."

"What about confidentiality?" Larry asked.

"This is a murder investigation. I'm afraid parents are going to get involved."

Larry said, "If this is going to become public, we're really scared. None of us is really out. My dad isn't happy about my being gay. If I was involved in some kind of murder case, he wouldn't let me out of the house until I graduate. Plus, I've got some good possibilities for athletic scholarships next year. If some universities knew I was gay, they might turn me down. No college team is going to tell me they don't want me because I'm gay, but a lot of sports are still pretty homophobic. A college could just say that all the slots are filled. That I'm not a 'match' for their program."

"The police aren't in the habit of making a list of witnesses public."

Larry asked, "Witnesses at trials aren't anonymous, are they?"

"No," I admitted.

Cliff said, "I saw an article in the *Trib* about how police in Chicago deal with witnesses. It said they treated them like suspects. Kept them locked away in rooms. I don't want to go through that."

The others nodded.

I'd read the same article. I said, "I'll do whatever I can to help you guys. I'll meet with your parents, or I can help be a go-between, if necessary, with another counselor at the clinic or my lawyer. I doubt if your names are going to be in the paper. I think talking to your parents is essential and setting up meetings with the police has to happen. Your parents will probably need to be with you."

Cliff said, "But we'll have to admit so much stuff."

"Lies and secrets aren't the best way to handle being gay or being a teenager or having information in a murder investigation."

I wanted to get these kids in touch with the police. Parents would have to be dealt with. I called Todd's pager. In a few minutes he returned my call. I summarized what the teens had said. He told me he was still involved with Lee. He said that he'd send over one of his associates whom he had total faith in. The teens agreed to wait.

As I went to get more coffee, Larry pulled me aside and said, "Mr. Mason, I know more." He gulped and blushed. Finally he mumbled, "I was there last night."

8

Jan couldn't hear what we were saying, but he looked like he was ready to leap at us. I was sure a conversation in the same room as Jan that he was not privy to would be enough to drive him wild. The budding drag queen hustled over.

"What's going on? Shouldn't we all be here for any discussions?"

I said, "Larry and I need to talk privately for a little while." Jan drew in a large breath. Whether he was preparing a hissy fit or quiet compliance, I chose not to wait for his response. I turned my back on him. Larry and I sat down in a corner of the restaurant away from the others.

I asked, "Were you with Jan last night?"

"Hell, no. Jan's not my type. He's an effeminate fag. I wouldn't be here with him now except Brenda likes him, and they both know you. They said you were the one we had to talk to." He smiled shyly. "I saved you and your lover's wedding announcement from the paper. I try to watch every game Mr. Carpenter pitches on television. I even went to one of those 'out at the ballpark' games."

Several gay groups had gotten together to sponsor gay days at Wrigley Field. The events were huge successes.

Larry was continuing, "I admire you guys so much. I never watch Oprah, but I did when you guys were on. You're like, masculine and normal."

His praise was almost embarrassing, but I was pleased we'd helped. A lot of the point of what Scott and I tried to do was to help gay kids deal with their sexual orientation. I wasn't particularly in the mood for a fan, but I said, "Thanks."

"When I found out you volunteered at the clinic, I'd hoped to meet you and even Mr. Carpenter." He shook his brush-cut head. "Everybody says you can be trusted. I've got to talk to somebody about this." He gulped. "Last night I was in the basement with a friend. A boyfriend. If there were some people around, it wasn't a big worry. No adults ever went down there."

"Sloan Hastern said he did."

"The guy in charge of volunteer stuff?"

I nodded.

"Some kids said he knew but that he was cool about it. I never saw him or any other adult."

The teenager rubbed his large red hands together. He'd bitten his nails to the quick.

"We never make noise when we're in the basement, even if it's after hours." He paused and when he resumed he spoke very softly. "I could hear Mr. Weaver in Mr. Fitch's office after everybody else left."

"Everybody else had left?" I had to make sure that the kid was clear and that I had the time sequence of what had happened the night before correct. Who was where when would be very important.

"We don't go down there in the middle of the day, but at night it's safe down there. As I was passing the clinic parking lot last night all the cars were gone. A few lights were on, but we figured they were mostly emergency lights. Mr. Fitch has that inside office. We can never tell if his lights are on or off. He's pretty oblivious most of the time anyway. He never goes in the basement. All the kids know that. They make us kids clean it. It's pretty ratty. Anyway, we heard Mr. Weaver."

"But Lee's car was gone a little while before?"

"Yeah. He must have come back."

Lee had lied to me. I was extremely pissed about that.

Jan flounced up to us. He put a hand on Larry's shoulder and said, "Did either of you need some coffee or anything?"

Larry moved his shoulder out from under Jan's hand. Jan didn't seem to notice. Larry and I said, "No, thanks." When Jan didn't look prepared to move any time before the passing of the next millennium, I said, "We're not quite through yet." Jan huffed away.

"How do you know which car is Lee's?"

"He's got the coolest yellow Corvette." An extravagance that I was sure helped keep Lee in all kinds of debt.

"What did he and Mr. Fitch say?"

"I couldn't make out everything." He blushed. "For a lot of the time I was preoccupied."

"Then how did you know they were arguing?"

"After we . . ." Now he was very red.

I said, "At some point, you heard them."

"Right. We were afraid to leave in case we made some noise and were discovered. Mr. Weaver isn't dumb. If he heard something, he might figure it out or at least investigate. Mr. Fitch is clueless. Our room is under his office. Somebody dropped a stack of CDs one time, and he didn't come down to investigate. I heard each of them say 'fuck you' and make threats. At the end they got really loud. They were screaming at each other."

"What kind of threats?"

"About other people losing their jobs. Mr. Fitch claimed he could fire anybody he wanted any time he wanted. He was being really mean. I can understand being tough on the football field, but not when you're talking to other adults. Aren't adults supposed to work things out or at least not be screaming at each other?"

I said, "Adults have disagreements, even people who love each other. Don't your parents fight?"

"My mom and dad have been divorced since before I was born. I don't remember my mom. I argue with my dad, but I figure that's teenage stuff. I guess I've seen adults fight, but not like this."

I said, "Unfortunately, all kinds of people don't get along. Did you hear anybody else?"

"No. My buddy and I were there until about ten thirty. Then we left."

"While they were still fighting?"

"Yeah."

I said, "I'm afraid you're going to have to tell the police you were there and what you heard. They're going to want to talk to the guy you were with. I'm sorry."

"I can't." He moaned softly. "I can't. He's on the team. No one knows he's gay."

"If you need an alibi, you're going to have to. Once you admit you were there, the police are going to want to know why, exactly when, and what was going on. If you lie, and they find that out later, the police will most likely get pissed and worse, be very suspicious. You could become a suspect. Your friend can back up your story. It's not going to help to lie."

He shook his head. "Yeah, but it could sure hurt a lot. It was our first date. It was the first time I kissed a guy. It took us both a lot of nerve to even admit to each other that we were interested."

"I'm sorry." I patted his arm. "Talk to my lawyer. He'll be better able to advise you. You've got to protect yourself and be honest."

He looked near tears. He said, "You have to understand. It's not me I'm worried about. I don't want to get Mr. Weaver in trouble. He's helped me so much. I told you because I figured maybe you could do something about it. I want to do what's right, but I can't tell on him to the police."

I said, "I'll do what I can. You're going to be talking to them about the Karek fight. Have you told anyone else about what you heard last night?"

"No."

"But your friend knows."

"He'd never tell. He's never been to the clinic. With all this happening I'm not sure he'll even speak to me again."

"Concealing this kind of information would be bad. I don't recommend lying."

"If they don't ask me, maybe I won't have to tell."

"Not the best policy."

"You won't tell, will you Mr. Mason, please? Mr. Weaver . . . he . . ." He wiped at his eyes. I saw the beginning of several tears. "I get pretty depressed sometimes. I've been better since . . . Well, Mr. Weaver, he saved me. I owe him a lot, everything. He helped me with colleges and scholarships and all kinds of stuff. I could never turn on him. Please don't say anything to the cops."

"It's not my story to tell," I said. I hoped that was true. More teen secrets. Not a good thing.

Larry said, "I figured if I told you, maybe you could, like talk to Mr. Weaver or something. Maybe you could fix stuff. Can you fix this?"

"I don't know. I'll try and use your information to help the situation." What I didn't say was that I intended to confront Lee with this new information at the earliest possible moment.

"Thanks. I appreciate your help."

"I'll do what I can. Try not to let it worry you."

"I'm worried about my dad, too," Larry said.

I thought he should be more worried about the cops. I tried to be reassuring. I said, "Maybe sometime Scott and I can trade coming-out war stories with you. The process of being who you are is seldom easy. This situation is more complicated than anybody would ever want, but you will get through it. Maybe Scott and I could arrange to meet you and your boyfriend. Or meet with your dad. I know we'd do anything to help. You're not alone in this. There are lots of people willing to help." He reached over and gave me a fierce hug. By the time Todd's associate arrived half an hour later, Larry wasn't looking quite so upset.

The associate, Frank Gebott, talked to the four of them. I'd seldom met Frank, but many years ago he and Todd had set up a practice together. If Todd had faith in him, so did I. Parents were called. When the kids and a passel of parents had been assembled, they met. Under Frank's tutelage, the whole aggregation trooped over to the police station. All this waiting, arriving, talking, and deciding took well over an hour. During much of that time, Jan kept up a stream of chatter that would have made Donkey in the movie *Shrek* look like a mute hermit. Thinking about Jan, the fleeting notion struck me that there was never a file cabinet drawer around when you really needed one. I know that's harsh, but the kid was a poster boy for annoying asshole of the year. As an adult he could easily rival Charley Fitch.

9

I wanted to get to the police station to see if I could find out anything about Lee. Todd had told me he thought he would be there for hours, and even then Lee might not be released today.

Before I could leave, a large man in a black business suit swung into the café. He had his hand clutched around Abdel Hakur's forearm. The adult elbowed his way to the front of the order line and leaned against the counter. He slammed his fist down next to the cash register. He just missed a stack of muffins. "Where are these clinic people?"

The teenager on duty stared at him. *Bang* went the fist again.

I walked up. I said hello to Abdel then held out my hand to the adult and told him my name.

He ignored my hand, glared at me, and said, "I know you. You're a teacher at my son's school. You're connected with this clinic?"

I said, "Yes, I am."

"I'm Abdel's father. I tried to find someone to talk to across the street. The police told me no one was there. They said try over here. They told me about the murder. My son went to that clinic for help. That is an outrage. My son is not gay. You people had no right to talk to him. You had no right not to inform me that he went there. I know all about you. You think your teaching job is safe because you've got that lover."

He spoke at full volume. People near us in the café turned to stare. I heard one say loudly, "Who is this homophobic asshole coming into our community?"

Mr. Hakur looked around. The place was crowded and the line to be served was eight deep. Patrons did not look sympathetic. Maybe he was getting the idea that he wasn't in his own personal little fiefdom filled with like-minded bigots.

I said, "May we sit down and discuss this?"

He wasn't quite as loud as he said, "There isn't going to be any discussing. There aren't going to be any more meetings. My son is not gay."

Abdel might have been two thirds his father's size. I give the kid credit: he wrenched his arm out of his father's grasp. He said, "I'm in love with a boy, a Jewish boy. You will not tell me what to do. I'm not like mother who you can bid and command. I'm a man."

The backhand Mr. Hakur used on his kid came so quickly that I didn't have a chance to block it. The kid stumbled backward several feet, knocked over a table. Patrons, cups, and coffee went flying. Abdel fell on his butt. He leapt back up. Tears didn't diminish his angry glower or his flow of profanity.

Several of the dumped-on and pissed-off patrons began to encircle us. The owner of the café hustled in from the back. Gordon Jackson was a large man in his late thirties. He used to wrestle on television. Patrons pointed and complained about a homophobic asshole. Gordon righted the table, mollified the patrons, and approached us.

Mr. Hakur was big, but Gordon towered over him and had a hundred pounds on him. Gordon had a deep, resonant voice. He looked down at Mr. Hakur. Gordon said, "There will be no violence in my café."

"I'll do what I want with my son."

"Not in my café you won't. Nor will you spout homophobic bullshit in here."

I heard shouts from several directions: "Yeah. You tell him."

Hakur looked around again. "I don't have to stay here for this."

"I'm not leaving," Abdel said.

"You will do what I tell you," Hakur said.

Abdel sidled around so that he was behind Gordon and myself. I glanced over my shoulder. The teenager was trembling and crying. The left side of his face was an ugly red.

I asked, "Do you abuse your child often?"

He started to raise his hand to me. I didn't flinch. He was only an inch or so taller than I, and his extra weight looked like it was mostly flab. I presumed I was in better shape than he was. I was certainly in a position to stop him from abusing his kid. Gordon stepped forward. "There's no abuse of anybody in here, ever."

Mr. Hakur looked rebellious, but he shifted from foot to foot, perhaps less sure of himself.

I asked, "Mr. Hakur, how did you know to come here?"

"I have no obligation to respond to you."

Abdel spoke up. "I said I was running in a track meet this morning. He came home early and decided to go. There was no meet. He's more concerned because he made a fool of himself looking for me. He called all of my friends. He thought people were laughing at him. They probably were."

Mr. Hakur said, "I searched his room as is my right. I found a brochure for this clinic and a phone number. I'd had suspicions before. This confirmed them."

Abdel said, "Bullshit suspicions. You're mad because I don't believe in that radical religious shit."

Mr. Hakur raised his hand, but Abdel remained behind us.

Abdel said, "He thinks I'm not masculine enough. I've heard him talking to my brothers. I know how he feels. I'm not ashamed of what I am or of coming to talk to Mr. Mason."

Detectives Lynn Stafford and Jason Abernathy walked in and strode over to the four of us.

"We need to talk to you, Mr. Mason." Nothing in their expressions led me to believe it would be a cheery session of jokes and good times.

"Arrest him," Mr. Hakur said.

"Who are you?" Stafford asked.

"These people at the clinic were trying to corrupt my son."

"Are you accusing someone of molesting your son?" Stafford asked.

"Nobody touched me," Abdel said. "Never at the clinic."

"My son has been to this clinic."

"When?" Stafford asked.

We looked to Abdel. He whispered, "This morning."

His father bellowed, "You stupid shit!" He launched himself at his son. Gordon had to physically restrain the man. Uproar followed.

When calm returned, Gordon permitted the police to use several offices in the back to conduct interviews in. I watched uniformed officers put Hakur and his son in separate rooms. The office I was in had a desk, halogen lamps, several well-worn comfy chairs, and shelves of ledger books.

10

“Friends of yours?” Stafford asked.

“Not likely. How’s Lee?”

“He’s being booked. We found another little problem since then. We need to focus on that.”

If they had a suspect, but were here again only a few hours later, that meant something was up, and I doubted if it was a small thing. And it had something to do with me.

Stafford said, “We found your fingerprints on your filing cabinet.”

“That doesn’t sound odd,” I said. “It was mine. They should be there.”

“They were the only ones,” Stafford said.

“But the killer must have left his.”

“Exactly,” Stafford said.

My stomach did an unpleasant lurch. I know that the one who finds the body, or in this case the first remnant of it, is always at least somewhat of a suspect. When I’d thought about it, I’d assumed there’d be lots of prints on the cabinet. At least five other people used that room as an office and dozens more had reason to use the filing cabinet. That all theirs were gone and mine were present was not a good sign. I certainly never took a dust rag to any surface or part of a piece of furniture. I doubted if any of the teens who performed the custodial tasks were fanatics about scrubbing or polishing. The staff made sure the public areas were reasonably pristine, but the individual offices were up to their tenants. When people shared an office, cleaning tended to be somebody else's job, not yours.

I said, "The killer must have wiped it off."

"Possible," Abernathy said. "Detective Stafford wasn't exactly accurate. We also found one other partial set of prints. They weren't on the handle or near the top of the drawer. We've got two sets, yours and someone else's. Only one other person. The rest of the thing was wiped clean. The place doesn't look like it ever gets touched by a janitor."

"Were they Lee's?" They kept silent. I said, "No, if they were, we'd be having a slightly different discussion. You don't know whose the others are."

Stafford ignored my observation. She said, "A logical conclusion would be that you and an accomplice put them there. Nothing else in the office was wiped clean."

"Another logical conclusion is that while I was reaching to put some files into the drawer this morning, I put them there. Then I found the head and had no notion that it was necessary to wipe up after myself."

Abernathy said, "Possible." His tone gave me no confidence that he was ready to accept such a conclusion.

I brought up my earlier point. "They aren't Lee's?"

"No."

"So there's a third person in your conspiracy theory?"

"That's what we're trying to find out."

"If I wiped it clean, why would I be stupid enough to put my prints back on it? And why wouldn't I have had the sense to make it look like everything had been wiped?"

"You carry around a lot of severed heads?" Abernathy asked.

I glared. They didn't wilt.

Stafford said, "Committing a simple murder would be enough to unnerve a normal person. Hacking someone to death and cutting their head off is the kind of murder that would unnerve anyone except the most demented criminal."

Abernathy said, "There's a small smear of blood on the outside of the filing cabinet. The other prints besides yours were on top of the blood. The blood matches Mr. Fitch's. The prints were put there after the murder. Who else was there with you this morning?"

"There is no logical connection between there being another set of prints and someone else being there with me."

"We don't believe in coincidences," Abernathy said.

Neither did I. Silence ensued.

Abdel had sat next to the filing cabinet. I didn't remember Max getting near it.

If I was uncomfortable with my silence, they looked as if they had all the time in the world. I'd dealt with police before. I could wait, too.

Finally, Abernathy said, "We understand that you and Mr. Weaver have known each other for a long time. You're good friends. He was fired last night. His prints are on the murder weapon. Yours are on the drawer."

"What was the murder weapon? Where was it?"

"Where is not as important as Mr. Weaver's prints being on it."

"But mine weren't, or you'd be booking me like you are him."

"We're not booking you, yet."

"Are you advising me of my rights?"

"We're not arresting you, yet."

I was moving from very uncomfortable to definitely worried. I thought it was just about time to ask for my lawyer. As Todd had told Lee, tell the truth. I hadn't killed anybody. I asked, "Were there other prints on other places where the killer put body parts?"

Abernathy said, "We've got yours at a significant point. The other print on that cabinet was not Mr. Weaver's or anybody else we've talked to so far from the clinic. You're the only one who admits to being there after the murder. Do you know who it was?"

"Maybe it's actually the killer's? Maybe he missed a spot when he was wiping up."

Abernathy said, "He wiped off the cabinet, put the head in, then touched the cabinet again?"

"It could easily have happened that way. He had to close the drawer. If I'm the killer in the scenario you're positing, then that's the way it would have happened."

Stafford asked, "Why use the hand without the cloth he wiped it off with?"

"You just tried to ascribe great nervousness to me because of the horrific nature of the crime. Perhaps your analysis is accurate for the real murderer."

Abernathy said, "We think the killer was calm and collected. He was distributing body parts, catching the blood. There were very few drops around the clinic. There are no other fingerprints on any surface near a body part. Just yours in that one spot."

"I didn't kill anybody. I wasn't there last night. You should be able to get an approximate time of death from the medical examiner."

Stafford said, "The man who was shouting when we came in got his son to admit he was at the clinic. He's not on any of our lists so far. Is he the one?"

"Ask him."

"Why don't you just tell us?"

"It's a minor thing, I suppose, but I don't break trust with teenagers."

Stafford asked, "Even if you could be accused of murder, or of being an accomplice to murder?"

"Why not just ask him?"

11

Abdel and his father were brought in. Abdel took a seat to my left, the farthest from his dad. Abdel wasn't crying, but his hands still shook. He had a lump growing next to his left eye. It was beginning to discolor. The cops asked him several direct questions. They got stubborn silence. When the teenager finally spoke, he said, "I don't want my dad here."

His father said, "I demand to be in the room when my son is questioned."

Abdel said, "I don't want you here."

"The law says a parent has to be present," Mr. Hakur said.

Since Abdel wasn't a suspect, I wasn't sure Mr. Hakur was right.

Stafford said, "We'd like Abdel to tell us his story. It might help us solve the crime."

Hakur whispered, "Are you saying he had something to do with this murder?"

"We just need to hear from him," Stafford said.

I said, "Abdel, I think it would be okay if you told the truth."

Abdel looked from one to another of the adults, his eyes

resting on mine last. He nodded, sniffled, then told an accurate story, leaving out Max. I didn't add anything.

Stafford said, "Why, specifically, did you want to talk to Mr. Mason? Why not just any counselor at the clinic?"

"People trust him. He's openly gay at our school. He's famous. Who else were we going to talk to?"

Neither of the cops made mention of Abdel's slip in saying *we*.

"How'd you know he would be here at an odd hour on a Saturday?"

He gave them the same answer Max had given me earlier.

"You didn't see Mr. Fitch at any time?"

"I don't know who he was. I don't even know what he looked like."

"My son is innocent," Hakur said. "You need to look to these unclean people."

"Shut up," Abernathy said.

"Did you touch the filing cabinet?" Stafford asked.

"I don't remember. I sat next to it. I guess I might have."

Mr. Hakur said, "You sat next to a filing cabinet with a head in the drawer? You stupid fool."

"I am not stupid," Abdel said. "Do you think I have x-ray vision and can see through metal? I'm not the stupid one."

"What you did was get yourself into this mess. If you'd have been at home where you belonged, you wouldn't be here now being questioned by the police."

"Shut up," Abernathy said.

"You can't keep saying that to me."

"Sure, I can," Abernathy said. "And if you annoy me often enough, I may decide to do something about it."

"You're not allowed to be prejudiced against Muslims."

"This isn't prejudice. I've found that being an asshole-blowhard pretty much crosses all national, ethnic, and religious boundaries."

Hakur said, "You just insulted me."

"Yes, I know," Abernathy said.

I said, "Neither Abdel nor I had anything to do with the murder."

Abdel said, "Mr. Mason didn't kill anybody. He just tried to help us."

"Who's us?" Stafford asked.

Abdel gulped.

"You said *we* earlier," Stafford pointed out.

Abdel had blown it. "I won't tell you who my boyfriend is."

Mr. Hakur said, "He's Jewish. Abdel let that slip earlier."

The cops looked at me. "Who was this other person you didn't tell us about?"

I kept quiet.

"You'll be in more trouble if you don't tell us," Stafford said.

I wasn't sure if she was referring to Abdel, me, or both of us.

Abdel said, "I didn't commit murder. My boyfriend didn't. Is Mr. Mason going to be in more trouble?"

"Just tell them," Mr. Hakur said.

"I won't." Abdel was adamant.

Stafford said, "We'll find out who all your friends are. If he's a boyfriend, someone will have noticed who you hang out with. You can't keep this kind of thing quiet. I'm sorry. We really don't want to bring trouble to you, but this is a murder investigation."

I said, "Look at it this way, Abdel. You were afraid your dad would know. He does. That part of the fear is over. This is something else entirely. They need to talk to everybody."

"Just tell them," Mr. Hakur said.

Abdel glared at his father. The teen set his jaw and crossed his arms.

I spoke directly to Mr. Hakur. "Don't you realize that every time you give your son a command, he just gets more stubborn and shuts down? When either the police or I talk, he listens and seems almost cooperative. Doesn't that give you a message of some kind?"

Mr. Hakur looked me full in the face and met my eyes for more than a second. When he finally looked away, he remained silent.

I said, "Abdel, it will help."

Abdel said, "It was Max Bakstein."

They got addresses and said they'd go out to talk to him to confirm Abdel's and my stories.

Before the detectives left, I said, "Have you been to the police station in the past hour?"

"We were at the forensics lab."

"There are some other kids who want to talk to you," I said. "I don't believe Lee killed anybody. They don't either. They heard a quarrel between Billy Karek and Charley Fitch. The two of them threatened to kill each other."

I gave the detectives the kids' names. I said, "They all went over to the police station with their parents and a lawyer. The whole crowd might still be there." I wanted desperately to add, Look how cooperative I'm being. I'm sending tons of witnesses your way to help you with your case. The police didn't pick up on the notion, though, and I had enough dignity and sense to keep my mouth shut.

"We've got a lot of people to talk to," Stafford said. "We've still got Mr. Weaver in custody. Prints on the murder weapon are pretty damning. On the filing cabinet is also bad, just not quite as bad."

The detectives told me in the strictest terms not to leave town. I wondered if the reason they didn't arrest me on the spot was because Abdel had been there that morning. I wasn't sure.

The detectives left. Abdel, Mr. Hakur, and I looked at each other.

"Let's go," Mr. Hakur said.

"I'm not leaving with you," Abdel said.

"And you would go where? No relative of mine will take you in. Nobody takes in other people's kids. You come with me."

I stood up. Mr. Hakur did also. I said, "Mr. Hakur, I'd appreciate it if you were more reasonable."

"You have nothing to do with my family."

I said, "Look at your son's face. He should probably have medical attention. In this state teachers are mandatory reporters of abuse and you just won the prize for the most direct observable abuse seen by a teacher this decade."

"I will do what I want with my son."

"Not bloody likely, you son of a bitch."

"You can't stop me."

Gordon wasn't there, but I was reasonably confident in my ability to keep Mr. Hakur away from Abdel.

I said, "Watch me. You will not do what you want. There are rules and laws. There are probably still half a dozen social workers within call."

"I don't care about your social workers."

"But I do, and you may not have a choice. They might not have much physical power, but the cops aren't far. If Abdel doesn't want to go, he isn't going to go."

"This is kidnapping. I'll call the police."

"They were just here. I'd be happy to have them take pictures of what you did to your son."

Abdel said, "I'm not going."

Mr. Hakur drew himself up very straight and said, "As long as you persist in this, you are not my son."

He walked out.

Abdel said, "I hate him."

I said, "We need to find a place for you to go."

"I can find my own place."

"Where?" I asked.

He sat there. Looked at me. Scratched his head. "I don't know . . . I guess . . . I'm not sure. I have some friends."

"I'd like to avoid dealing with the foster care system. Can you appeal to your mom?"

"I told you this morning, it's my dad who's the problem. My mother is not the solution. Not in my house. My brothers would probably beat me or worse. I can't go home."

I wanted to make sure he was safe, but I was worried about Lee and obviously the police were very interested in what my role was in all this. I needed to take some action before I was arrested. Just because they hadn't, didn't mean they wouldn't.

Gordon, the owner, entered. He said, "You okay?" Gordon was a friend. After coming out publicly, Scott had done one of his first talks to the gay community to a crowd that filled the café and blocked traffic in the streets around it.

I said, "I need a place for Abdel."

"I can watch him for a while. He could even earn a few bucks working in the back."

Abdel said, "I'd like to work in a gay place. It would be okay. I'm going to call Max and tell him what happened. He was going to tell his parents everything. I hope he's okay." Abdel pulled out a cell phone. I wondered how long it would be before his dad pulled the plug on that.

12

Back out in the café Evan Smith, who often shared my office, came up to me. He was in his mid-twenties. The slight roll in his midsection said he'd need to start going to a health club in a year or so. He had a pleasant sense of humor. He said, "Can we talk?"

"Depends. Were you the last one to see Charley Fitch alive?"

He looked confused. "No."

Irene Kang, the receptionist with the glorified title of executive assistant, came out of the back and swept toward the bakery counter.

As she passed us, Smith asked, "What's going on?"

Kang paused next to us. "Who are you?"

Smith said, "I'm one of the volunteers at the clinic."

"I don't remember you."

"I stuffed envelopes for the last several fundraisers."

She lowered her glasses on her nose and glared at him. "I do know you," Kang shrilled. "Charley had it narrowed down to only a few people who could be the reporter who was trying to cause a scandal. He thought you might be the one. He said you asked too many questions."

"What questions aren't there to ask about a place when you newly volunteer?" Smith asked.

"Nobody's going to talk to you. Are you a reporter? If I ask, you have to tell. You can't lie."

Smith said, "Whether I'm a reporter or not, you don't sign my pay check, you rude jerk. I'm sick of putting up with the incessant nastiness from you people. Frankly, I wish you'd eat shit and die."

Kang drew herself up. "Well!" she said. "Well!" Smith glared. Kang said, "You're probably the one who caused all this. Why don't you go chase an ambulance or do whatever it is you people from the gay press do? They arrested the killer."

I said, "I don't believe Lee did it."

Smith said, "I agree."

Kang said, "No journalist is concerned with the truth. They're all out to smear and harm."

"Go away," Smith said.

Kang stomped off.

Smith said, "I am a reporter for the *Gay Tribune* here in Chicago. I heard Lee was arrested. I know you're good friends with him."

"Yes."

"What can you tell me about what's going on? I don't think he's a killer. I like Lee. If we could sit quietly for a few minutes, it might help. Would you mind?"

I hesitated. I was used to reporters because of all the publicity with Scott. That didn't make me like them any better. It didn't make me dislike them immediately either.

"We really need to have a private conversation. I know things about the clinic. Maybe I can help prove Lee didn't do it."

"I never knew you were a reporter. You hid that information. Why should I trust you? I don't know you." I'd had a vague notion that he was a college student.

"You don't need to trust me to listen to me."

An eminently reasonable statement, and one that made me feel just a bit abashed.

"Of course," I said. "I was being silly."

Smith said, "I think there was stuff going on at that clinic that a whole lot of people would commit murder over. None of these staff people are going to talk to me. They barely acknowledged my existence when I volunteered. When I tell them I'm a reporter, they'll react like Kang just did. I'd like to do whatever I can to find out who did it. I'd love to prove it was one of these asshole staffers. At the least, I'd like to prove Lee didn't do it. I'd think you'd want to do the same. Sure, I'd make a name for myself if I found out who did it, but that's not what I'm in it for."

Another reporter dedicated to the cause of truth and right. I've met too many reporters to not keep a healthy heap of cynicism handy when dealing with them.

I said, "Before I answer any questions, I want to know exactly what was going on at the clinic. Why was there a need for an investigation? No bullshit. No holding back."

Smith said, "If you'll respond in kind."

"If what I say doesn't get printed until we find out who killed Charley Fitch."

We agreed. Did I trust him? I wasn't sure. He could give me information. It might help clear Lee and by extension me. I wasn't worried, really, but I wasn't as calm about my being a suspect as I had been before the cops told me about the prints.

Smith said, "How come they arrested Lee?"

"The cops didn't tell the reporters?"

"They didn't express an inclination to confide in me. There's supposed to be a press conference later tonight or early tomorrow morning. I heard a rumor that they found the murder weapon."

"How'd you get the rumor?"

"I was hanging around with a bunch of other reporters. You never know if what you hear around them is useless drivel or real facts. Most often it's something in between. Whatever it is, Lee's in trouble."

I agreed. I said, "I've got to find out more about this clinic, the dirt. I've never paid much attention before. I was just trying to help the kids. I didn't know Charley Fitch personally or intimate details about his life. Did he have a lover? What was he like outside the clinic? Not how he sucked up to donors, but him as a person."

Smith said, "I've been hunting around in his background since I started on this. The owner of my paper doesn't like Snarly Bitch. Snarly tried to buy the paper some years ago. Why he would want to buy it makes no sense. All of us were terrified he'd succeed."

I said, "I heard he heavily funded the clinic."

Smith said, "Actually, that was his family foundation's money. He had a vote in how it would be spent, but it wasn't like he was dictator. But they never turned down what he wanted to do."

"Who inherits his money?"

"I don't know," Smith said. "He didn't have offspring. I don't know if he had a will. I do know he had at least one sibling, a sister. It might go to her or back to the foundation. I only began working on that last a few days ago."

"So what happened with the paper?"

"Snarly tried to get the employees to organize against the owner. Tried to get them to just walk out with all the equipment and everything."

"That sounds odd."

"Wouldn't be the first time that happened in this town. It didn't work. We like the owner. He's a great guy. He works hard. He gives us great benefits. He gives us a lot of latitude. He pays the advertising staff the best rates in town. The more ads they sell, the bigger the percentage they get. They're really motivated. So Snarly Bitch tried to go through a third party. He got somebody to make a bid. Our owner turned it down. We heard Snarly was going to start up his own gay paper, but this town already has several. There isn't room for another. The advertisers wouldn't respond to Snarly. The gay ad budget in this town is limited. Snarly's paper never got off the ground. My boss was willing to do anything to get back at him for trying to sabotage his paper."

"Commit murder?"

Smith gazed at me as if this was a brand-new thought. "He wouldn't do that," Smith said.

"You sure?" I asked.

"We're lovers. I know him. Lots of people didn't like Snarly Bitch."

"Somebody must have liked him. Did he play cards on Saturday night with friends? Did he go to the movies? Did he give razor blades to little babies, kick puppies?"

"I don't know anybody who ever referred to Snarly as a friend. He could have haunted leather dungeons nightly or sat home reading books. Sorry, I don't know."

I wanted to find out. I asked, "What were you investigating?"

Smith said, "Possible embezzlement. Maybe fraud. I talked to Ken Wells. I was working with him. Ken says he didn't notice any problem for the longest time. He was involved in getting the money in. Snarly could schmooze with the best of them, but you had to have the basics intact. Snarly was good at what needed to be done for an event for it to be successful, the right caterer, that kind of stuff. Wells probably wouldn't have noticed anything at all, but he was in New York meeting with some fundraising people there and they were telling him how much they were clearing in terms of percentage of profit on their events. Everything Wells did here was earning less, not always significant amounts less, but less. Like if there was a dinner. Someone in another city might clear eighty-five percent and the clinic would only clear eighty. For a while you can put that down simply to differences in practices, but it kept up."

I asked, "Who actually handles the clinic money?"

Smith said, "Everything is supposed to be accounted for, but in a small group it's tougher to move things around. Wells organized events, but the checks come into the clinic. As far as I can tell the chain of custody was Kang took in the money from whatever fundraiser. She counted it up. Snarly Bitch made the deposits."

"Kang would know if there were any irregularities?"

Smith said, "Kang might have been the cause of them. She might have been doing them without Snarly's knowledge. We'll never be able to tell what Snarly knew. He might have been suspicious of her. They didn't like each other."

I said, "Every time I saw them together, she did nothing but suck up."

"You should have heard him bawl her out."

"I never did."

Smith said, "Her favorite expression was, 'It's not in my job description.' I think he was going to fire her."

"Can you prove that?"

"Not anymore."

"So it was her, not Fitch, who was cheating? If he knew she was cheating, if she was, that might give her a strong motive for murder."

"She might have been cheating. Snarly almost certainly was. Two nights ago I found evidence that there were two sets of books. I found receipts that weren't accounted for in the books that were there. I found different reports of income from the same fundraiser. I uncovered receipts that had obviously been doctored. I couldn't find a second set of books. I'm sure two sets exist."

"Isn't it all just a matter of computer records?" I asked.

"Fitch was being dragged howling and screaming into the twenty-first century. To be fair, the computer upgrades he needed would have cost a lot. They couldn't spare the cash."

"How'd you find this stuff?"

"I volunteered to answer the phones after Kang's nine-to-five stint was done."

"Were you there last night?"

"Yep. While they were having that prom meeting, I had another chance to snoop in Snarly's office. I'd managed to do that in small bits and pieces. Nothing gets locked up too well in that place. I'd been through small sections of his office. I used to offer to do the filing. Kang hated filing. After a while, I figured out which things needed to be filed in Snarly's office. I could get in there fairly regularly. Most of the stuff I hunted through was a waste of time. Some of their record keeping is pretty haphazard."

I asked, "How late were you there last night?"

"I left just before the prom meeting ended."

"Did you know Billy Karek had been there late recently?"

"No."

"Did you know the kids used the basement as a hangout after hours?"

"No. What I did find out was that the board itself was investigating Snarly Bitch."

"They had the nerve to do that?"

"One of the board members hinted about somebody on staff watching the till."

"What were they investigating?"

"The board member wouldn't tell me. I presumed the same thing I was."

"Did you tell the board member what you were investigating?"

"No. He didn't ask. He wasn't confiding in me. I put two and two together. Last night I also found Snarly's personal check book. I know what he makes as the head of the clinic. There were other unaccounted-for deposits. I found a set of deposits into accounts with the clinic's name on it, but which were not part of the official records."

"What did you do with the knowledge?"

"I didn't confront Snarly. I have a single-use camera. I took photo copies of everything. The copy machine at the clinic always jams. I couldn't risk taking things there and having to fight with the damn machine."

He was right about the clinic's copier. The damn thing jammed more frequently than the Kennedy Expressway at rush hour.

Smith was saying, "I need to get the records to my boss and to Ken Wells. We need to have our accountant go over them. I'm sure what I found proves that something criminal was going on."

I asked, "Why would he just leave that kind of thing out where people could find it?"

"He didn't. There's a safe that they keep money in if they don't have time to get to a bank or make deposits. I'm surprised the damn safe didn't fall through the floor. It's heavy and that place could blow over in the next gale. Kang had the combination. It took me a few months to find out where she kept a record of it."

"Do you know who the board's investigator was?"

"No. I wish I did. What did the kids say about Snarly's fight with Karek?"

"That it happened. That they threatened to kill each other."

"Son of a bitch," Smith said. "How often were those kids down there? This wasn't some kind of coincidence?"

"As far as I can tell, they were down there quite often. It was like a haven for them."

Smith said, "Some of those kids were pretty screwed up. That Jan needs a team of therapists."

I said, "I'm afraid he's going to try and hurt himself if he hasn't already. You can't be as perversely and willfully manic as he is without eventually paying a toll. Either you become the star of every musical in your high school and college and go on to a career on the Broadway stage and make enough money to afford all kinds of therapy, or, my guess is, you try to hurt yourself. He desperately needs attention."

Smith agreed. "Are these kids talking to the police?"

"Yeah. There's a lot of coming out to parents. Murder trumps hiding your sexuality."

"Which kids?" Smith asked. "I'd like to talk to them."

I said, "Talking to me is one thing. They confided in me. I got them to talk to the cops. They're going to be talking to their parents about some basic emotional issues. I don't think they need a reporter intruding on that."

Smith said, "I've got a right to get my story."

I said, "What you need to remember is they're kids. Gay kids. You work for a gay paper. I assume you're gay. You need to have some loyalty to them. You need to leave them alone. Do you think their parents are going to want you intruding on their lives?"

"No, but this is a murder investigation."

I said, "But it isn't your investigation, not technically. That's the cops' job."

"Yeah, but Lee is your friend. Don't you want him exonerated?"

"He'll get off. I'm not going to sacrifice some kid's life to get you a headline or to save my ass or a friend's ass. These kids are our trust. We don't break it. Not for any reason. They are not cattle to run over on your rush to fame."

"I'm not a monster," Smith said. His voice was soft. "You talked to them. They might be the key to this."

I said, "They only heard something. That simply means that Karek can't deny anything. Karek is going to be the one with the problem. Not the kids. They should be out of it by this time. My suggestion would be to leave them be. If something comes up with them that's important to the investigation, I'll tell you. I told you this part." I held back what Larry had told me about Lee returning a second time. I wasn't about to reveal the fact that I knew that to anybody but Lee. I hoped he had a good explanation. If he didn't, he could very well be a killer. I just didn't believe that. He was a good man. Who'd left out a big piece of information. I still wanted to trust him. I hoped I was right about him. I'd known him too long to distrust him.

I said, "And I can give you more information. I'm a suspect."

I told him the story.

When I finished, Smith said, "You're in deep shit."

"I didn't kill anybody. I barely knew Fitch. I'm not sure I cared whether he lived or died. Yeah, I helped the clinic employees, but that was using my expertise in a delicate situation. Dealing with him was a seldom thing. What I want to know is, who knew this guy? Did he have friends outside the clinic, or better yet, enemies? Who hated this guy? Who'd want him dead?"

Smith said, "He lived with his sister, who is a lesbian. As far as I've been able to tell, while she's on the clinic board, she never has much to do with the place. She works for one of those groups that finds things wrong with your food and scares you about it. I've seen her give interviews on television. She's intimidating in the way a ten-ton locomotive coming straight at you is intimidating. I wouldn't cross her."

"Maybe Snarly Bitch crossed her. Where they close?"

"I don't know."

I decided to try to pay her a visit. Daisy Tajeda had said she knew her. I'd try asking her for an introduction.

13

I was beginning to think about lunch.

Max Bakstein strode into the café. He was in the company of a smiling bear of a man, round and bearded. Max saw me and nodded. The two of them joined me. We all got coffee.

Max introduced his dad. Max wore a bulky black turtleneck sweater and tight blue jeans.

Mr. Bakstein said, "You're at that clinic." His voice was deep and rumbly.

I nodded.

"I didn't know Max was going there. I'm not opposed to being open-minded. He has to learn about many different things in this world. I'm glad he had a chance to talk to someone."

The man sounded unctuous and smarmy, the opposite of what Max had described.

"You're okay with him being gay?"

The suave slipped for an instant as he said, "My son is not gay."

Max looked very pale.

"I've talked to him and talked to him. He knows better. We

communicate, Max and me. We always have. We do men things together. He's not gay."

I looked at Max. He fiddled with the sleeves of his sweater. I thought the thing was at least three sizes too big for him.

"Why are you here?" I asked.

"I want to be sure there are no misunderstandings. I want to be sure that anyone connected with the clinic knows they don't need to talk to my son. We'll take care of that in my family. We don't need to burden the clinic staff with problems that don't exist. Max isn't gay."

Maybe if he said it enough times, he'd convince himself.

I said, "That isn't quite the same story I heard from Max this morning."

"Well, really, he's a changeable teenager. What do they know?"

I swallowed my standard answer to this comment—more than we'd like to admit, and less than teenagers think.

Max leaned over and put his elbows on his knees and his hands on his head. His sleeves of his sweater gathered at his elbows. I saw several deep bruises.

I said, "Max, where'd you get those?"

His father reached to move the sweater up. Max jerked his arm away. He looked at me. He whispered, "Help me." Max reached up and moved the collar of his sweater away from his neck. He had purple welts and bruises around his throat. The kind hands leave when someone is trying to strangle you.

Mr. Bakstein said, "We don't need any help. Everything is fine."

Smarmy like Bakstein or shouting like Hakur, the effect was the same. The kids were in extremis.

I said, "Max, who did this?"

All three of us knew, but Max had to say it. Max had to make the accusation. I could offer to have Mr. Bakstein arrested and investigated on what I saw, but Max had to speak.

Max dissolved in tears and whispered, "He did it. He did it. He did it."

Mr. Bakstein stood up. "We're going to leave. This is so traumatic for my son. He hurt himself. That's all those are."

"No," Max muttered. "No. It was you."

I said, "I'm calling the police." I took out my cell phone.

"You're calling nobody." He reached across the table. His meaty hand clutched my right arm. All his smarmy suave was gone in an instant.

I'd had just about enough. I took my left palm and jammed it up and in, pushing his nose back and up. He bellowed, loosed his grip on my arm, flopped backwards, grabbed his nose, and shook his head back and forth.

His nose might have been broken, but not his spirit. Seconds later he hurtled toward me over the table. I turned. He missed. As he passed, I picked up the back of his jacket and his belt and, with the help of his momentum, pitched him to the floor. Crockery, furniture, and patrons went flying. He lay there moaning.

Gordon came out. He asked, "Is there anybody you're not at war with today?"

"There must be someone left on the planet, but not in this time zone."

"You need help?"

"Just another homophobe biting the dust."

Several of the patrons had helped Mr. Bakstein to his feet.

"He attacked me," Mr. Bakstein said. "You all saw it."

Max held out his arms. The bruises showed vividly. "You've beaten me black and blue for the last time. I'm never going anywhere near you again. Gay kids don't have to put up with this."

The patrons who'd been helping Bakstein a moment ago saw the marks. They quickly moved away from him. Mr. Bakstein swayed from side to side. He clutched a table to keep from falling.

"I will press charges," Max said. "I will."

Bakstein said, "Never come back to my house." He left. Max watched him go. When the door closed, he began to blubber. I had another sobbing teenager on my hands. At this rate I might be able to declare myself in charge of the weepiest teens on the planet. Max hugged me tight. I patted his back until he calmed down. Between snuffles and tears, he said, "I am such a coward. I just caved in. He found out I hadn't gone to Abdel's when Mr. Hakur called. He was waiting for me when I got home. I'm not brave. I told him where I'd been. I'm such a coward. I couldn't stand up for the guy I loved. I am such a shit. I've fucked everything up."

I looked up and saw Abdel. He saw us and loped over. The two boys clutched each other in a fierce embrace. Abdel added his tears. A little more dampness and we'd have more water than the characters had to deal with in the movie *The Perfect Storm*.

"What's wrong?" Max asked. "What are you doing here?" They untangled themselves from the intense embrace. They sat holding hands. Max put one leg over Abdel's knee.

Abdel told him about his dad.

"He was here?" Max asked.

"Yes. He threw me out. I don't even have a change of clothes."

Max said, "I'm not sure where I'm going to get any stuff. I don't have access to money. Before we got here, my dad said he'd take away my college fund. My mom asked what she'd done wrong. She was worse than my dad. She tried to pile guilt upon guilt. I hated her reaction more than my dad's. I can understand getting hit. I can deal with that. Her bullshit is worse. They both wanted to know how I could throw my life away. I told them Abdel was Muslim. I just told them everything including about using the clinic." Max looked more sad then defiant. All his bluster of the morning was long gone.

"Have you talked to the police?" I asked.

"No," Max said. "About my dad?"

"That's one thing we'll have to handle," I said.

"Abdel told me about the murder when he called. My dad had heard a news report about the killing here. I think that's partly why he was so angry."

I said, "The police are going to want to talk to you about it."

"Why?"

Abdel said, "We were there. They think Mr. Mason might have had something to do with it."

Max said, "That's stupid. I'll talk to them." A little of his earlier unrealistic ego strength resurfaced. He spoke with all the confidence of a blissfully illogical teenager.

"I'm more worried about you two right now," I said. "I don't think either of you can go home."

Max said, "I didn't get thrown out until I got here. At home the whole scene was emotional dynamite. They forbid me to ever see Abdel again. They forbid me to date anybody. We went at it for two hours. You called near the end of the whole thing. It was nuts. What are we going to do?"

I said, "First, we're going to eat lunch. Then we've got to find some place for the two of you to stay."

Max said, "I wish we had a place to go to together. Even if I could I wouldn't go back to my parents' prison."

Abdel said, "I called several of my friends. A few of them said maybe, but they'd have to talk to their parents. I'm not sure anybody's going to take both of us. My friend Mike's parents are cool. I could stay at his house tonight."

I said, "I need to talk to Mike's parents."

I called. I explained what was going on. They wanted nothing to do with the situation. I expected most parents might have the same reaction. As we tried to figure out what to do, I bought us some lunch. Max and Abdel spent the time dreaming up strategies each more wildly unrealistic than the last.

Daisy Tajeda walked in. She and I moved a few feet away from Max and Abdel. I filled her in about the two teenagers.

She said, "I can handle it. I can find them a place to stay. Possibly we can find someone in their community who knows them who can handle them temporarily. I will not let these kids rot in a hostile foster system."

"Their dads have to be reported for physical abuse." I gave her the details about what I'd seen.

"Bruises and direct observation. Those two are toast. Taking care of this will get my mind off the horror of the past few hours. Helping somebody will do that."

"Max needs to talk to the cops, too."

"I'll make sure everything goes smoothly."

I brought her over to introduce them. She shook their hands. I explained that she was a social worker from the clinic and knew how to help. The kids looked reasonably relieved. Their last scheme had been that they would go to California where it was warm and sleep on the beach.

As they were leaving, I managed to get Tajeda to one side. I asked her if anyone had said anything significant after I left the clinic group.

"Nobody confessed to murder, if that's what you're asking. It's all confusion and chaos."

I said, "I'd like to talk to Charley's sister. Earlier you mentioned you knew her. Could you get me an introduction? I've got to try and clear Lee. I think she can give me information."

"She might not be willing to talk at this moment."

"Will you give it a try? I know you like Lee. I know you don't think he did it. We've got to help him."

She agreed to try and set up a meeting. She left with the teenagers. I went to find out what was happening with Lee.

14

They had taken him to the Area Three police station. In Chicago they have police districts staffed with beat cops. Those handle minor crimes. The Areas cover homicides and major felonies. With enough grudging rudeness to make Charley Fitch proud, the cop on the desk informed me that Lee was inside. No other data passed the cop's lips. I sat down to wait. I tried not to think about the hideous face in the filing cabinet.

About half an hour later a heavyset, balding man walked up to the desk and asked for Lee. They didn't tell him any more than they had me. I walked up to the man and introduced myself.

He was Walter Truby, the chairman of the clinic's board of directors. In real life, I'd heard he owned a used car dealership in the Northshore suburbs. It was the kind of place that advertised itself as having pre-owned luxury vehicles. He said, "I know you. You found the head. That must have been awful. How are you?"

"The more I think and talk about it, the less pleasant it becomes."

He nodded. Walter Truby was the kind of guy who kept his hair longer on top to try and cover an expanding bald spot. At least his head was still attached to the rest of him. He said, "Your lover's that baseball player. Everybody thinks that is so hot. Everybody is so envious and jealous. I hope I'm not giving offense."

I muttered, "It's okay."

He wasn't the first man or woman to say this to me, my sister having been among the first women. To me, Scott's looks were kind of like frosting on a cake. I presume we were like most successful relationships: it was the depths within that made the difference. An all-frosting diet would probably be a bad thing—although it might depend on how much chocolate was in it.

"We were hoping when you volunteered that we'd be able to get some big donations from him." I had no intention of discussing anything to do with cash at this moment, but I was a little startled at his willingness to be that honest.

I said, "I'm worried about Lee."

Truby turned a little red. "I'm sorry for being crass. This has been an awful day. Charley Fitch is dead. Lee's been arrested. This is so awful."

I mumbled agreement.

He ran his hands across his balding pate as if to check how many hairs were left at the moment. He continued, "What's the board going to do? Are the members of the board going to be held responsible for all this? I didn't join the board to get involved in this kind of thing."

"Responsible for the murder? Responsible for the arrest? Responsible for how rude Charley Fitch was?"

"Just everything. I've never had the slightest connection to a murder. I've never even gotten a parking ticket. Now my name is going to be in the paper. I'm involved with this horrible mess. That's terrible. This isn't the way it is supposed to be."

Once again I was struck by the lack of sorrow over Charley Fitch being dead.

I said, "Times like this are tough."

"How can you be so calm? You found that thing."

"I'm worried about Lee right now. I haven't had time to worry about myself. I will."

"Do you think Lee did it?"

"No. I've known him since he was in high school. He's a good man."

"I was told you were friends. He's the best counselor at the clinic. Kids have faith in him. The board knows what a hard worker he is. We wish they all were like him."

"It's not really my business," I said, "and it's an awful time, but I've heard all kinds of nasty things about Charley, not just today but ever since I volunteered. Why didn't the board get rid of him?"

"I never referred to him as 'Snarly Bitch.' I'd heard the nickname. I thought it was odious. The board wasn't happy about it." He took a deep breath. "We didn't get rid of him because we thought he was doing a good job." He shrugged. "It was also a matter of cash. Pure and simple—he had lots of it. And he had a lot of the people intimidated. He's been involved in the community for ages, and he founded the damn clinic. He knows powerful people. The wealthiest bar owners support him. Charley was out there working before most of us dared to come out of the closet. People who didn't have to deal with him as their boss respected him. People he sucked up to liked him. You should have seen him at fundraisers. He knew how to work a crowd. He was charm personified. If he had malcontents working at the clinic, there were other jobs they could get."

"I had heard he sucked up to big donors."

"You say that as if it was a bad thing. How was he supposed to act toward big donors? I wouldn't want him to act any differently. How did he treat you?"

"Pretty okay. Even when I went and talked to him about his style of management, he wasn't all that hostile."

"Money. He knew you and your lover might be a source of big bucks. We all know your lover supports lots of gay causes. Charley might have thought he could at least latch onto your lover as a draw for a fundraiser. We heard about when you went in to talk to him representing the employees. Even though you didn't work at the clinic often, people trusted you. That kind of word gets around. It's valuable to have someone like that on the staff."

I didn't bother to tell him I didn't think it was a matter of trust that I was the spokesperson. It was more like enlightened self-interest on the part of the other staffers. If I was the one sticking my neck out, the rest of them didn't have to.

I said, "I was just trying to help out."

"I don't know why the people he worked for couldn't get along with him better."

"Pardon?"

"People on the staff just never seemed to get the idea. This is a service-based organization with a limited budget. Everyone has to pitch in. Charley did the best he could with a bunch of prima donnas."

"They thought he was a jerk."

"Not all of them, and the board didn't see it that way, most of the time."

"Besides disliking the boss, the employees were always at each other's throats. How could the board not see that? Do you mean they did see him as an asshole some of the time?"

"The board seldom heard about any dissent. Remember, we got all our reports from him. The employees never brought their complaints directly to us. Charley would report that everything was fine. We might have heard rumors. Every organization has problems. He was a boss. All bosses get criticized. None of them are perfect. If every boss with a discontented employee was fired, there'd be no bosses."

"I've worked with a lot of administrators. Charley seemed to deserve the employees' dislike more than most. He seemed to create a lot of his own problems."

"I wish employee relations were the only problems Charley had." He glanced around nervously. "There were big problems at the clinic."

"What was wrong?"

Truby sighed. "I wish you were willing to take on the job as temporary director. It would put a known face on the organization. A neutral face, one that hasn't been caught up in intracommunity fights. You'd have to be aware of these things if you did. I realize you turned down our request, but maybe if you saw how vital it was to the community. I'm so worried. The board would like to make you the next director. I know right this minute might be a terrible time to talk about this, but we've got to look out for the clinic's future, the lives of these kids. Maybe it's crass to bring it up now, but your lover is rich. Your presence might make a big difference."

"I can't imagine taking the job."

"Will you at least listen? I don't know who to turn to."

"I won't make any promises."

"I can say this much. It was money. It always comes down to money. You've heard about the scandals with gay fundraising on both coasts?"

"Yes."

"Well, we've had somebody investigating here. We had a ringer on the staff. We were trying to find out what was going on."

"Why not investigate the rumors about him being a lousy boss?"

"Him having poor people skills wasn't our problem. Money being missing would be."

"Charley was raiding the till?" Were they looking for the same money as Smith? Should I tell him about the other investigation? I wasn't sure which of these people to trust, or if I owed much loyalty to any of them.

"Charley *might* have been raiding the till. Money was disappearing. We'd ordered an independent audit."

"Who was doing that?"

"One of the volunteers. I can't give you his name."

"Who else knew about this?"

"Only the board and our mole in the organization. Charley didn't even know about him. The board is ultimately responsible for financial management. I've been saying for years that the board had to be more hands-on in watching how funds were managed, both income and expenditures. I've also thought we should gear ourselves so we'd be less dependent on one major source of funding. Too late for that now. Charley dealt with all the money. He knew every aspect of the operation."

"Is anyone really that indispensable?"

"He might have been, but his money wasn't. I find it hard to believe he wouldn't know about mismanagement. And if he knew, then there may be criminal charges to be filed. Do they file charges against dead people?" He shrugged. "The heart of the matter is nobody on the board was willing to go to jail or get our butts sued because of financial mismanagement. The local gay press had gotten a whiff of something wrong, despite our strongest efforts to keep a lid on it. They had sent someone sniffing around. It was one of the volunteers. Charley knew about that. He watched the volunteers carefully, but neither he nor anyone else could figure out who it was. A few of the other board members thought it might have been you."

Or maybe Charley Fitch did find out who one or the other of the investigators was and confronted him, a confrontation that had gone horribly wrong.

I said, "I've never worked for the gay papers. Since Charley used so much of his own money, maybe he was simply taking from himself. Then again, why would he have to steal? He could just give less of his money."

"It wasn't his money. It was his family's. There could be a huge scandal. This death makes questionable finances more awful. The killing is going to harm the clinic. It can't help but generate negative publicity. And it was a terrible way to die. Who would do such a killing? And in that awful way? Can you imagine carrying a head around?"

"No." Not since the last performance I'd seen of Macbeth in Stratford, Ontario, had I even thought about carrying a head around. It's not the kind of image that comes readily to mind: mom, apple pie, Disney, severed head—doesn't have the down-home kind of ring to it you'd hope for. I said, "But nobody had any proof?"

"We didn't have any. We never found out which of the volunteers was from the gay paper."

I didn't bother to tell him that I knew who it was and that I had talked to him not more than a few hours before. I felt only a small pang of guilt for not adding my knowledge to his.

He was saying, "We get so many volunteers from the community. Sloan Hastern was in charge of that part of the operation. He wasn't as cooperative with the board as he should have been. Charley was eager to get someone new in that position. No, our spy was auditing the accounts at odd moments when he could get a chance."

"Was he there last night?" I asked.

"I presume so. He was supposed to gauge his schedule carefully. That's what was taking the investigation so long. Charley sometimes worked ten- and twelve-hour days, and when he wasn't around that Irene Kang person hovered like a vulture. The best times for him to look were when they had those staff meetings. He knew he'd have time then."

"Was your guy there last night?" This time I added impatience and insistence to my tone.

Truby hesitated then said, "I talked to him. He says he didn't see or hear anything. I thought mentioning his presence would look suspicious to the police. We don't want them to know there was any kind of scandal."

Obviously he didn't want to give me the name. So much for trust. I said, "The police will want to know if he found something wrong with the books or even saw or heard anything. They've got to be told if he was there. I'm not sure it's a very good idea to try and conceal evidence from the police. Do you really think you're going to be able to keep that kind of thing from them?" I knew I was a hypocrite after a fashion on this. I hadn't told about Abdel and Max being there.

"Public knowledge of an unofficial audit will make the whole clinic look bad. We can't afford that."

"Don't you think having someone horribly murdered makes the operation look bad?"

"Well sure, I suppose, but not in the same way. I mean one person killed someone. Even if they worked for the clinic, it's one person. I'm sure the auditor wouldn't have committed murder."

"How are you so sure?" I asked.

"I've known him for years. He's a good friend."

"Friends can do some pretty awful stuff."

"He didn't. You believe in Lee's innocence. I trust the auditor."

"Why did the auditor have to be a volunteer as well?"

Truby said, "If he ever got caught, he might be able to make a plausible excuse for being around."

"Why not just tell Charley there was going to be an audit? Why the extra secrecy?"

"Every time any member of the board ever suggested the slightest change to Charley, he'd go nuts. It wasn't worth the hassle. Plus, we're not a public company. If we found out something embarrassing, we could keep it quiet."

"You're not really a private company. You solicit donations from the public. People want to know what's happening to their money."

Truby said, "I know. And we give excellent quarterly statements. It's the best we can do."

"Maybe someone on the board tipped off Charley that he was being investigated."

"I've thought about that. I'm afraid it's possible. We had a tremendous fight about whether we should permit the audit. We never took a formal vote. We couldn't have anyway. He was at all the meetings and his sister is on the board."

"Some of you were trying to cover your asses."

"Yes. My personal lawyer was insistent that something had to be done. On the other hand nobody wanted to offend Charley. Even with us he could be short-tempered."

"Then why didn't you fire his rude ass?"

"We couldn't. We just couldn't. He could just pull his family's funding. That would take care of that. Plus, he has a lot of supporters on the board. I wasn't about to go against them. Some of them are my friends. I've known these people for years, but Charley worked with some of them for more than three decades. It's all terribly incestuous. Those activists from the Sixties and Seventies are now in positions of power in organizations. They aren't about to let anything threaten that."

"Doesn't anybody just believe in doing a good job, doing the right thing?"

"They all have such different definitions of what the right thing is."

I said, "At some point in an organization, someone's got to take responsibility."

"We were trying to. The board was concerned. After that

embarrassment on *News Forum*, several of us tried to get the board to at least discuss Charley's behavior. Frankly, I thought that blow-up with Billy Karek would cost Charley at least some of his support. I was wrong. People saw him as a put-upon martyr. His supporters rallied around him and donations poured in. Nothing ever seemed to touch that man."

"That chair almost did."

"Maybe it would have helped." He shook his head. "No one thought death would happen. But it has." He sighed. "I wonder if the police have talked to Karek."

I said, "I'm sure they will. If they didn't have firsthand knowledge of the incident, I'm sure someone would have told all about it when they asked if Charley had any enemies."

"It's just that he had so many."

"What was the deal with him and Karek?"

"Charley feuded with all the homocons. Not just those in town, but around the country as well."

"Who else in town?" I asked.

"Gosh, I'm not sure. I knew both him and Karek. I run with the political left and right. I try not to take sides. I try to get along with everybody."

"What is Karek like?"

"He has far fewer rough edges than Charley. He went to Yale for his college degree. He liked to let people know he graduated *summa cum laude*. Hell, I graduated from Harvard, but Karek felt the need to mention his academic credentials."

"Where'd Charley graduate from?"

"He didn't. He always felt people were looking down on him for that."

I said, "Maybe he resented those people who did graduate. Maybe that's why he was rude to them."

"I couldn't tell you about that."

"Can you get me an introduction to Karek?"

"Sure."

"I'd like to talk to him about Charley, get some background, see who else had personal animosities toward him."

"I don't think Karek was angry at Charley. I could be wrong. I think their fights were political, not personal."

Sure sounded personal to me.

I asked, "Did you know teens were using the basement as a hangout?"

"What! Really?"

"Yep."

Truby shook his head. "We could get sued for that, too."

"I don't see how."

Truby said, "If they were unsupervised, and something happened, it might be negligence. What if somebody got pregnant?"

"It's a gay clinic," I said.

"Or diseases?"

"You don't teach safe sex?"

"These are horny teenagers."

I knew the type. I said, "It strikes me as more breaking and entering than the responsibility of the board."

"That's mostly what the responsibility of the board seemed to be, to worry about whether some action or another would get us sued. Or some lack of action getting us into hot water. Dealing with gay teens is a dicey business in the first place. Everybody is always suspicious that you're 'recruiting' or 'endorsing the homosexual lifestyle' or molesting them. Half the time it seemed like the board was running from one fear to another. I wish I hadn't gotten involved." The plaint of every single person who I knew who'd ever volunteered for a gay group. If mismanagement and confusion or lack of focus on the part of the organization didn't do the volunteer in, then attending a few meetings did.

He slapped his hands on his thighs. "I can't stay any

longer. When you know what's happened to Lee, will you give me a call?"

I didn't want to be this guy's messenger boy, but I couldn't think of a way to gracefully refuse. I said, "Depending on what his lawyer says, I'll do my best. You might want to try and contact him yourself." And I wanted him to help me get in touch with Karek. "And you'll give Karek a call?"

"As soon as I get home."

15

An hour and a half passed before Todd came out to talk to me. I spent the time making phone calls. Thoughts filled with the image of the severed head caused bits of nausea to appear in my throat at unpleasantly frequent intervals. I tried to get in touch with Lee's lover several times. Scott and I had attended social events with them occasionally. I got no answer. I called Scott. He was still in his hotel room in Los Angeles.

He was very concerned. "Do you want me to fly back today?" he asked.

"I think I'm okay. I know I will be eventually. It's when the thoughts come unbidden that it's worst. It doesn't help that I've got nothing to distract me here in the police station. I don't want to leave and then have Todd come out. I'm not sure they'd deliver my messages if I asked them to."

"Call Todd's cell phone."

"I bothered him once. It's not an emergency. I'd rather wait."

"Maybe you should call someone to come sit with you. I wish I was there."

"I do, too. You're scheduled to pitch tomorrow. There's nothing you could do here."

"I could be with you."

"And that would be enough, but the phone is okay for now. Hearing your voice helps. I found the head and that's awful, but it's not a member of your family or mine. He was little more than an acquaintance."

I asked about the trip so far, places he'd gone to eat. "You really want to hear about this?" he asked.

"I'd rather have a minute-by-minute account of the slightest thing you've done. Anything rather than think about that thing."

We talked for quite a while. When we finished, I tried again to get in touch with Lee's lover. Dustin Larkin and Lee had met in college. They'd dated and finally moved in together two years ago. This time he answered.

Dustin was shocked and promised to get to the police station as soon as he could.

Todd emerged about ten minutes after I talked to Dustin. He said, "Your young friend is in deep shit."

"I know," I said. "They found his fingerprints on the murder weapon. The cops said so when they told me they had my prints and only mine on the file drawer that had the head."

"Hell, I'd arrest you for that."

"It took them a few minutes to add that they had someone else's, too. Turned out it was probably one of the kid's, Abdel Hakur's, on the damn file drawer."

"Whose presence you didn't tell the police about."

"Which they now know."

"My expert legal advice is don't find any more bodies until this gets sorted out."

"I'm willing to agree to that."

"Good."

Todd explained that he'd spent most of the past couple

hours trying to get Lee to shut up. "He doesn't listen. He thinks the truth is going to make him free."

"You told him to tell the truth."

"There's a difference between essential facts and an entire life story told in the most lurid and unflattering light. If I hadn't been there, he might have talked about every fight he ever had with Charley Fitch. Probably confessed to every unsolved murder in this jurisdiction since 1837. Why can't they ever just shut up?"

"Lee is a good man. I've known him a long time. He's been through a lot, but he is not violent. He overcame the same things a lot of gay guys did as a kid. I trust him."

"Good for you. The police don't. The murder weapon was in his office. It was an ax from a fire truck. He claimed it was a gift. You know anything about an ax?"

"Yeah. I've seen it. It *was* a gift."

"An ax? What a moronic gift."

"It wasn't moronic until today. One of the first teenagers Lee helped at the clinic went on to become a fireman. At one of the first fires the kid responded to, he used an ax to break into a burning building. He saved the lives of three children under the age of seven. The fireman felt Lee had saved his life. He gave Lee the ax as a remembrance. Since the ax was Lee's, it would make sense that his fingerprints are on it." Lee had saved the fireman's life, and the guy had wanted to give Lee something symbolic of life being saved. Lee kept it on the wall a behind his desk along with a citation from the mayor and a letter from the fireman.

Todd said, "Well, it's also got a boatload of blood on it now. There's little doubt it's going to be the dead man's."

"Any fingerprints in the blood?" I asked.

"Not a one."

I said, "The killer put it back in Lee's office?"

"For Lee's sake, I presume so."

I asked, "It had to be a weapon of convenience, a spur-of-the-moment crime. Does a killer leave home and conveniently pick up an ax? Does he say to himself, 'I think I'll do some dismembering today'? Or 'I've got a lot of hacking up of dead bodies to do today, better remember the ax'? Does he carry his lunch in his other hand?"

"Do ax murderers eat lunch?"

"We could ask Lizzie Borden."

"She's dead."

"If Lee was the killer, why would he put it back in his own office? It's not that difficult to take a murder weapon and drop it into a distant trash can or flip it off a bridge into the Chicago River. Hell, even one of those overpasses along the lake between the lagoons and the open water would do. Plenty of opportunity all over to get rid of the thing. Only someone who wanted to implicate Lee would put it back in his office."

Todd said, "Maybe Lee thought it would be suspicious if it was missing."

"It would be more suspicious hanging on his wall covered in blood. Lee isn't stupid. He'd have had the brains to wipe off blood and fingerprints."

"He wasn't displaying great levels of intelligence when I was talking to him."

"He's just been accused of murder. How many of your clients are accused of murder?"

"Very few. Unconnected to you, even fewer. The cops may say they're keeping an open mind and covering all angles. I don't believe that. They think Lee is their killer, and I'm sure they'll try to interpret every new fact in that light."

If there was a gloomy angle to take on a case, Todd would take it. His view of cops was negative but his opinion of his clients was usually even lower. His suspicion of both sides came from his deep distrust of the human race in general. He often said that he thought "one strike" for felons was plenty. Despite his gloomy outlook and his jaded view of his clients, he was an excellent lawyer. Lee would get the very best representation.

I said, "We couldn't dare hope they'll find any other fingerprints on the ax?"

"They'll check it," Todd said. "They have Lee's. It's his ax. It's covered in blood."

"He kept it sharpened?" I asked.

"Sharp enough."

I said, "Another thing the killer had to do: remember to wear gloves in case he decided to hack someone to death. I wonder where on the ax they found the prints."

"*Where* isn't going to help Lee."

"But if the killer wiped the haft only where he touched it then . . ."

"A print is a print," Todd said.

"Are you going to be able to get him out on bail?"

"I don't know. This is going to take quite a bit longer. You don't need to stay."

"I helped Lee in high school. I'm not going to abandon him now. His lover is going to be here any minute. I want to talk to him. I'll stay with him if he wants me to."

Todd shrugged. "I've warned you about the road to hell."

"You can't leave someone alone who's been told his lover's been arrested on a possible murder charge."

"I suppose. You'd be the one to know more about that than I. Don't let the boyfriend talk to the police. Did all these people really hate the dead guy?"

"You never heard of Charley Fitch, or as most of the people who worked for him called him, Snarly Bitch?"

"I don't read the gay papers. I don't follow gay community gossip. I have enough to do to keep up with information directly related to my life."

"They hated the man with a passion. I didn't like him. Not many people did. When they find out who did it, a lot of the people who worked for him might want to give the killer a medal. If the jury has one person on it who was abused by a boss, they'll never convict."

Todd said, "That assumes someone in the office did the killing." He left and returned to his client.

Dustin, Lee's lover, arrived about fifteen minutes later. I intercepted him before he asked at the admitting desk about Lee.

"What is going on?" Dustin asked.

I told him. Dustin was in his late twenties, as was Lee. He was much taller and heftier than Lee. He tended to affect leather outfits at parties. Perhaps in the privacy of their home, they indulged in S-and-M games. If they did, I doubted if it would be a good idea to blab this information to the police. S-and-M games at home would easily give the police the idea that Lee was prone to violence. I'd never seen any master/slave activity between them. Then again, I'd never asked. I wasn't interested in their private sexual practices. Nor did I think that private S-and-M activity between adults gave any indication about the practitioners' proclivity for inflicting their predilection outside the home.

When I finished he whispered, "Somebody really cut his head off?"

"Yep."

He put his hand on my arm. "Are you okay?"

"Yeah, thanks. I'm more worried about Lee right now." And I wanted to talk to the son of a bitch about his return visit to the clinic. That thought nagged at me, second only to finding the head in the dismay category, but leading in the frustration and irritation sweepstakes. I told him everything I knew so far.

When I finished, Dustin said, "I know he didn't do it. Lee is the most gentle man on the planet. He's always caring. He's always the quietest one in a group. We almost never fight. He always wants to work things out. He gives in a lot of the time just to keep the peace. He hates fighting, but he does want to talk and talk. He sticks to his guns about that. He says we have to communicate to make the relationship better. I know he's right, but sometimes I wish he'd just shut up."

"He exploded last night at his boss."

"That is so not him."

"How was he when he got home?" I'd seen tears of rage and frustration ten years ago, but Lee had never struck out at his antagonists.

Dustin said, "I was exhausted. I'd had three hours of overtime at work. I was asleep when he got home." He was a welder and worked long hours. There were a few in the gay community who looked down on his profession as a trade, and a sweaty one at that. There was another faction who thought it was terribly butch. I figured it was his job. It wasn't any of my business whether he was happy or not in it or whether it met some snobbish queen's expectations of what a gay person should do or if he was the epitome of a wet dream for the leather-lust faction.

Dustin said, "Funny thing. He was proud of that ax. I guess when you're a social worker, you don't always get feedback that things you're doing make a difference in a person's life, a positive difference. The guy was one of his first clients."

"But he hated Fitch."

"So did I. Didn't everybody? I want to be first in line to congratulate the killer. I remember clearly a confrontation with Snarly Bitch once a few weeks after Lee started at the clinic."

"What happened?"

"It was so stupid. I'd come to pick Lee up. I walked up to the receptionist at the clinic and asked for him. The receptionist, that Kang person, got all huffy and rude. I'd come straight from work. I'd been finishing a major project that afternoon. I guess she wasn't interested in grime and sweat as the signs of a legitimate occupation. I probably didn't look rich enough to please her. Snarly Bitch was standing several feet away. First, he told me this was a youth services clinic, and I was obviously too old. I told him I wasn't there to use the clinic. He said that he hoped I wasn't there for any kind of personal business with any of the staff. After the secretary being condescending, his attitude pissed me off. What he was saying was nasty enough, but the tone he was using was deliberately insulting. It was as if he wanted to make sure I was aware that he was older and more sophisticated than me, and I was some snot-nosed interloper, and a dirty one at that. He demanded to know if this was something personal. I remember exactly what I said to him: 'You are not my boss. You do not sign my paycheck. Fuck you, go to hell, drop dead.' He did neither of those last two things. He told me to get out. Lee walked in at that moment. Snarly got mean toward Lee, told him to keep his personal life out of the office. Lee was conciliatory, like he always is. I wish he'd stand up for himself more. I guess I understood. It was a new job. He really couldn't do much. Snarly Bitch was such a shit. Many's the time I met Lee and some of the people from that clinic for a drink after work. They couldn't stop complaining about the guy. Lee and I even got our hands on a copy of the tape of the fight on *News Forum*. We'd show it at parties. We began to run it backwards and forwards. Backwards without the sound was even funnier than forward with the sound. Lee and I worked out a routine where we shouted out the lines. Over time we added new ones or altered the old ones slightly. We could keep the thing going for half an hour. Anybody who knew Snarly Bitch even slightly would roar with laughter. It was a lot of fun."

I guess that depended on your definition of *fun*.

Dustin continued, "It got to the point where Lee and I had a system of signals if I was going to meet him at work. I'd call just beforehand. If the coast was clear, I'd come into the clinic. If not, I'd meet him on the corner of Addison and Monclair."

I said, "I didn't think a lot of the clinic workers socialized very much. Most of them seemed to be at each other's throats."

"There were three or four who were kind of close. Lee said he invited you once or twice."

I remembered him asking. I hadn't been much interested in socializing with the bunch from work. "I never went."

"It wasn't always the same ones who went out drinking. There were a few good people, but there were a whole lot of rats in that ship. Then there were the shifting alliances, the backbiting, the double dealing, the sophomoric intrigues, just all kinds of stupid shit. Didn't you see it all?"

"As little as possible. I kept to myself, stayed in the back, had as little contact with the rest of them as I could."

"But they got you to represent them."

"That might have more to do with a fatal flaw in my personality rather than anything else. I cannot resist trying to help people out. I volunteered at that clinic, for god's sake. I guess the other big reason they asked me to represent them is that I was the only one they all assumed was neutral. They could have faith that I wouldn't try to use what they'd told me against them. And I've had experience in my school district with negotiations and union business. At the time, Lee hinted that I was a compromise candidate. Then again, they might have all been hoping for big contributions from Scott."

Dustin said, "All I know is that there's a lot of people who would make better suspects than Lee. Everybody at the clinic. Everybody. And that Karek guy. And some of those kids. That Jan! I'd be most suspicious of that neurotic drag queen. You know Jan?"

"Everybody at the clinic does. Why be suspicious of him?"

"Lee didn't tell you?"

"He doesn't discuss his clients with me."

"I'm not sure Jan was a client. The kid kind of flitted back and forth between whoever would listen to him at the moment."

"Put up with him is more like it."

Dustin nodded. "I know that just this week Snarly Bitch threw Jan out and told him never to come back."

"That I heard. I have Jan's version of why he got thrown out. What did you hear?"

"I think Snarly just got sick of how obnoxious the kid was. Lee never gave me the full explanation. I'm not sure he knew it. I wouldn't cross Jan."

"Why not?"

"You know he looks all soft and doughy."

"Yeah."

"Well, he goes to the same gym Lee and I do. The kid bench presses over two hundred fifty pounds. He takes boxing lessons. Jan is really strong. One time I saw him have a confrontation with three straight guys. They'd taken Jan's feather boa, a pink and mauve one that day. A bunch of us rushed up to help Jan. Stupid place to try a gay bashing. Half the damn gym is gay. But the kid was doing okay by himself. He had knocked one guy out, the second was so woozy he could barely stand, and Jan was starting on the third. Jan has a temper. He was shouting and hitting. I'd never heard such outrage or anger. There wasn't a hint of effeminate mannerisms in sight as he bellowed at his attackers. The drag queen persona was not in evidence as he battered them one after the other. If it got around that every gay guy fought back with that kind of intensity and that much finesse and ferocity, there'd be a lot fewer gay bashings. The first guy had to be taken to the hospital. I'm sure he'd have tried to sue, but we all saw them teasing Jan, trying to push him around, and harassing him. Lots of times his locker got vandalized, his clothes strewn around. They could never catch who was doing it. The guys actually confronting him was the most blatant. Maybe they thought with the three of them, they could get away with it. Jan took it for maybe all of a few seconds and then he just let go."

Several other of Lee and Dustin's friends came in. They joined the vigil. It was nearly ten before Todd came out and said they were in the middle of the booking process, that they'd be taking Lee to court. Todd didn't know about bail yet. Privately, I told him that Scott and I would pay Lee's bail. I was pissed at Lee, but I still believed he was innocent. I'd known him too long. He just wasn't the kind of guy to commit murder. Dustin and several friends said they'd go down to court. I decided to head home.

16

As soon as I arrived, I called the answering service. I had twenty-two messages. Most were kindly friends inquiring if I was okay. A few were reporters. One call was from Billy Karek. The answering service woman said, "He begged and pleaded with me to have you call him as soon as you got in, no matter how late, but he wouldn't say what it was about." I wondered if Truby had gotten through to him.

I was tired and out of sorts. In the quiet, high above the city in Scott's penthouse, the clamor of the day seeped into my consciousness. I put off the call. I read most of the early edition of the Sunday paper while I had some ice cream and an ocean of chocolate sauce. I'd have to work out an extra hour tomorrow.

Scott called from the West Coast just after I finished reading the QT column in the paper. He was loving and understanding. After I started talking, the words began to tumble out. I included more of the gruesome details than I'd told anybody else. He listened attentively as my reason began to catch up with my emotions.

Scott again asked if I wanted him to come back as soon as

he could get a flight. It was silly for him to miss a start for this. The team wasn't scheduled to be back until after a night game on the Coast on Monday. I told him it wasn't necessary for him to come back.

When I mentioned Karek, Scott said, "My agent got a call from a friend of Karek's. He asked me to try and convince you to talk to him."

"I already want to talk to him."

"My agent begged me to convince you. I guess he and this friend are pretty close."

"I wonder what the urgency is on his part."

"I don't know. Obviously Karek is pulling out any stop he can think of to get you to call. It's gotta be something important."

"You'd think. I'm not so worried about him. I'm far more concerned about the kids who use the clinic. I'd hate to see them lose such a valuable resource. Whether from financial malfeasance or parental fears, the place is in trouble."

Scott said, "Any parent would go nuts if their kid was involved, no matter how peripherally, in a murder investigation. The kids didn't see anything last night?"

"They claim they didn't see anybody. Larry might have been there last. I can picture Jan sneaking back to catch a glimpse of Larry making love."

Scott asked, "Are you sure Larry's not trying to implicate anyone he can? The cops might not know about what those kids were up to, but you do. You need to check into all of them. You need to talk to Larry's boyfriend even if nobody else does. You've got to be sure you have all the facts."

He was right. I had a fleeting worry that the teenagers might start distrusting me if I asked them tough questions. That was absurd. This was a murder investigation.

"I'll talk to them," I said.

"Or," Scott said, "Larry and the rest of them are telling the truth. I understand about Larry and sports. After this is over

I'd be happy to meet him or with him and his dad. If it'll help, I'll do it. I feel sorry for all those poor kids, even Jan."

"Me too. What do you think I should do about Karek?"

"Call the guy. What can it hurt?"

"The message says he called about nine this evening. After the kids told the police about him being at the clinic."

Scott asked, "How did the killer do it?"

"I told you, chopped him up."

"Yes, but how? You don't just say to someone, 'Would you please hold still, I'm going to decapitate you.' "

I thought for several moments. "Good question. The cops have got to know. I'll ask them. I'm not sure they'll give me much of an answer."

"Were there signs of a struggle?"

"The police didn't say. I'll ask that, too."

Scott said, "Maybe it's sort of one of those eternal conundrums, what came first, the chicken or the egg, death or decapitation?"

"Todd was doing attempts at feeble humor earlier. He wasn't very successful."

"I'll bet mine was more feeble than anything he tried."

I appreciated Scott's attempts to ease my stress with a little humor. A very little. For quite a while we talked about my feelings in dealing with the dead person, as well as with Lee's seeming duplicity, and about the kids at the clinic.

Then we had phone sex. Well, what did you think we did when we were apart? When we finished, I told Scott I loved him. He said the same.

It was a little before one. I called Karek's number. I told the male voice that answered that the message had been to call no matter what time I got in.

"I'm his lover, Reece. Would you be willing to meet us tomorrow for breakfast or an early lunch?"

It was a little late to beat around the bush. "Why?"

"Billy's got to talk to you. It's important."

"If it's that important, tell me now what the hell this is about. More secrets aren't going to help."

"I honestly don't know why. He's not here. If I knew, I would tell you. Please, he's my lover. I think he's in a lot of trouble. He's still out meeting with his lawyer. If you knew someone who could help your lover, wouldn't you plead for help? Well, I'm pleading."

I thought he and Karek might be grasping at straws. I wasn't going to let on that I was just as eager for the meeting. We set up a time and place.

17

I had trouble falling asleep. When that happens I like to reread a favorite book. This time I picked *Early Autumn* by Robert B. Parker. Some may not consider it the most mysterious of his fine books, but I find it comforting as Spenser works at domesticating a recalcitrant teenager. I fell asleep as Spenser and the boy were driving back from the ballet.

The morning brought Easter Sunday. I didn't feel much like rising. My first thoughts were of the severed head. Not good. I showered and called the answering service. Daisy Tajeda had left a message with the service giving me a time that afternoon for a meeting with Charley Fitch's sister.

Before driving to my meeting with Karek, I checked Albert Bergland's website. He was one of the homocons Tajeda had mentioned. I didn't find anything on it that would lead to murder. It seemed to be your normal personal rant site that has become so popular these days, a mixture of blog and blather. The main points seemed to be the elimination of taxes and the abolition of all government. I scanned it carefully. No clues to murder leapt out at me. After that I left a message with the gossip columnist who I knew that I'd like to get together that afternoon.

It was a wet, rainy morning, but the traffic was light on a Sunday. We met at the Melrose restaurant at the corner of Broadway and Melrose. Karek insisted we sit in the farthest back booth. It was only eight o'clock so there was plenty of space.

Karek was in his early thirties, tall and muscular, with broad shoulders, jeans that clung to his hips, a blue work shirt and heavy boots, construction worker drag which looked very good on him. His lover, Reece, was a six-foot-six blond Viking. He wore a blue dress shirt and khaki pants.

The waitress brought coffee and took our order. I got toast. Karek ordered pancakes. Reece stuck with coffee.

I asked, "Why did we need to meet?"

Karek said, "You're the one who knows everything at the clinic. The one everybody trusts. Your lover has clout in the community. I can't think of anybody else to turn to. You guys are the most prominent gay guys in the city. You can help me."

"Help you what?"

"You talked to those kids that ratted me out."

"They told the truth."

"I didn't kill anybody. The police were not nice."

"They've got a murder to solve."

"You're taking the part of the police?"

"I don't know you."

"I'm not the bad guy here. I presume you want to clear your friend Lee. Everybody knows he was arrested. I'm willing to help you as much as I can."

"Why? The police have a suspect. If I clear Lee, then you're back on the list."

"Because I'm afraid you will clear your friend. You're right. If you clear him, I'm a very logical suspect. I'm not stupid. I'm not going to sit on a powder keg with my eyes closed and hope everything just goes away. I know I need help. I'd like to know who killed Charley. We had our differences, but he didn't deserve to die. Other things are going to come out about the clinic. I'm worried that this is going to be a smear on the community. I'm worried that prejudiced people are going to see this as another instance of gay violence."

His comments reflected a fairly standard bit of prejudice, which was that if one person who was part of a minority committed a crime, then all the persons in the group were capable of said crime, or tainted by said crime, if they weren't actually implicated in said crime. Guilt by stereotype. I thought it was a crock, but I'd seen the right wing use that bit of logic against any number of groups and causes.

Reece had mostly sipped coffee, nodded occasionally, and looked at Karek with a worried frown. Now he spoke. His voice was soft and mellifluous. He said, "We really need your help. I don't want there to be antagonism at a time like this." Was he referring to me or his lover?

I didn't know what to make of Karek. I didn't trust him. At the same time, I was certainly very interested in what he might be able to tell me. I had to be more careful and less hostile.

Karek said, "I think people will use anything against gay people. I'm one of the ones who's against permitting drag queens in the Pride parades. I think we've got to meet the culture, not rebel against it. One of the things that Charley never figured out was that the Sixties were over. That 'us against the world' crap is passé. I think we have to be conscious of our image."

I said, "I'm just worried about Lee. I'm interested in any information you can give me."

Karek said, "I instigated an investigation of the fundraising activities at the clinic. I wanted to avoid a scandal if I could. Charley and I might feud, but real damage could have been done to harm some very good work. At the same time the truth had to come out. There was real fraud going on. Nobody wanted to believe me. Charley Fitch was a goddamn icon in this community. I've never been able to figure out why. How someone congenitally rude can be so powerful is beyond me."

"Everybody knows he was rude," I said. "If rudeness were actionable, half the planet would be in jail."

"I'm trying to explain the dynamics of the situation. I'm trying to do good for this community. Charley Fitch was siphoning off the community's money for that clinic. There's only so much cash available in this town for donations. He was taking a huge chunk."

"And you were envious, jealous, spiteful? You hated him because he was successful?"

"Don't you get it? The fight between us was symbolic."

"Of what? Rampant stupidity?" I was afraid I'd gone too far.

Karek looked pissed, but he tried to explain. "It's the same in every gay community in this country: who gets to be spokesperson, who the media talks to, who sets the agenda for the community, who gets the cash. A lot of us were afraid when your lover came out that he, or both of you for that matter, might try to take over from those of us who have worked so long. Neither of you did, so we could go back to fighting among ourselves."

"It seems like an awful lot of fighting over a very small piece of pie."

"But it's our pie. Look at the fight after Daley finally appointed a gay alderman."

"If infighting is so typical, why would it all of a sudden become a cause for murder?"

"It might not be, but the fact that Charley was taking people's money and misusing it could be."

"Are you sure he was stealing?"

"Yes."

"How did you find out?"

"By accident. A check of mine made out to the clinic had been cashed through someone else's account."

"You were donating to the clinic?"

"I believe in minimal government interference in our lives. People should take care of themselves or their own. I was helping gay kids. I know they need help. So I wrote this check, a large one. You know how with checking accounts some banks don't give you the actual checks back anymore unless you pay for the service?"

I nodded.

"Well, I made some stupid error in my account, so I had them return the actual checks. I happened to look on the back of the one I wrote to the clinic. It had been countersigned by Charley."

"So what?"

"It wasn't supposed to be. He's not the treasurer. He'd put it into his own account. That made me suspicious. I got the ball rolling. We were starting to get more proof, but I think Charley had begun to catch on. I had to be careful that the investigation didn't look like a ploy to discredit him or simply some kind of personal vendetta or smear campaign. I had to have real proof. We've disliked each other for a long while. He couldn't stand it that I was being listened to by people outside the community. Reporters were coming to me for quotes now, not him. What's worse, he was a remnant of the old gay socialist left. He was rude and out of step. He had to be replaced."

"So some of the feud was about politics. Some was about ego. Some was about violations of the rules of etiquette."

"It was a mixture of a lot of things. He and I disagreed a lot personally and politically."

"What about the other prominent gay political conservatives in town, Mandy Marlex and Albert Bergland? Was it personal or political with them?" Marlex and Bergland were the other homocons in the community that the people at the clinic had mentioned yesterday.

"Mandy has fought for years to become a person listened to in this community. When she finally got on a few cable shows, she thought she'd arrived."

"And hadn't she?"

"Mandy never met an illogical argument she didn't like. I know one time she argued that what we did in this country to the Native Americans was the same as what we did to the Germans in World War II."

"What?"

"I'm not trying to defend her position. Most of the time she was reasonable, at least with me. She did believe in the free-market economy. On the other hand she had a string of businesses that went broke. She refused to take any kind of government money to help her out. She was very independent."

"But not very businesslike?"

"No."

"When did she meet Charley?"

"They went way back. I heard Mandy and Charley's sister Susanna were lovers back in college. I think Mandy used to volunteer at the clinic as well."

"What can you tell me about Bergland?"

"Albert is a bit odd, kind of a gadfly, but he has a first-rate mind. He's a professor at Minooka Technical Institute, a small liberal arts college. He's got tenure and has been around since god. Wants to canonize Milton Friedman."

"What about his connection with Charley?"

"I'm not sure. They met a few times. I know they weren't friends or anything, but I don't think they were active enemies."

"I'd like to talk to both of them. Can you get me an introduction?"

"I'll do what I can."

"And both of them fought with Charley?"

"Charley fought with everybody."

"How'd you know Charley was suspicious about there being an investigation?"

"Questions he began asking around the office got reported back to me."

"How'd you know he was asking questions?"

"I had a contact in the office."

"Who?" I asked.

"Jakalyn Bowman."

"The press secretary was a spy for you?"

"Jakalyn is a friend."

"Did Charley know that?"

"Jakalyn never told."

"Why was it your job to be investigating?"

"How could I ignore what I learned? I've got a responsibility to this community. I've also been in contact with Ken Wells, the guy who had all the problems with his latest fundraiser."

"I still don't get why Fitch would sabotage his own employee."

"Ken was furious with Charley. It was more than one fundraiser. It turns out, Fitch tried to ruin Ken's reputation around the country, a very nasty, underhanded smear campaign. Ken is a very honest man."

"Why'd Charley keep Wells on the staff if he was trying to ruin his reputation?"

"Charley was no fool. He recognized competence."

"Wells hinted yesterday that he was looking for other work."

"He told me he was. He was very quiet about it. He'd been to several interviews, but if anything came out about financial irregularities, he'd be under a cloud. He was in the middle of all the financial workings of the clinic."

"Maybe he was incompetent. Maybe he was committing fraud."

"I got no sense that it was Ken. My source never mentioned him."

"If your source was Jakalyn, maybe she just never figured it out."

"Jakalyn may have been my source, but she wasn't investigating for me."

His lover said, "Doesn't anybody in this town get tired of secrets and conspiracies and holding back information?"

Karek said, "Shit happens. I don't want it to contaminate me. I've got to protect myself."

"Did you ever ask Fitch directly about possible financial irregularities?" I asked.

"I tried talking to him once, very obliquely. I barely got the first question out. He said I had no standing to interrogate him about what went on in the clinic." Karek put his elbows on the table, leaned forward, and lowered his voice to a whisper. He said, "Okay, here's the deal. I talked to a reporter for the gay press."

"Evan Smith?"

"You talked to him?"

"He didn't tell me who his boss was, but that he had some connection to Ken Wells."

Karek said, "He agreed to volunteer at the clinic and to investigate. I actually got more from him than I did from Jakalyn or Ken. From Jakalyn I got more gossip than actual data. But there's more. Much more. Let me explain." He took a sip of coffee then began. "First of all, those kids were right. I'd been to the clinic a couple weeks ago. I guess half the planet knows about that now. They need to keep a tighter rein on those kids."

"I doubt if there's going to be much to rein in after this killing. I suspect the place is simply going to fold up."

"Oh. I guess you're right. They'll have a hard time getting funding."

"They do good work."

"I know. I went there a few times when I was in high school. Charley Fitch hadn't changed."

"You knew him then?"

"He never really spent much time with the kids. He talked to our group a couple times. He mostly seemed interested in getting away as soon as he could. We were introduced to each other once. When I met him as an adult, he never said he remembered me. There was no reason he would. Back then the clinic was just as crazy as it is now. This was fourteen, fifteen years ago."

"When you went there, did the kids use the basement for trysting?"

"Yeah."

"You just said the kids needed to be reined in."

"Well, yeah, I guess I'm older. I guess I'm a hypocrite. Sue me."

"Did you listen to adult conversations back then?"

"Nah. In those days we could roam through the whole downstairs. It hadn't been renovated, and they hadn't started using it for storage. It still had dirt floors and rats and who knew what else. The adults avoided the place. But teenagers are kind of nuts and desperate. Only a few brave souls ever dared to enter the basement. It was sort of like those scary movie things with people staying in a haunted house. We only used the room in the first building far in the back nearest the alley. No one wanted to listen. People made out, but nobody stayed all that long. I guess after they renovated, it wasn't so bad. Old, dank, and miserable or new, dank, and miserable, the kids still found a way to use it for their trysts."

I pointed at Reece. "Did you two meet back then?"

Reece said, "No. We met on one of those gay cruises in the Caribbean. I've never been in the basement."

I asked, "Did Charley Fitch have enemies back then?"

"Us kids heard about fights. I saw one guy, Arnold something, who almost had a physical fight with Charley. I didn't pay much attention. I was a teenager. Mostly I worried about getting my dick sucked. Isn't that why gay kids go to these groups? To get laid?"

"At least to meet others like themselves."

"You're not one of those idealistic ones who thinks they're having meaningful discussions? Charley Fitch was like that. Boring. I bet Charley has given that same Gay 101 sociology lecture since the invention of dirt. It was useless when he gave it more than a decade ago. Through most of it, I was wondering if the kid sitting across from me would be interested in having sex. Isn't that the way with most gay groups, especially gay teens?"

"I worked at the clinic to help kids."

"Well, we'll declare you a saint. How many people have gorgeous, rich, famous baseball players as lovers? You live a fantasy life."

I said, "My life doesn't include being insulted by you, putting up with your observations, being interested in you as a human being, or in helping you not be a suspect." I figured that pretty well blew any further discussion with him.

Reece put his hands on his lover's arm. His voice thrummed a gentle remonstrance. "Billy."

Karek pulled back some and then drew a deep breath. He said, "Sorry, I apologize. I get so passionate. I don't know when to keep my mouth shut. I get angry so quickly at gay groups. I'm sorry. I can really give you information that might help solve the murder. Your friend has been arrested. You want to help. I don't know if Charley got along with any more people back then than he does now. Other than with that Arnold guy, I never saw anything close to a physical fight. I also never saw him with a date or anything. I wasn't paying much attention."

"Did you have an appointment to meet the night the kids heard you?"

"No. I knew from years ago that Charley often stayed very late. I was embarrassed about what happened at the television station. I wanted to apologize. I was at least half at fault. I wanted to try and reach a truce with him. For the good of the community. It had been months, but we were scheduled to be on that show again. I wanted to avoid more fireworks. That night at the show wasn't our first fight, and maybe it wasn't even our worst. But there's also a big foundation fundraiser coming up, and we're both on the planning committee. We were put on it before we had the public brawl. The organizers begged me to make peace for the sake of their group. I thought I could talk to Charley. I went to him that night to try to reason with him."

I said, "Maybe you should have scheduled a fight and sold tickets. You might have made a fortune for everybody involved."

Karek almost smiled. "I'm afraid there's more. I don't know who else to turn to. The people in this community are cut-throat creeps. I need you to trust me. I'm willing to give you valuable information, but you have to promise not to take it to the police."

"If you confess to murder, I am not going to keep it quiet."

"I have nothing to confess to. I didn't kill him. Maybe I can help you figure out who did."

"Why not just trust the police?"

"I see them as agents of a collectivist state."

"That's a bit strong."

"I am not fond of the police. Anybody who knows gay history is wary of the cops. I'm offering to put my fate in your hands."

That sounded awfully melodramatic. Still, I would be stupid not to listen.

Reece said, "Billy, are you sure you want to tell this?"

Karek patted his hand. "I've got to trust somebody."

I said, "I won't make unconditional promises. If you confess to a crime, I will turn you in."

"Fair enough." He drew a deep breath. "We'll be working together for the good of the community."

Please. "Isn't that rather collectivist?"

"Touché. I was there. At the clinic. Last night. We fought again. Why that man couldn't see reason, I don't know."

"You were there last night? The kids said the other night."

"I was there last night as well."

"What time?"

"About nine. I was going one last time to talk to him."

"Why not just call him on the phone?"

"It did no good to try and talk to him on the phone. He loved to be able to hang up on you before you could hang up on him. It was childish but effective. At least he thought so. You met him face to face or not at all."

"Did you see anyone else?"

"I thought I saw a short blond guy at one end of the alley behind the clinic, but I didn't get a good look at him. Maybe a little pudgy."

Jan was short, blond, and a little pudgy. "So, you've got no alibi."

"I do for when I got home. My lover can vouch for the time I arrived home, just before ten."

"How'd you get into the clinic?"

"Charley opened the door for me."

"How could you be sure he was there?"

"I'd called Jakalyn."

"She knew you were planning to go there?"

"Yes."

"She lied to the police for you?" I asked.

"I guess."

"Not 'guess.' You got somebody else mixed up in this."

"She's not 'mixed up' in anything. I didn't kill him. I swear to God he was alive when I left. He looked red enough in the face to have a stroke, but he was breathing."

"Have you told the police this?"

"No. You're not going to, are you? I'm trusting you here, in the hopes of getting information."

"Or making me an accessory after the fact. Why didn't the kids hear you last night?"

"We didn't scream and carry on last night. Maybe none of them was down there when I was around. Maybe they were preoccupied. When a date and I were down there, I usually was. Maybe they were too involved in intimate activities and didn't give a rat's ass. I was determined not to yell last night. I'm really worried. I was there. If this gets out, my reputation is ruined. I'd be a suspect. The goddamn news shows are already replaying that goddamn fight scene with Charley." He shuddered. "I was no saint at that interview. He may have started it, but I tried to belt him with that chair. And I look like a fucking wimp, cowering there and him swinging that microphone at my head."

I said, "This was all about image and reputation, trying to be more butch than the other guy?"

"Anything connected with Charley is going to be tainted. These cops are being very thorough. Charley Fitch knew the mayor and other politicians. Charley may have been controversial in the community and nearly universally hated, but he was the token gay person they put on all their committees. Before me, he was the one the straight politicians and media people turned to. The police don't want any mistakes. The mayor's got an election coming up next year, and he wants Democrats elected in Springfield this November. Gays have lots of money and plenty of votes."

As Glen Poshard, a downstate Democrat, discovered when he ran for governor and wouldn't endorse anything pro-gay. The gay community had deserted his gubernatorial candidacy in droves. The demographic comparison between his race for governor and the senate race that year made it clear how important the gay voting bloc was. If you wanted to win as a Democrat statewide in Illinois, you alienated the gay community at your peril.

I said, "The police interrogated you, and you didn't admit to any of this?"

"No."

"Even if you didn't do it, you should probably be talking to a lawyer."

"I've met Lee. He's a good guy. I can't believe he'd kill anybody. I can't believe I would. That night at the television station, I think I was capable of anything. I never thought I was that kind of person, but Charley Fitch's goddamn arrogance just drove me nuts."

"We all fantasize about doing a lot of stuff we'd be arrested for if we actually did. I understand you're worried about being a suspect, but I still don't understand how I come into this."

"You know things. People tell you stuff. Can you keep me up to date about what you find out about anything? I want to make sure I don't become a suspect."

My "Why should I?" came out as, "I don't understand what you want from me."

"I can't be under suspicion for murder. I'm sure Lee didn't do it. I know I didn't. I think I need to find out who killed Charley. It's protection for myself. Can you snoop around?"

"Frankly, you're my next best suspect as the murderer."

"I'm willing to risk you thinking I'm a suspect for your willingness to help me."

Karek was a conduit to Mandy Marlex and Albert Bergland. I didn't want to be Karek's friend, but I didn't want to lose him as a possible source for further information.

He said, "Knowing about the finances might help you clear Lee. I think this shows how much I want the truth to come out. The more truth there is the less likely I am to be a suspect." He pulled a cell phone out of a black gym bag that was sitting on the seat next to him. "I'll call now. I can get you introductions. I can get people to talk to you." He held up the phone. "I'm willing to help."

Everything about this guy set off suspicion bells in my head, but he knew people. I wouldn't tell the police about him unless I needed to. I almost hoped I needed to. I did not like this guy, but I said, "Okay." I didn't get a sense that he was dangerous. I hoped I was right about that. For now he was being helpful. I needed that.

He made the calls. He set up meetings for early that afternoon with Mandy Marlex and Albert Bergland. Karek stood several feet away from the booth to make his calls. Reece leaned over to me and put his hand on my forearm. "Please," he said, "I know Billy's in trouble. Please, help him."

"What do you know?" I asked.

"Nothing for sure. I'm worried. That's all I can say."

He either didn't know or was unwilling to say more.

Karek came back and gave me the details on what he was able to set up.

18

It was the middle of the morning. The rain had let up. The day was cool and humid. For the moment the clinic was off limits. Gordon Jackson, the owner of the Rainbow Café, had agreed to let the staffers use the meeting rooms above the café to do business. I had agreed to stop over to see if they needed any help.

The largest upstairs conference room was filled with volunteers, staff, kids, and a few parents from the clinic. Todd sat quietly on the dais reading a legal-looking document. He told me they were still processing Lee, and it would take quite a while longer. Daisy Tajeda was at the front of the room preparing to address the crowd. I saw a number of kids I recognized clustered together in chairs on the left near the back.

Jan hurried up to me. "What's happening with the investigation?" he asked. He was in a yellow zoot suit and a pink fedora. He was flipping his wrists and lisping worse than a drag queen who had just swallowed a bottle of speed. I wanted to slug him.

"What time were you in the basement with your friend?"

"Why would you even ask?" A flip and surly teenage drag queen.

"What time?"

His eyes shifted. Picking a time he hoped nobody else was there so no one could destroy his lie?

"Eight, I think."

"What time were you in the alley that night?"

"Did someone say they saw me?"

"What time?"

"I wasn't *in* the alley. I was hanging around the café around ten, I think. There was so much going on. I don't wear a watch. Can you tell me if someone saw me? What's going on?"

I said, "Nothing." I put as much short, clipped *go away* as I could into my tone. He looked like a hurt puppy. I felt a little like a heel. The kid was being inquisitive, maybe even trying to help in his own inept way. Or the son of a bitch was in that alley or in the basement and knew something.

Tajeda was saying, "The clinic will remain open. The board of directors will meet later today to name an interim director." She began to explain the details of how various programs would continue. She finished, "The prom is still on. No matter what, it is going to happen."

"Is that good in an atmosphere of violence?" a woman near the front asked.

Tajeda said, "We will do everything possible to ensure that the kids are going to be safe."

"You can't guarantee their safety," the same woman said.

"You can't guarantee they're going to be safe crossing the street," Tajeda responded. They began to wrangle about details for security for the prom.

Larry, the football player I'd met the day before, sat down next to me. He whispered, "Can I talk to you?"

We went downstairs and found a quiet table in one of the rooms near the back. I had coffee, black. He had a mocha calorie something.

He took a sip of his drink, put it down, and placed his hands flat on the small table. He said, "I think I'd rather be dead."

I put my hand on his. He didn't move. I met his eyes and didn't look away.

"What happened since last night?"

"I called the guy I was making out with in the clinic basement. He won't talk to me. He hung up on me."

"You told the police about the night when you heard Karek, but not last night."

"Yeah."

"Somebody's going to need to talk to the guy you were making out with. The police wouldn't be my choice."

"Maybe he'll talk to you. If I can even get him to talk to me." He sniffled. "My dad blew up at me last night. That lawyer guy of yours was really nice. He was great, but once he was gone, my dad went nuts. That's how he's always been. Like he was nice to teachers, then he'd get home and scream at me. I told the cops everything. Turns out, that was the easy part. This coming out is for shit. Your lover's a baseball player. How does he do it? I wish I had somebody like he does. I want to be an athlete and be gay. I don't want to fight any causes. I want a boyfriend like everybody else. I just want to be touched, to make love without any hassles. I want to be normal." He started to cry. He whispered. "I just want to be normal." A lament that young gay kids and older gay people too often make. Gay guilt. Some of us never get over it.

I held his hand. He gripped mine tightly. I patted his arm. He slowly pulled himself together. One or two people looked over at us.

I handed him some napkins and he blew his nose and wiped his eyes. When he was done, I said, "If it ever comes to a moment when you think you might hurt yourself, please call me." I wrote down my number on a slip of paper. I said,

"Tell the answering service who you are. I'll leave your name with them. They'll put you straight through."

"Thanks." He sniffled and said, "Does this ever get easier?"

"Yes," I said. "It does. My guess is, you'll fall in love, perhaps more than once in your life."

"Everything seems kind of hopeless."

"The impression you gave me yesterday is that you're a good guy, sensible, with a grasp on what's real. You can get through this. There are good people who can help you. Especially don't give up on yourself. Please don't hurt yourself. I care. When I was talking to Scott, my lover, last night, he'd said he'd be happy to meet with you. He's willing to help. In a couple years I'd like to come see you play in a college football game. You've got a lot to offer the sports world, but even more, I think you've got a lot to offer everybody."

"Thanks, Mr. Mason."

"Promise you'll call me."

"I will."

"Good." I breathed a sigh of relief. "How was talking to the police?"

"That's how the thing with my dad started. He ragged on me last night after we went to the police station. He started in on me again before breakfast this morning. He wanted to know how I knew anything connected with murder. I could have tried to lie, but I'm tired of lies. I wanted him to know the truth. I wanted him to know that I could make decisions. That I could be honest. That I wasn't just some big dumb kid."

"Your dad thinks you're a big dumb kid?"

"He rags at me constantly about my grades. He always puts me down. He calls me stupid. He laughs at me. He wouldn't let me be in any help programs when I was a kid. He said they were all dummies in those classes. Well, I am a dummy. I needed help, and I didn't get it."

"Do you want help now?"

"It's too late."

"No, it isn't. You could work out tutoring things with people from the clinic."

"Then they'll know I'm stupid, too."

"Getting help isn't stupid."

He hung his head for several moments then muttered, "Well, maybe. I'm afraid of my dad. He's three inches taller and fifty pounds heavier than me. He was a linebacker for Michigan State. He thinks gay guys are sick."

"Does that bother you?"

"Yeah, a lot."

We talked until I was as sure as I could be that he wouldn't hurt himself. At the end I asked, "Can I get you to talk to one of the counselors?"

"I'm not going to kill myself. Don't worry. I promised I'd call."

I said, "It's important that someone talk to the guy you were with."

"I know."

"It'll have to be soon. I'm sorry to push you into talking to a guy who's backing off, but it's necessary."

"I know. I'll talk to him. If he won't see me, I'll give you his name."

He left. In the normal course of events, I would have reported the conversation to Lee. I didn't think Larry needed to be on a suicide watch, but I thought it was best to be careful.

19

Karek had set up my meeting with Mandy Marlex for noon. I heard her before I saw her. A motorcyclist roared up to the café on a black Harley Davidson. Before shutting it down, the driver revved the immense motorcycle to its loudest possible roar. A diminutive figure stepped off. At first I couldn't tell if the rider was male or female. The driver unzipped a leather jacket, and mostly unclad mammary glands appeared. The helmet came off and soft blond hair cascaded to her waist. I thought it was a little precious that a woman barely five-feet-two was riding a motorcycle bigger than she was. The black leather pants and black boots were set off by a pink cashmere torso-hugging garment under the leather jacket. The bit of cloth clung in ways that I didn't usually notice. If I was noticing, then her figure was truly remarkable.

Karek had described Marlex and her motorcycle to me. I met her just inside the door and introduced myself. Up close I could see well-concealed lines and furrows on her face. She was nowhere near as young as her biker persona pretended her to be. In another Sucaryl-drenched precious bit, when we got to the table, she swung her leg over her chair, sat down, and began to plunk helmet, goggles, gloves, and scarf on the marble top.

She ordered tea and biscuits—the British cookie kind of biscuits, not the American biscuits-and-gravy-breakfast kind of biscuits. Her soft, mellow voice came with a downeast Maine accent. She said, "Billy Karek suggested I talk to you. He says I could give background on Charley Fitch. I love it that his employees called him Snarly Bitch." She did a flip of her blond hair with her right hand. It struck me as an affectation, just like Jan's. Maybe they were related. Or maybe she had an uncontrollable arm/flip twitch. Maybe not.

"How well did you know Charley Fitch?" I asked.

"Since college. He was not a pleasant person back then. His family was rich. He was putting in his time and getting his paid-for degree." She snorted. "He never even graduated. I think I saw him studying once. Charley's had it easy his whole life."

"Did that bother a lot of people?"

"Sometimes, but I don't picture that as a motive for murder. That is what you're doing here, looking for a motive for murder? I assume you must be. What with your famous lover I'm sure you feel entitled to ask questions and presume the rest of us will simply answer them. How does being rich qualify you to stick your nose in where it doesn't count?" I swallowed several nasty retorts about her rudeness. I'd see if she could be of any help and then retort in kind if the moment warranted it, and if she was worth the effort.

While I was irritated, I knew I was basically an amateur sleuth who had to rely on the goodwill of the people I was talking to. I swallowed most of my ire and said, "I'm simply helping out a friend. I imagine you've done that before, helped out a friend in a tough spot. Is that so hard to believe?"

She fiddled with her helmet, toyed with her tea, rearranged her glove, scarf, and goggles. Then did the hair-flip thing again.

"Why should I help you?" she asked.

"If you help me, you help Billy Karek."

"You presume I want to help him."

"Don't you? He gave me you as a reference. You aren't a friend of his?"

"An acquaintance more than a friend. We have worked on a bunch of projects together. He was more ideological than I. He always had to come up with a fresh argument in favor of or against a point. He kept thinking up new reasons to be negative. He got me on a few talk shows. I guess we agree more than we disagree politically, but it's presumptuous to extrapolate from that that we are friends."

"It's not much of a stretch."

"We're certainly not enemies."

"Did he and his sister get along?"

"They did have occasional quarrels about money. Even in college Charley was a spender, not a saver. Of course, with that much cash, why bother to save? They certainly never fought to the point of murder."

I asked, "Can you give Billy Karek an alibi for Friday night and Sunday morning?"

"Did he say I could?"

"No."

She asked, "Where were you then?"

"Asleep in bed."

"And can you prove that?"

"No."

She said, "I was having sex with my partner." Another hair flip.

Good for the two of them. I wasn't ready to give up, although a few more of those hair flips and I might call the Annoyance Police. I asked, "Do you know anyone who would want to kill Charley?"

"Lots of people disagreed with him, but I can't imagine it was over anything important enough to kill for."

"Disagreed about what?"

"Tons of stuff. Maybe the Pride parade is the best example. The lewd behavior and foul language at that thing are a disgrace."

"Which parade? New York, LA, here, or someplace else?"

"All of them are embarrassments."

"To whom?" I asked. "The hundreds of thousands of people who come to watch? The several thousand who are in the parade? Is someone counting obscenities? If so, why? Don't they have a life?"

"The parades around the country are our largest single public event. People should behave. And no, I don't want everyone in business suits. I want to be represented by normal people. You and your lover qualify."

"I thought you were pissed at us because we're rich."

"You're normal in a non-capitalist kind of way."

I wasn't sure that made a whole lot of sense, but I avoided sounding annoyed. I said, "I'm getting frustrated. I thought Karek gave me your name because you were a friend of his who could back him up. Either I seriously misunderstood him, or he is clueless as to the real nature of your relationship."

"Billy's kind of dense. He's so naïve about the way the world really works."

"And how is that?" I asked.

"Greed. It works on greed. Give people what they want or what they think they want and they'll be happy."

"Is that what someone did to Charley, kill him to fill their acquisitive impulse?"

"Probably not."

"What about your fights with Charley?"

"They were never violent. Never. I knew when to back off. So did Charley. I think Charley never got as angry with me as he did with others because I'm a woman. He didn't take me seriously. He said several times that I was an illogical woman. I was dismissed out of hand."

"You didn't find that frustrating?"

"You think being treated like that is odd for a woman? We all have to put up with that kind of shit. Karek's the one who got violent publicly."

"Billy Karek said that you and Susanna Fitch were lovers in college."

"And that has something to do with what?"

"A former lover getting even?"

She smiled. "You must be desperate. If that wasn't such a pathetic piece of analysis, I'd be pissed."

"Former lovers have been known to be angry."

"Sorry to disappoint you. I'm not."

"Karek gave me Albert Bergland's name as well."

"I think Charley was actually close to Albert. They were boyfriends at some point."

"Karek didn't think they were close."

"Wrong again for Billy."

"Did Charley have a boyfriend recently?"

"I don't remember any boyfriend, not in a long while. I wouldn't know about any kind of sex, for that matter. We weren't sexual confidants. The thing with Albert was over years ago. Albert didn't commit murder. He doesn't have the temperament."

"I think all of us have violent thoughts." For example, I had no intention of actually tying her by her flipped-back long blond hair to the back of her motorcycle and driving off at ninety miles an hour, but it was a tempting thought.

She said, "Maybe you're projecting. But most of us don't act on our violent impulses, and I have a witness and an alibi."

I asked, "Do you know of any enemies he might have had?"

"His whole staff. Everyone who worked at that clinic past and future. They hated him. Mostly he hated them, too."

"Didn't he do the hiring?"

"Pretty much."

"So who's fault was it that so much hatred existed?"

“I suppose it was mutual. Charley would go on and on about them, and he could be very funny, but he wasn’t a good judge of people. He just wanted to do some good in this world, and he had the money to make the attempt.”

I said, “Maybe cash isn’t everything.”

“In Charley’s hands it wasn’t.”

She reclad herself in her motorcycle regalia and swaggered out to her machine. Before she drove off, the violent revving continued for an impressively annoying length of time.

20

I had an appointment that afternoon set up by Daisy Tajeda with Charley Fitch's sister. She lived in Lake Shore Drive East, one of the high rises between where the Lake Shore Drive S-curve used to be and where Lake Shore Drive currently is. The security guard called up to ask if I was to be admitted.

I didn't hear the answering voice, but I was told to go up.

Susanna Fitch had short hair, weighed three hundred pounds, and wore a black jumpsuit.

The plush condo had high ceilings with ten-foot-by-ten-foot abstract paintings on every wall I saw. The artist must have gotten a special deal on red, because he or she didn't seem to have used any other color. We sat in low swivel chairs with a view north toward the Chicago River.

I said, "Thank you for agreeing to see me. I'm sorry for your loss."

She said, "Thank you. I know your name. You found him. I'm so sorry. And I've seen you on television with your lover. Did you know Charley?"

"Not well."

"Charley was a good man. I loved him. And to die in that

horrible way." She shuddered. "All the money in the world can't change what's happened, but I'll spend whatever I need to make this less painful. This whole mess has got to be cleared up." She shook her head. "I'm still numb. Charley was trying to do a lot of good. Helping gay kids is so important. Daisy Tajeda asked me to meet with you. Walter Truby mentioned you as well. I know you're being considered for interim director. They both said you were a good person who might have some questions. I'm not sure I'm up to a lot of questions."

"I'm flattered by their interest, but I'm not going to take the job. Being a school teacher is plenty enough for me. I know this is a tough time, but my friend was arrested. I'm trying to find out information that would clear his name and help find who killed your brother."

"I'm not sure I'd be able to help. I don't know who the killer could be."

"Did Charley have any enemies?"

"Oh, my. I suppose you're referring to those ugly rumors about employee dissatisfaction."

"I saw some of that dissatisfaction firsthand."

"I don't listen to rumors. I guess there might have been some truth to these. I never heard there were any fights that became personal."

"Many of his employees and most of the volunteers referred to him behind his back as Snarly Bitch."

"Well, people often snipe at bosses."

"Somebody could have gotten angry enough to get even."

"I don't know those people. I don't want to know those people."

I said, "Mandy Marlex claimed you and Charley had disagreements about money."

"Mandy and I were roommates in college. We were lovers once. She's quite bright. She has no animosity toward Charley."

"What about toward you?"

"After the initial break-up we became friends. We're not as close as we once were, but that's more due to separate paths in life, not old lover's quarrels. Mandy and I haven't been close in a long time. Her knowledge is limited. Charley and I disagreed occasionally. Charley's eyes were always bigger than his budget. You're not suggesting I had a motive for murder?"

I was, but I figured a yes answer would get me pitched out on my ass. I said, "Mandy didn't impress me much."

"She doesn't impress anyone. While we were breaking up, I wanted nothing better than to stop her doing that stupid hair flip. Ripping it out from the roots seemed appropriate."

I couldn't argue with that. I asked, "Do you know of any particularly strong political enemies Charley might have had?"

"Charley was a confronter, not a calmer. I don't know who really took any of that seriously. To me, it was just a bunch of little boys fighting over a very small piece of a political pie."

"Did he have close friends? Maybe if I talked to them, they might have a notion if he'd quarreled with anyone recently."

"Charley had a lot of contacts. I'm not sure he really had a lot of friends."

"I understand your brother's financial records at the clinic were being investigated."

"I think it would have been an excellent thing for there to be an investigation. The board never took any formal vote that I was aware of. I didn't go to many of the meetings. Charley attended all of them. They wouldn't have voted such a thing with him there. After I heard the rumors, I talked to a few of the board members privately. I was pretty angry at first. Nobody would admit to anything. I know Charley did nothing wrong. An independent investigation, open or secret, would have proven that my brother had done no wrong. Only now that he's dead are these accusations starting to surface. Those vultures had to wait until he died so he wouldn't be able to challenge all that baseless bullshit. I told him about the rumors. He dismissed them. He knew he had nothing to hide."

"Maybe he should have taken them seriously."

"Are you saying because he didn't, he was killed?"

I thought that was a bit of an overreaction on her part. I said, "I don't know why he was killed."

"I agreed to see you because justice needs to be done. I agreed to see you because Daisy said you're the one who has knowledge. You're the one that people talk to. You're the one the kids trust."

"Do you think Lee did it?"

"Him I know. I don't think Lee would have the balls to kill anybody. I don't think he's got the brains god gave to a demented termite. The guy is a wuss. But the police arrested him. They must have a reason."

I swallowed several snappy rejoinders, especially the one about rudeness being an inherited genetic trait in their family. I figured I still needed her good will. She also had the heft to wield an ax. She could be the killer as well as anybody. I said, "I was told you didn't have anything to do with the clinic."

"Charley ran the day-to-day operation."

"But you're on the board."

She said, "I've never crossed the doorstep of the place. I'm on the board to protect the family's interest, which means the family money."

"Did it need protecting?"

"Charley could spend money like a trooper. His personal habits were fairly spartan, but the money he plowed into that clinic was enough to start his own third-world country. He did not have unlimited access to the family money. All the different projects he wanted cost a bundle. He really had to do fundraising for that clinic. By no means did he get a free ride."

"Who did he have the biggest fights with?"

"Just the big ones?"

"I've been told the little ones were innumerable."

She said, "If you're going to talk to people, you could start with those homocons. The rivalry for the gay market's money in this town has been intense. It seems every other week some do-good group was having a fundraiser in a wishfully posh hotel not quite in the most fashionable part of town."

"Do you know of any personal animosities?"

"Mostly all he had were personal animosities." She thought for several moments, then said, "Some were worse than others. Karek and his lover were awful to him."

"What was the problem there?"

"That confrontation on the television show wasn't their first fight. They'd come near to blows several times over the years. Their animosities went quite far back. They were lovers a number of years ago."

"Karek and Charley?"

"Yes. It was a rocky relationship. They lived together for a short time."

Somehow Karek had left out this little detail. I wondered why. I said "I've talked with Mandy Marlex. I'm going to be talking with Albert Bergland. How was Charley's relationship with him?"

"I don't like Albert. I think Charley was mostly indifferent to him. Albert didn't have a lot of money. If there was one thing you could count on Charley for, it was that he would know how much people were worth. He may have been my brother, but that doesn't mean I was blind to his shortcomings."

"How about in Charley's past? Any conflicts there?"

"He had occasional boyfriends. I never heard there was any lasting ill feeling after he broke up with them."

"Do you know why they broke up?"

"Charley never really discussed his relationships with

me. He'd bring a lover to a family event once in a while. Not often. All of us get together to vacation in our place in Aruba every year. He bought one the last time."

"Do you remember any names?"

"I'm sorry, no."

"I was told he hired call boys."

"That sounds like vicious gossip. People are envious of the rich and famous."

"Were you worried last night when he didn't come home?"

She gave me a thin smile. "He kept very late hours. We own half of this floor. He could be gone for a week, and I wouldn't notice. Half the time we didn't know if we we're in the same city. Our secretaries coordinated most family things."

"Did everybody in the family get along?"

She said, "I appreciate that you're concerned for your friend, but my family and my trust fund and our company are off limits to you." She stood up. "I have a great many things to take care of."

"Of course. I'm sorry to have intruded. Again, I'm sorry for your loss."

21

I met Professor Albert Bergland at the Rainbow Café.

Bergland was about four-foot-ten. He had blue eyes and a white goatee. He looked about as tall as the ax that had been used in Fitch's murder. He may not have been big enough for the part, but I figured anybody with an ax can sneak up on someone and do plenty of damage.

After our orders arrived, Bergland dropped a dollop of something from a hip flask into his coffee. "Brandy," he said. "Would you like some?"

I declined.

I said, "I checked your web site."

"You were shocked?" he asked.

"Not particularly. Is there something there I was supposed to be shocked about?"

"Well, it's not the usual liberal gay palaver. I've seen you on a few shows. I assume you believe all that commie line about what gay people should do, how they should toe the left-wing line."

I said, "I'm more interested in your relationship with Charley Fitch."

“Pah. Charley still believed that gay rights laws were a good thing. We need less government, not more.”

“Yes, but if you’re dedicated to less government, why don’t you concentrate on important parts of less government? Why concentrate on having there be less government connected with protecting people’s rights? Why not fight about having less of the kind of government that takes away people’s rights?”

“We do that.”

“Funny, I didn’t see it on your web site or in any of your arguments.”

“Did you want a philosophical discussion, or are you here about Charley’s murder? Billy Karek begged me to talk to you. I’m not sure I like you.”

“Seems to be a lot of that going around the past two days.” I was the one who needed information here. I said, “I’m sorry if I was offensive. I’m trying to help my friend. I was hoping you could help.”

His look became a little less hostile.

“Did Charley have enemies?”

“I’d put it that he didn’t have many friends. He had lots of acquaintances. He had intimacy issues.”

“Political issues between him and everybody else or psychological issues with intimacy?”

“Maybe both. The main thing is, he didn’t have a lot of people skills. He had trouble being close to people. I don’t think he’d been on a date in a long time.”

“Maybe he didn’t find anybody who was his type to ask.”

“That may have been true, but nobody asked him either.”

“Maybe they did when you weren’t around.”

“He confided in me.”

“I’d heard you and he had a relationship, but also that you had strong animosity toward each other.”

“Our differences were strictly political, not personal. We have been friends for years. He and I would talk on the phone. Charley wasn't a bad guy. Our friendship transcended politics. I think he was closer to me than I was to him. He needed me more than I needed him. I have friends. He was kind of lost, lonely. When he wasn't talking about politics, he didn't have much to say. Kind of the ultimate Sixties-type radical, not much personality outside of his politics."

"But no specific quarrels? Karek said you weren't friends."

"Karek hadn't been close to Charley in years. They were lovers once, you know?"

"I'd heard."

Bergland said, "As far as suspects go, I think you should try that family of his. I heard there was all kinds of intrigue. That sister is a piece of work. She's odd. I've only met her a few times. She seemed more aloof than Charley and totally without his passion. She never seemed to have many people skills either. Charley was overtly hostile, very verbal. Mostly she radiated hostility and disdain, as if the rest of us weren't worth the time it took her to tell us how useless we were."

"She seemed okay when I talked to her. I had an introduction from a friend."

"That helped break the ice."

"Did Charley and his sister fight?"

"I heard she called the tune for that trust. She had the largest percent of the voting block, and she knew how to work the bunch of total loonies in that family. If Charley wanted something, he had to kowtow to her. The rest of the family didn't care much for Charley."

"Because he was gay?"

"Because he was a prolifigate left-wing commie. He spent all that capitalist-earned money on all these silly do-good causes."

"If the government isn't supposed to help them, and those who get rich shouldn't be helping them . . ."

"That leaves them to pull themselves up by their boot-straps."

Scott has more patience for debating people than I do. I ignored the opening for a politically correct back and forth and said, "I heard he hired call boys."

"He may have. I saw him with a few young things once in a while. I knew they weren't dates. I also was too discreet to ask how much they cost."

"How'd you know they weren't dates?"

"I'm not stupid."

I said, "Who benefits from Charley being dead?"

"I wouldn't know. I won't have someone to debate on talk shows, but that's not much of a benefit."

22

I met with the writer of Blithering Bullshit. He'd responded to my message of that morning. The columnist printed reams of blind items about feuding local gay politicos, nearly famous gay business people, and the not-as-famous-as-they-wished-they-were gay hangers-on. Even including all these categories, this was an extremely limited bunch. I figured these folks must all know each other in at least a peripheral way, and that writing a column about them was kind of an incestuous thing to do. His column appeared in the newest bar rag, *Party On*, which had more blank space on its pages than ads. The publication was the personal whim of a group of gay doctors who decided that investing in a gay newspaper was a good thing. Being nuts or taking poor investment advice is not limited by one's sexual orientation. The editor's lover was the writer of the column.

Fortunately, Scott and I had had the good sense to invite everyone in the Chicago gay media, including the editor of the rag and the columnist/lover, to our wedding. A dubious decision at the time, now turning out to be fortuitously helpful.

The writer of the column was Benjamin Awarjak. We met

at the Starbucks coffee shop on Broadway at Roscoe. We sat in the comfy chairs in the back. He squirmed with anticipation. He said, "I've wanted to talk to you so much since the wedding."

Actually, what he did for the next ten minutes was give a stunningly boring monologue about how tough his job was as truth teller to the community. I let him ramble. He was about five-foot-eight with hair died yellow on top and presumably naturally black below. He was overweight but wore loose clothes to cover any bulges. He might have been in his late twenties or early thirties.

When he finally wound down, I asked, "Did you know Charley Fitch?"

"Did I know him? Well, I'm here to tell you, there is dirt, dirt, dirt there to be known. Everybody's saying you found the head. Did you really?"

"Yep."

"The *Chicago Tribune* doesn't print that kind of thing, but I've heard it from several sources."

I said, "I haven't been keeping it a secret."

"What's it like finding a head?"

"Not nearly as much fun as people seem to imagine."

"Oh." A snippet of a pause. "Was there a lot of blood?"

"I guess I'm a little reluctant to talk about the details. The memory is still pretty raw."

"Of course. It must have been awful for you." He sounded about as sympathetic as a hooded cobra might just after it struck its victim. He sipped his drink.

"Can you fill me in on Charley's fights in the community?"

"Oh, yes, yes, yes my dear. I'm sure you're investigating who did it. I heard you were friends with Lee Weaver, the one the police arrested. I hope if you find anything out, you'll give me a call. I'm helping you here, and it would be great if the scoop came out in our paper."

"You'll be on my list of people to call." I didn't say how far down the list he would be. Most likely right after all the people in the Chicago phone book. Did he really think the news would wait for a weekly paper? Lack of a grasp of reality didn't seem to be limited to any sexual orientation, either.

He said, "Well, Snarly Bitch, and everybody loved calling him that, was hated, hated, hated. I've never heard a more perfect nickname. Once, I heard someone call him 'snarly bitch' to his face. One of the more enjoyable moments of the past party season. It was a vicious fight."

"When was that?"

"Last winter at a big New Year's Eve party. One of the lovers of one of the workers at the clinic made the crack. Marty Bennet, ex-worker, I might add."

I barely remembered Bennet. My memory said he worked as one of the underlings to Ken Wells.

Awarjak was gushing forth with the story. "Drinks were thrown. Tears were shed. It was the hit party of the winter season. Everybody talked about it for weeks."

And this is the world I was getting the gay kids ready to join? Although I knew the drama queens were in the great minority, they sure thought they were in the vast majority. And you were to respect their feeling of superiority. I didn't give a rat's ass. I swallowed all this critical claptrap. I wanted information, and I knew a cue when I saw one. I said, "What exactly happened?"

"Well, Snarly just walked into the party and started attacking people, although not anybody who might be a big donor to the clinic. He attacked under the guise of humor. Picking on people's outfits, or sneering at older gentlemen who appeared to be with someone significantly younger. Just rude, rude, rude. Marty Bennet's lover, Spike or Butch or some other hyper-masculine name, responded to Snarly in this deep, deep, deep rumbly voice almost too soft to hear. You know, like the bass on the stereo on high but the volume low." Awarjak leaned toward me and whispered. "I almost came in my pants just listening to him."

"You were that near to them?"

"As close as I am to you right now. The lover was in this fabulous leather outfit. Had the perfect build for it. So few people who wear leather really wear it well, don't you think?"

Scott looks fabulous in leather. I didn't mention this. I said, "The exact correct fashion can be difficult for the unwary."

"You are so right. So in that deep voice, he says, 'Why do you feel such a need to be so rude to those who are in your employ.' Snarly just went ballistic. He said, 'I'm busy. I don't have time to deal with daily drivel.' And the leather guy said, 'Everybody's busy.' And Snarly said, 'My job is more important than everyone else's.' And the leather guy said, 'Not in the larger scheme of the universe, it isn't.' Snarly was getting redder and redder in the face. Marty Bennet said, 'Let's just leave.' And the leather guy said, 'No.' So Snarly said, 'I do more good for this community in one day than all the others in this town have since Stonewall.' And the leather guy said, 'That doesn't give you the right to be a rude, egotistical, snarly bitch.' Well, drinks flew. Snarly threw first. I think half the people at the party wanted to dump their drinks on Snarly. Some were too polite. Some didn't want to get in the middle of a fight. The few clinic employees in attendance were probably terrified for their jobs."

"How did it end up?"

"Well, Snarly insisted the couple be thrown out. He fired Marty Bennet on the spot. Although I heard he rehired him a few days later. He was mercurial like that. The host got them into separate rooms. Everybody cooled down. Snarly left soon after. Marty and his lover stayed to the bitter end. Trying to prove a point, I suppose."

"Any other big fights?"

"Well, there was all that gay right-wing brouhaha. It was

even more delicious, delicious, delicious. The old gay left and the new gay right hate each other. It made great grist for my column. Their spats were guaranteed to make good copy. I could almost always count on one or the other side for some kind of dirt for every issue. Lots of times, I'd get one to make a comment and then trot over to the other. They hate each other personally and passionately."

"Anyone specifically?"

"Anybody who I think might be a suspect? Well, there's the fella the board had as a ringer investigating the fundraising scandals."

"You knew about that?"

"Everybody knew about that. They had this hot, hot, hot guy volunteer." If he repeated another word three times, I thought I might rip his tongue out for him myself.

"Who was he?"

"Timothy Chong. Very slim. Very smart. He got in and I heard the scandal he discovered was going to rip the roof off the secrets in this community. There wouldn't be a gay community organization that wasn't touched."

"That sounds a little strong."

"We'll see soon enough. There's a lot of big money in this town. Gay money. One report I heard was that the clinic was going to be revealed as one of the groups that spent the most on overhead and the least on meeting the needs of the clients."

"But a lot of it was Charley Fitch's own money."

"Yes, he did add a lot, but he didn't have near enough to keep such a large organization going. The renovations a few years ago cost a fortune. He's got nearly half the block on that side of the street. The mortgage payments on all that properly have got to be immense."

"Why not just move to a smaller building in a less expensive suburb?"

Awarjak said, "Prestige. You want an office in a decent

neighborhood in Chicago or be exiled to luxury in Berwyn? Please, Berwyn? There is no luxury in Berwyn. It would be humiliating."

I wondered if the people of Berwyn would agree.

I asked, "Did you know someone from one of the gay papers was investigating?"

"No. Which paper? Who?"

It wasn't as if the knowledge was going to harm Charley. And telling Awarjak might get him to give me more information. I said, "A guy from the *Gay Trib*. Evan Smith."

Awarjak snorted. "Evan Smith is this young, desperate kid. He's got more student loan bills to pay from Northwestern than any three other people. He doesn't strike me as very bright. He was investigating? Did he find out anything?"

He might be willing to sneer at Evan Smith, but he didn't want to be scooped by Evan Smith. I said, "He agrees with you. There might have been fraud."

"I wasn't investigating per se, but I snooped as best I could into everything in this community. It was all grist for the mill. If it was delicious gossip, I wanted it. I knew what the board was doing because, Edward, my lover, is also on the board. He got me all kinds of inside information. There was more intrigue with those people than there were official votes to take action."

"What about the other gay papers?"

"The *Gay Trib* likes to think they're a real paper. I guess they resemble it more than most of the gay rags in this town, but really, gay papers like that are passé. You can find most important news about gay people in the *New York Times* now."

I didn't mention that a lot of people probably don't catch the *Times* every day. I asked, "What do you know about other right-wing people who hated Snarly?"

"You mean Billy Karek. Everybody saw the clips of their fight on the news. Karek and him had a history. Did you know they were lovers?"

"I'd heard a rumor."

"They were. It started when Karek was a senior in college at Yale. They met at a Pride parade about ten years ago. It was going to be true love and happiness forever. It was the talk of the gay world at the time."

I always kind of wondered how I managed to miss all this vital "talk of the gay world." Either it was a very, very small world, or I had a real life and they didn't.

"Karek was this handsome, up-and-coming star of the gay firmament. They traveled the world together. Well, one night, Snarly came back to find his true love in the arms of the president of the Log Cabin Republicans. That was before Karek converted to the right wing."

"Converted or not, Snarly had a right to be pissed."

"The television show wasn't the first time furniture was thrown."

"They had a history of violence?"

"No S and M that I know of, but domestic violence, abuse of some sort."

"Are you sure of this information?"

"Well, one puts two and two together. I never repeat gossip unless I've got it confirmed from at least two sources."

I doubted this. Frankly, I figured he just made up most of his crap.

"Did you ask Karek or Fitch about this?"

"Snarly ignored me completely. Karek confirmed it. I met him at an exclusive gay fundraising cruise on Lake Michigan."

"Why would he confirm it to you?"

"I try to be a friend to everyone who is someone in the gay community. But he was not the only right-wing person who fought with Snarly."

"Really?" A variation on my standard comment—how interesting, tell me more.

"Each side would plot against the other. Karek and his lover would make all kinds of elaborate plans. Each side was like a group of unsupervised little kids in a sandbox, but with chemical and biological weapons. There was no holding back. It was a frightful mess."

And a boon for you, I thought.

"What about Benton Fredricks, the guy whose show they had the fight on?"

"It is not true that Benton is a closet gay. So it is even more not true that he was or is Karek's lover."

"Did people think that?" I guess I miss all the good stuff.

"All kinds of people think Benton is gay. He is not married. I made it my business to find some of the women he dated in college. According to them, he was a hell of a lover."

"Until further notice we'll move him into the heterosexual column."

"But Karek isn't the only homocon in town. His lover, Reece, who is hot, hot, hot . . ."

The file drawer never looked so good to me.

"He's been in several porn magazines. Made a ton of money as an escort and in the video biz. You know how these young porn stars are supposed to waste all their money on drugs and circuit parties?"

"I've assumed the cliché to be true."

"Well, Reece saved every penny. He's very rich and very conservative. Has a degree in philosophy from Stanford. Supposedly had a professor from there as a client, which made matriculation much easier. I have no idea about that. I do know that he is bright, bright, bright. And big. Six-foot-six. The original blond Viking. Big, strong, handsome, and smart, hell of a combination. Reece and Karek were the toast of the town. No love lost there with Snarly. Some people say Reece is the brains in that household. I think he and Karek are both really bright."

"Did this Reece appear on any talk shows?"

"A few. Not as many as Karek. Reece was kind of the manager, setting up speaking engagements around the country. I don't want to imply that gay men are shallow, but the shows sometimes had Reece play Mr. Eye Candy. And he is. People responded to that. More importantly, do you think the homocons were at war with the leftists and that's why Snarly was killed?"

"I'll believe it if it helps get Lee out of jail."

"Personally, I think you need to look into the internal affairs of the clinic itself. Maybe even Snarly's family. You may know enough about the clinic, but do you know about the family?"

"I've talked to the sister. She doesn't like the gay press."

"She hates all of us. She felt we unfairly portrayed her brother. She always stood up for him. But I hear there's skeletons in that closet."

"What skeletons? They were openly gay and rich. Where's the problem?"

"There are other siblings, and I heard one or two of them were"—he leaned closer and whispered—"you hate to say this in polite company, but they were Republicans."

I figured he must be kidding, but maybe not. I said, "I'm not sure what that has to do with anything."

"The other siblings wanted the family money for their own projects. I don't think they were homophobic particularly. I just heard there were some feuds about how the money was spent."

"Exactly how many people were voting members of the family trust?"

"There were five besides Snarly and Susanna. They didn't have equal voices. I think that caused resentment. In their father's will he gave out odd percents. Susanna got thirty-nine point something. Each of the other six got nine point something. There was one uncontrolled percent that could break ties among them."

"Who was in charge of that?"

"I don't know. I do know that the two brothers and three cousins are supposed to be rich brats and eccentric loonies. I've never met them. Walter Truby had some connection there. He might be able to get you an introduction."

"How did the family make its money?"

"Started out in snake oil, real, genuine, fake snake oil, back in the 1880s, graduated to Colpers Products today."

"*The* Colpers?"

"Yep. One of the biggest drug manufacturing companies in the world. Makes a ton of money, especially in third-world countries."

"A pharmaceutical company operating in the third world? That's got to be ripe for traffic in illegal drugs. Hell, even illicit prescription drugs. A perfect motive for murder."

"That may well be, but Snarly had nothing to do with that part of the family's money. The foundation existed for this generation of kids. Old Man Fitch didn't trust any of his offspring. He left sensible business people in charge of the company. I've never heard a whiff of scandal about the company. The kids and cousins got a percentage of the profits every year, but they had no say in the running of the business. From what I heard, Snarly never even spent his percentage of the profits on himself."

"How much money are we talking about?"

"The profits? Millions but not billions. Eight figures, maybe nine."

"More than enough money to kill for."

"I don't think this is about money. Besides, I never heard that Charley had any interest in being in business. Their trust, along with the company itself, combined with overseas holdings, is one of the top twenty in the world. That's comparing family trusts. They've got plenty more than enough cash to play with. Nope, I think you have to look to that clinic or people who worked with him to find a killer."

"I'd like to try and talk to the rest of the family." I didn't know how I'd get an introduction. Certainly the sister didn't seem very open.

The reporter said, "I really think you need to look to the clinic. How many spies for how many different groups were working at the clinic?"

"I'm not sure." I figured there were at least two, Smith from the Karek/Wells faction and Timothy Chong for the board. Then again, maybe all the volunteers were spies for someone else. Although if they were, you'd think they'd go out of their way to be polite to each other and not make waves. How the hell can you hide that many spies? I had this vision of a Marx Brothers comedy with one investigator going out a back door while another came in a side door.

He said, "The clinic is a huge organization. It does all that youth work, and a great deal more. And Snarly has been an activist for a long, long time. He knows everybody. And they had that outreach program to let other organizations meet in all those rooms. He was planning to use that two-story office building they just bought to set up a woman's clinic. I think that was to mollify his sister Susanna."

"But you don't think this is about cash?"

"No. Who was it that said the rich are different? Hemingway, Fitzgerald? I don't remember, but it's true. These people weren't worried about money."

"But they had to scramble to get donations for the clinic."

"Well, yeah, but not for personal money."

I said, "If it's not about money, maybe it's about sex. I heard Charley Fitch used call boys."

"Yes, he did."

"You seem awfully sure of that."

"He and I used the same escort service."

It was such a casual announcement that it took a moment to register. I managed to say, "You did?"

"Yeah. It wasn't that big a deal."

"Could one of the guys from the service have been planning to meet him Friday night?"

"I have no idea."

"Could you help me find out?"

"Sure, but none of the guys from the service are violent."

"You're the one who says this isn't about money. It's got to be about something. That's a place to ask questions. Are you saying that none of the guys for this service did S-and-M scenes?"

"I guess they must have, but they are not a violent lot. They're very professional."

"Yes, I suppose they are." I think I kept the sarcasm out of my voice.

Awarjak said, "I can try and find out who he had dates with recently."

My cell phone rang.

It was Larry Mullen. "Mr. Mason, you better get here. I need your help." He gasped and gulped several times, as if he'd just got done running a two-mile sprint and was trying to breathe, drink fluids, and talk simultaneously.

"What's wrong?"

"You gotta help me."

"Where are you?"

"In the clinic basement. Please hurry here."

"What's wrong?"

"There's a big problem."

"Are you going to hurt yourself?"

"No."

"If you're in danger, call the police. Now. Do not wait for me." I wasn't going to be responsible for him being dead when I got there.

He said, "I think the danger's over. Please hurry."

I left.

23

The front door of the clinic had been padlocked. Yellow crime-scene tape flapped in the cool breeze. I rushed around to the back where I figured the kids' entrance had to be. It was solidly boarded up.

I hurried to the back door I'd used the morning before. Night sounds of the city drifted into the alley: an ambulance siren, passing traffic on Addison, the rumble of a bus, the slurred song of a reveler who'd revelled too much. Broken bits of light from a distant alley lamp caught on various pieces of metal in the darkened entry. The padlock hung from a broken hunk of metal. This crime-scene tape lay strewn and broken on the ground. As I approached, the door began to inch open. I saw a hand reach out of the blackness. The padlock fell to the ground. It clattered for an instant or so. The door slid open. I could make out Larry's face. Light fell on the pale beige of the sleeve of his letterman's jacket. I saw several dark stains on it. I smelled piss.

I rushed forward.

"Help," he mumbled and grabbed me fiercely. I held him several moments, then moved out of the dim light to just inside the clinic's doorway. He put his hand on my arm and leaned toward me. He still breathed heavily. I could smell cheap burger on his breath. With his other hand he wiped his eyes. He said, "In the basement."

I didn't move. "What?"

"It's Jan."

I led the way to the basement stairs. Any crime scene-tape we encountered was lying on the floor. At the top of the stairs, I found the light switch, flicked it on, and then proceeded down. It was my first time in the basement. The first room we entered had remnants of blood stains along the walls and floor. Here's where Snarly's killer had done his work. Thick wooden beams crossed the ceiling. Pipes of different circumferences trailed along the ceiling and walls.

Larry pointed. He led the way through a second to a third room. Jan hung from a center beam. His face was deep purple. The room smelled acrid. His khaki pants were stained. He'd soiled himself. I held my breath and walked up to him. No question. He was very dead. His feather boa was tight around his neck and tied to the beam. They must make feather boas industrial strength if they didn't break under the pressure of a dangling body.

I heard Larry start to cry. I led him back upstairs. We sat in my office. As good a place as any. I decided I wanted to be in a space that was comfortable and familiar to me. The filing cabinet was gone.

Larry snuffled a long while and used the tissue from the box on the desk. When he was under sufficient control, I asked, "What happened?"

"My dad was really angry with me. Really angry. I've never seen him so mad. I was supposed to go to football camp starting early tomorrow. My dad said he wasn't sure he was going to let me go. Then coach called. Word had gotten around school already about all this shit. Kids blab. He told me not to bother to go to the camp. So I went kind of nuts. My dad demanded I tell him what was going on, but I just walked out. I went to my boyfriend's house. At least, I thought he was a friend. His dad wouldn't let me see him. I don't know if it was because I was gay or because of all this murder stuff. I had nowhere else to go, so I came here. I figured I could find a spot in the basement away from where it happened."

He started to cry again. I patted his shoulder and waited for him to compose himself.

"How'd you get in?"

"The kids' entrance was blocked up. I used a piece of concrete from the alley to bust the padlock on the back door. I got here just after sunset. I couldn't turn on any lights. The shadows spooked me. We keep some candles and matches hidden behind one of the ceiling tiles in that first room. I managed to get a couple of those. I lit a candle. When I got to the third room, I saw Jan. I was shook up, but I managed to get close enough to be sure he wasn't breathing. I've never been so scared or so frightened, but if I could've I would have done something to save him." He held out his stained sleeves. "I tried to lift him down. I called his name. He wasn't breathing." He started to bawl. He reached toward me. I awkwardly held him and patted his back and made soothing noises.

After several minutes he muttered into my shoulder, "Why'd he do that?"

"I don't know," I said.

Larry sat back in his chair. He stared down at his hands folded in front of him. "All of us think about killing ourselves," he said. "We talk about that in our group sessions. When I finally asked my boyfriend to go out, I was petrified. I know you don't die from embarrassment, but I thought about offing myself if he said no. He could tell everybody."

His face was a mess. He blew his nose.

I said, "I'm going to have to call the police. I'll call my lawyer. You're going to have to tell your dad."

"What happens if I just leave? Can you keep me out of this?"

"I'd have to give a reason for breaking in here." I had the fleeting thought that the kid could leave, and I'd be stuck without an explanation.

"Maybe we could both leave."

"Then why bother to call me over here?"

"I had to tell somebody."

I said, "Neither of us has done anything wrong. We don't know for sure if Jan committed suicide."

"Sure looks that way."

I said, "It's not an easy way to commit murder, but the police always treat every unexplained death as a homicide until it's proved otherwise. If it was suicide, why would Jan do it?"

His voice got very low and I barely heard his whisper. "I came down here to kill myself. Didn't you think about killing yourself when you were a kid?"

Painful memories welled to the surface. I didn't want to talk about my feelings of fear and loneliness as a teenager. Not with a kid I barely knew. I wasn't comfortable with those feelings then, and remembering them does not meet my definition of fun. But the kid needed an answer. And gay teenagers are still far more likely to try suicide than their straight counterparts. I told him about my discomfort discussing painful feelings. I added, "I never tried anything. I never really got close. When I got really depressed, I'd either sleep, work out for extra hours on the football field, or try to deny my feelings. I didn't deal with them in the best way, but they never overwhelmed me. My parents loved me, and I always knew they would. I wasn't picked on by the other kids. I was a football player, like you. I was athletic. I hid pretty successfully most of the time. Your dad might have been angry tonight, but my guess is he loves you. And you know you have a group of people who would be willing to do anything they could to help you."

He didn't look convinced. I was speaking to a hope, not a certainty. Larry said, "That's why I came here tonight. I didn't see a way out."

"I'm not sure there's always a perfect solution to our problems, but for coming out there's always someone to call or talk to."

"I wasn't thinking real well," he said. "I'm not going to hurt myself. I wish I was older and was on my own with a lover."

"Both gay and straight kids have that same kind of desire. For now, for this situation, the truth is going to be better. We've got calls to make. It's not going to look good us being in here. We'll have to tough it out. I'll stay with you. Neither my lawyer nor I will abandon you."

"My dad might."

"We'll get through it." I tried to infuse my tone with confidence. Yeah, we get through things. Time, whether we like it or not, does pass. Sometimes what we go through hurts a lot and for this kid, it might hurt a great deal.

I dialed my lawyer.

Todd said, "A what?"

"You heard me."

"I know what I heard, and I'm stuck believing you. That's two this week."

"Technically it's one last week and one this week."

"Are you planning on finding any more?"

"I wasn't planning on these two."

"That's what they all say."

"I'm not some demented Miss Marple."

"We'll have to try that."

"What?"

"The demented-Miss-Marple defense."

"We could try the client-pushed-the-lawyer-off-the-cliff gambit."

"Never works." He sighed. "Who is it?"

"Jan, the kid who . . ."

"I remember. Maybe somebody wanted to shut him up. Of course, that would limit the suspects to only the people who ever met him."

I said, "I think that would be funnier if I hadn't just found the body."

"It's not the first gay kid committing suicide in the city. It won't be the last."

"Doesn't make it feel any better."

"You sure it's suicide?"

"I'm not sure of anything except I'm nervous and uncertain."

Todd told me he'd be down. I phoned the police. Larry called his dad. I spoke to him briefly. How could he sound anything but unhappy?

After the calls, Larry said, "Your lawyer sounds like kind of an odd guy, although he was nice to me."

"Todd thinks sarcasm and wit are the highest art forms. He likes to tease. He's great."

"I didn't tell the police or the lawyer about Mr. Weaver coming back."

"It hasn't come up in my discussions with them."

"Maybe I should have just run like hell and not told anyone."

"Could you really have kept silent?"

"I guess not. It was awful."

I said, "If this one is suicide, and it sure looks that way, then the deaths probably aren't connected. If somehow it's not suicide, we know Lee didn't do it—he's still in jail."

"I don't want it to be Mr. Weaver."

"Neither do I," I said. "Tell me what you can about Jan."

"He was a jerk. I already told you how I hated that effeminate shit. I don't get that. I'm interested in guys. I don't want to be a woman or dress in woman's clothes. If I wanted a woman, I wouldn't be dating guys. I don't want to get in touch with my feminine side. I don't even understand what they're talking about when someone says that. Is that a gay thing?"

"Some people confuse being gay with gender identity issues. Others seem to think particular emotions or the ability to be in touch with them belongs to one sex or the other. Then there's the whole drag queen phenomenon. In Jan's case, my guess is, he assumed that persona to get attention."

"It sure seemed like an act. He used to zero in on me at meetings. He always wanted me to talk more. I think he thought if I shared my feelings, he could claim he was closer to me than he was. Getting my attention seemed so important to him. I didn't understand it. It annoyed me more than anything."

"I imagine he's been picked on for a very long time. Most likely jocks have played a part in that."

"I never pick on anybody. Ever."

"Do you intervene if somebody else is being picked on?"

"Yes."

A brave young man.

"Or speak up when somebody makes harmful gay jokes or gay slurs?"

He hesitated. "Usually."

Perhaps as brave as many of us.

He asked, "If it's not suicide, why would someone want to kill Jan? He was an annoying asshole, but I don't see why anybody would want to kill him. It doesn't make sense."

"Unless it's connected with Charley Fitch's murder."

"You think it might be?"

"I think it could be. I don't know. I'd like to find out where Jan was all day today. I wonder if he knew something about what happened Friday night and Saturday morning."

Larry said, "He asked me once if I wanted to do a three-way with him and another guy. I think the other guy wasn't very interested in him but was interested in me. The whole idea was creepy. It was like, maybe Jan wanted to watch."

"Or he thought it was the only possible way he could get physically close to you."

Larry said, "What if he saw me? Maybe he came back that night to try and watch me and my friend. Maybe he didn't leave. Jan is the kind of guy who'd get his kicks out of watching. That's kind of sick."

"How could he get down there without being heard?"

"We were always very quiet down there. Lots of kids used this place when there were adults upstairs. No one came down. The basement is kind of bleak and miserable. There's no real heat in the winter. From late spring to early fall, it's not so bad. It can be spooky. Some of the kids got off on it being scary. We'd talk about doing one of those teen slasher movies with gay characters. It was kind of a joke. Everybody was so tired of Jan walking up behind them and shouting boo. He could always beat a joke to death."

The police showed up. It's an understatement to say that Detectives Abernathy and Stafford were not happy.

Larry's dad arrived. The police took the two of them to a separate venue for questioning. While I waited my turn, I had time to sit and reflect.

I was miserable about Jan's death. I was horrified if it was murder. If it was suicide, and it sure looked that way, I felt guilty as well. I remembered Dustin, Lee's lover, saying Jan was a strong kid. From what I'd seen, there were no signs of a struggle. I could ask the cops if there was any forensic evidence of one. I know I'd disparaged Jan often. Not to his face, but perhaps I and the other adults could have reacted differently, somehow saved him. The poor kid didn't deserve to die. I could imagine the world being a quieter place without Jan, and that thought made me feel worse. His being dead didn't make me like him, but if his death was a suicide, it was a tragedy. If it was murder, there was little question in my mind that it had something to do with Charley Fitch's death. A logical, but unproven assumption, was that Jan might have been investigating and got caught up in something way too big for himself. Whether he actually did know anything, or the killer just thought he did, Jan might have had to be gotten rid of. It was possible that finding out who Jan had talked to and why he was dead would go a long way toward answering a lot of the questions about Fitch's death. Two deaths in two days in the same venue not being related? I found that hard to believe.

24

I met Jan's parents. They looked like a perfectly ordinary suburban couple. Their faces showed strain and tears. I only talked to them for a few moments.

"You found him?" Mr. Aiello asked.

"Yes, I'm sorry." They were led away.

Larry's dad turned out to be a decent enough guy. Mr. Mullen certainly had the remnants of the heft required to play college sports. He had sandy brown hair turning to gray. We talked for a few minutes. He neither yelled nor blustered.

Mr. Mullen said, "What kind of world is it that makes it so hard for kids like mine, that gives them so many obstacles?"

I said, "Larry is worried about how you're dealing with him being gay."

"Hell, I'm not happy about it, but he's my kid. I do my best with him. I just think it's harder for him being this way. I don't want him to change. I do want him to survive. Who is this kid who's dead?"

I told him about Jan.

Mr. Mullen said, "Yeah, I don't get that effeminate crap. My kid didn't know him, did he?"

"He'd met him here at the clinic. I haven't heard of any fights or problems between them. Jan might have had a mild crush on Larry. That's not a crime." I doubted if it would lead to murder, but I'd have to check out Jan's feelings.

"What are the police going to do?" he asked.

"I don't know."

He said, "He called you and not me."

What could I say to that?

Into the silence, Mr. Mullen said, "At least he had somebody to call."

I didn't ask about his earlier fight with Larry, the one that drove him out of the house. He was here now. That's what counted.

After Larry and my lawyer finished with the cops, they stopped by where I was waiting to be interviewed. Larry's shoulders didn't look like they could droop any further. I hoped he'd recover from the horror of what he'd seen. His dad thanked me for helping out. Larry hugged me tightly and whispered, "Thanks." They left.

Abernathy and Stafford badgered me for a bit. Todd kept the worst of their attacks at bay.

When they seemed to have run out of questions, I asked, "Did Jan commit suicide or was he murdered?"

Abernathy said, "You've got the nerve to ask us questions?"

"Yeah. It's not illegal to ask."

"Yeah," Stafford said, "it's also not legally required for us to give you any information."

I asked, "Can you give me any details about what happened to Charley Fitch?"

I got a lot of silence from the cops. I decided what the hell, I had a bunch of questions, why not go for broke. Anything beyond silence would be a plus, right? I asked, "How did the killer get Fitch to hold still? Did he lure him to the basement? I haven't heard anything about blood anywhere else in the clinic. Why kill him down there? What difference did it make to the killer where he killed him? If he was upstairs getting the ax from Lee's office, why go back downstairs?"

"Excellent questions," Abernathy said.

I said, "I appreciate the positive reinforcement, but am I going to get any answers?"

More silence.

I said, "I'm up to my nipples in this. If I was the killer I'd already know the answers to these questions. If I'm not, what does it hurt to tell me?"

Todd said, "Please tell us what you can. Perhaps if we knew more, we'd be able to help."

Stafford said, "Charley Fitch was killed by a blow with the ax from behind. That would need somebody large and strong, such as yourself."

Todd said, "Or a very lucky or very strong smaller person."

"Maybe," Abernathy said.

Undaunted, I asked another question. "Did Charley Fitch struggle? Where there signs of a fight?"

Instead of answering, the police tried to have me go through everything again. Todd said, "Once is enough."

When the police were done with me and I was outside, Daisy Tajeda walked up. She said, "Are you all right, Tom?"

"I'll be okay."

She said, "They made me temporary director of the clinic. I'm sorry this had to happen to you, but I'm glad Larry Mullen had someone to turn to."

I nodded.

Todd said, "I know it's late, but Lee is in the Rainbow Café. He said he'd wait for you. I don't know if he's still there."

"Is he okay?"

"I'll let you decide."

"Did he come with you?"

"I was picking him up when you called. This is my first chance to talk to you without the police around since I got here."

Tajeda said, "I was over there. He very much wants to talk to you, Tom."

I said, "I need to talk to him as well." I was glad Lee was out. I was tired and would have preferred to go home, but I was also still very pissed at Lee for lying about going back to the clinic. I wanted some answers.

The Rainbow Café was a twenty-four-hour operation. Late night in winter, watching snow gently falling, with books and wood and warmth around you and the soft flakes filling the night was a joy to look upon.

Lee looked like hell. He said, "Tajeda told me about Jan. Christ, what is wrong with this world? Jan would be one of the last kids to commit suicide. What the hell happened?"

"No one knows for sure. It looks like suicide, but with one murder already at the clinic, I presume they're being extra careful."

"You found him?"

"Larry Mullen did. He called me."

"How is he?"

"Not so good."

"I should try and talk to him."

"He says he went down there to commit suicide himself."

"Ah, jeez, the poor kid. I like him. He and I have talked a lot. I had hoped he was past that. His dad has strong ambivalent feelings about Larry being gay. Did Larry cry for you?"

I gave him a quizzical look.

Lee said, "The kid is a crier. For such a big kid, it is a little odd. His dad is one of the those guys who goes to every one of his kid's games."

"That's good."

"And bellows and screams and constantly points out faults. I went to one of Larry's games. The kid was not exaggerating. There's lots of verbal abuse in that family, most of it connected with athletics."

I said, "Larry is afraid if he's openly gay, he'll lose his scholarships and his chance to play football in college."

"He probably would. Football is almost that kid's entire world. He sublimates most of his desires into sports. I'll try and call him tomorrow. Did he seem okay when you left him?"

"About himself, yeah. About finding the body, no."

"Why would Jan want to kill himself? His confidence was real. What you saw was what you got. He was up so much, it was hard for people to see there was a down side there."

"I always assumed there was. I assume this was not his first attempt."

"I don't know about that. I can't believe he'd do it. Jan would spew his highs on anyone. He'd be more likely to talk himself to death. Any of his friends who listened long enough might suffer the same fate. All Jan all the time is not a pretty thought."

I said, "If somebody killed him, it was a clumsy way to commit murder."

"So is chopping somebody up with an ax. When did this happen?"

"They didn't tell me."

"If it was murder, at least they can't accuse me of that one. Your lawyer is a saint."

"That's how I usually refer to him, Saint Todd."

"The cops told me not to leave town. I thought I was in a lousy television crime show. How'd your lawyer have that much money for bail? Dustin and I don't have that kind of cash. Did you and Scott pay?"

"Yes."

"We can't pay you back."

"There isn't going to be a need. You didn't do it. We need to do everything we can to prevent a trial. We need to find out who did it."

"Thank you. A thousand times, thank you."

"Have you seen Dustin?" I thought it odd that he hadn't gone home first or called Dustin to pick him up from jail. Perhaps Todd was convenient, but I know my first impulse after such a horrific experience would be to be with Scott. Maybe all wasn't well in their relationship.

"I haven't been home yet. I called him on my cell phone while your lawyer drove me. I came to see you because I wanted to find out what was going on. Your lawyer said people had been congregating over here. What's happened since I was taken away?"

I told him. When I got to the part about the kids in the basement, I said, "You were pretty quiet when that was brought up in the café. Did you know about them using it for trysts?"

"Hell, I used to use it for trysts when I was a kid. And it had been in use for years before that. It was a known place to meet. It's probably been used since the weekend after they opened the clinic. Kids are resourceful."

"But as an adult you felt no need to do something about it?"

"No. Hell, it was fun. You could make out, and you could listen to the adults sometimes. Snarly always used to stay late. One time he was entertaining some guy, probably a call boy. It was hysterical. Us kids laughed about it for ages. That night he was begging the call boy to ride him like a stallion. We thought that was gross and funny."

"Snarly being sexually odd would be amusing to repressed teenagers."

"I guess. The basement was an outlet. A safe haven. I was not about to take that away from the kids. As long as they used condoms and common sense, I didn't care."

I sort of agreed. "But you took a job knowing about the fights and about Fitch's peccadilloes."

"There's no better place for accomplishing what I wanted to. Every place has a boss. Every place has oddities."

"The kids were down there the night of Fitch's murder. Two of them heard you go back a second time to talk to Fitch." I watched him carefully.

He had the grace not to attempt to deny his presence.

"Who heard me?"

"Not relevant."

He wouldn't meet my eyes.

I said, "I don't like being lied to."

"I'm sorry. I should have told you. I was wrong. I was worried about being accused."

"Did you tell Todd?"

"No. Did the kids tell the police?"

"No."

"Have you?"

"No."

"Why not?"

"They like you. I like you."

"Still?"

"Yes. A little less than I did forty-eight hours ago, but this is a murder investigation. Things can get very screwed up very fast."

"I wasn't thinking. I'm so sorry. You've been a friend for a long time. I treated you like shit. And you're a suspect. And the kids are in trouble. I've betrayed who I am and my profession."

He was miserable. In a lot of ways I thought he should be. I don't like being lied to, but I had history with him. I'd helped him as a kid. While that didn't obligate me forever, there was a bond he had strained but had not yet broken.

Why was I helping him? Because I looked at him and saw the seventeen-year-old gay kid who came out to me when he was in high school. And up to now he had been a genuinely nice guy.

I said, "You came to talk to me yesterday when you were worried you might have been the last to see him. Why didn't you tell me about the second visit?"

"I figured no one had seen me. It was so late. I was ashamed of how I'd acted. I really was petrified of losing this job. I've got a lot of heavy bills. My student loans are crushing, but I'm in this for the kids. I know I can do a lot of good for them."

I knew that was true. I was also aware that he was financially strapped. After he announced he was gay, Lee's parents had refused to spend a penny toward his college education.

Lee was saying, "Dustin's in no position to pick up the slack for all our bills. I wouldn't want him to if he could. I'm not in a relationship with him so I can be supported." I didn't bother to remind him that he could sell his expensive yellow Corvette.

"But you didn't tell me about the second visit."

"I am very, very sorry about that. I took advantage of you. I'm sorry. I wish I'd thought more clearly. I didn't. I really need help now. If you found out about that second visit, the police could, too."

"Yep."

He rubbed his hands across his face. "I'm in deep shit. You're not telling and that puts you in deep shit. You're making a hell of a sacrifice I'm not sure I deserve. I've put the kids in an awful position. I don't know what to do." He had the forlorn look on his face he had when I first saw him in high school—vulnerable, lost, and a little bit desperate.

"The important questions are, why did you go back and what the hell happened?"

He said, "I made the fatal mistake of believing that if I was eloquent enough, I could convince him of anything. I was so wrong. He was meaner than ever. I talked and talked. He smirked and smirked. He kept caressing that damn cast-iron poodle. For the millionth time I wished I could take both sides of that smirk and stretch them from here to pain and gone. I was stupid to go back the first time, even stupider to try again."

He wouldn't look at me and his eyes shifted. There had to be more. I said, "Why did you go back?"

"I told you."

"I'm not buying it."

He finally looked at me. His eyes were wet. He said, "When I got home, Dustin wasn't there. We'd fought earlier in the day. About Snarly. Sometimes he comes to meet me without telling me. Usually he calls. Dustin said he was sick of me being a doormat. I was afraid he might try something stupid. He wasn't home. I didn't know where he was. I haven't had the nerve to ask him. When I got home the second time, he was in bed. I thought he was pretending to be asleep."

"Did you ask him later where he'd been?"

"I was afraid to." That he was sleeping next to a killer, that his lover had been out with another man?

"Would he kill Fitch because your boss was mean to you?"

"I don't know. I don't think so. Dustin is an aggressive guy, but he wouldn't do that."

"Are you sure?"

He shook his head. I waited until he was looking at me and then I spoke very softly, "Did you kill Charley Fitch?"

His eyes didn't waver. "I deserve that, I suppose."

"Let's suppose you do."

He looked away for several moments then looked back at me and held my gaze. He said as softly as I had asked the question, "I did not kill him. He was alive when I left. I swear to God."

"He didn't say if he was going home or going out?"

"No. At the end he just stared at me with that fatuous

smile on his face. I swear to God, I could have killed him at that moment, but I didn't."

"I'm sure lots of people have wanted to. What's worse is now you've put these kids in an untenable position. They know you and don't want you to get in trouble, but they have information about a murder investigation. Do you want to leave the kids in that kind of position? I know you said you thought you should call Larry. I would suggest you not do that."

He looked at me. "I've got to do something." After a few moments' pause he said, "If I tell the police, I'll be arrested again. I didn't get raped or anything, but the prison was awful. I never want to go back. I guess I could tell Todd."

I said, "I'm not sure you have much choice. At the least, you've got to take pressure off these kids."

"I promise I'll tell Todd." He twisted his fingers together. "I know you don't owe me anything, but do you have any possible suspects besides me?"

"Dustin."

Lee blanched.

I said, "I'll have to talk to him."

"He didn't do it."

I just looked at him.

He gulped. "Anyone else?"

I said, "I'm trying to get an interview with one of the call boys he was currently seeing. Maybe there was one there this past Friday."

"As an adult, I never asked about his sexual escapades. I never cared. I haven't used the place since I was a kid. Dustin and I stick to our apartment." He took a sip of coffee. "I feel bad that the kids are in the middle of this. Is Larry the only one who heard me? Is that why he was back there? He wasn't trying to hurt himself because of me?"

"He heard you."

"Shit. I'm supposed to be helping kids, not fucking them

up. I've got to help find out who did this. I've got to clear my name. Sitting in jail was twenty-four hours of pure hell. I know you're pretty angry, but I need your help."

I remembered the first time I'd met Lee. I'd found him in the boy's washroom on the second floor of the high school. I'd heard moaning from out in the hall. He'd been severely beaten. I found out later he'd been trash canned and given a shit-infused swirly topped off with the beating. His injuries put him in the hospital for a week. He'd come back to school looking like a martyr. Back then he'd held his head up and kept going.

I agreed to help.

"Who could have done it?" he asked. "Not one of the kids."

"I don't think so. My guess is one of the employees or volunteers at the clinic or one of the people Charley feuded with in the community. Plus there's the brewing financial scandal."

"You think that's really true?"

"I hope so for your sake."

Lee said, "I had as little to do with fundraising as I could. I hate that shit. It's like begging for your supper."

"Other people had to do work to pay your salary. It paid your bills." I knew it was harsh, but I wasn't quite ready to add reality checks to my list of things I wasn't going to say to him.

He looked abashed. "You're really angry."

"Yes."

"I'll apologize as many times as necessary and do whatever it takes to get you to trust me again. You were my teacher. You were my friend in high school when I had nobody. I'm so sorry."

I didn't need for him to be groveling, but I didn't think a healthy dose of guilt would hurt much either.

"I'm going to help you," I said. "We can work on our relationship after we find out who did this."

"Thanks. Whatever you can do, thanks." He took a deep

breath and then sipped some coffee. He said, "Have you talked to the homocons? That's a place to look, although I have a hard time picturing any of them wielding an ax."

I said, "I can picture a number of people I know doing great violence. There's a line we usually don't cross. The police think you were capable of crossing it."

"Do you?"

"I think any of us is capable. I don't think you killed Charley Fitch."

"Thanks." He paused. "Why not?"

"I've known you for a long time. I watched you grow up. It might sound sappy to call it instinct, but I don't think you did it. That you lied pisses me off, but it doesn't make you a murderer."

"Thanks for that. Is there anything I can do, we can do?"

"I think you should keep a low profile. The police won't be happy about me investigating. The actual arrested suspect getting involved in asking questions might really piss them off, but you can help me. Do you know Karek and these other homocons, Albert Bergland and Mandy Marlex?"

"I know Mandy a little bit. I've met her at a few events. Albert I only know from comments Snarly made. Snarly hated them both. I think the feeling was mutual."

"Bergland told me he and Charley were close."

"Not from what Charley told me, but then he could rip somebody one minute and be their best friend the next. He was such a hypocrite."

Brenda Hersch, Jan's closest friend, walked in. Her face was a mass of tears.

25

Brenda scanned the crowd, spotted us, and rushed over.

"Is it true?" she gasped. "Is it true?"

"I'm sorry," I said.

She didn't stop sobbing for five minutes. We brought her napkins to clean up with. Lee held her hand and patted her on the back.

"Is it true you found this body?" she asked.

I nodded then asked, "Do you know why he would commit suicide?"

"No. No. No. Jan would never do that. Never. I hotmailed him off and on today. He was investigating Fitch's murder. He was talking to all the kids who used the clinic. He was trying to find things out. He was excited. Sure, we all talked about depression. Sometimes with the counselors. Mr. Weaver, you were great. We all trusted you. Are you okay? The police let you go. They don't still think you did it do they?" She clutched his arm.

"I'm afraid so. I'm out on bail."

"Oh, but I know you didn't kill anybody. I know you wouldn't ever."

"Do you know if Jan actually found out anything?" I asked.

"He wanted to meet with me, but he couldn't get out of the house during the day. He was supposed to call me this evening. His parents were going to a play. They took his cell phone away, but we still had the Internet. Jan wasn't one of those gothic depressos. Jan was always 'up.' He never got down. But he could get serious. None of you ever saw that side. Everybody thought the drag-queen stuff was an act, but that was Jan. He was pure. He wanted to be exactly what he was. Everybody at the clinic kept telling us to be ourselves. Well, Jan was himself. That's exactly who he was. Why do so many people think that if we just be ourselves, we'll all be calm and sensible and reasonable? I can't believe he's gone. He was so vibrant. I could talk to him better than anyone else."

"How did you get out of the house?" I asked. "Weren't your parents angry about you being involved in all this?"

"My parents are pretty liberal. When I told them last year, they took my being a lesbian surprisingly well. They found about the clinic before I did. They drove me here for my first meeting. They thought it was a good place for me to meet people. It was outside the school environment. They were right. They always told me they would help me any way they could."

I asked, "Did Jan say where he was going tonight?"

"Jan wanted to help Mr. Weaver. He also wanted to be the great detective. He said he was going to get out of the house as soon as his parents left. They always had places to go and people to meet for dinner. They were out of town half the time on business or visiting his brother at college or his sister in Little Rock. Jan was left on his own pretty much. He got away with a lot more stuff than I did. My parents are liberal, but they check up on me pretty closely. His parents didn't have much of a clue. Jan kept saying he wanted to get his face on television. He always said he was going to get more than fifteen minutes of fame."

Lee said, "He shouldn't have been investigating."

"If Jan got an idea in his head, there was no stopping him. He wrote me that he had some ideas about what had happened. I know he didn't commit suicide. Which means it had to be murder."

"Have you talked to the police?" I asked.

"I'm not talking to them. Us kids don't trust cops. I was hoping somebody from the clinic would be here. Maybe you guys can do something."

"Tell me exactly what Jan e-mailed to you today."

"He wrote that he liked the way that you asked questions. He made some obscene speculations about you and your lover. Sorry. Jan was like that. He'd say or write the most outrageous things. That's what I so liked about him. I'm so ordinary and conservative. I was a great audience for him. I preferred being an audience. I could never be a star like him."

I didn't try to correct her perception of herself.

"What else did he write?"

"I'm trying to remember everything. He said stuff about you. He talked about Larry. He had a crush on Larry."

"Were his feelings about Larry strong enough that if he were rejected, it might cause him to kill himself?"

"I think his feelings were more in the stage of being attracted to Larry and wanting Larry to notice him. Larry was pretty oblivious. It's hard to ignore Jan, but Larry managed. Larry wasn't mean, just clueless. Jan expressed his feelings as more of a wish, more, this is a hot guy and I'd like to cuddle with him."

"Did he say anything about the murder?" I asked.

"He was obsessed. He figured the police had missed some clues. When his parents left for the evening, he called me."

"His parents left on the day he'd gotten into all kinds of trouble?"

"He hadn't done anything. They never talk about him being gay. Never."

I asked, "Did he say anything specific?"

"No. That's another reason I came down here. He wanted an audience. I think he was going to confront whoever he was suspecting. He didn't know precisely who, but I think he had it narrowed down."

It was possible he had hit on the killer, who may very well have perceived him as a threat. Although I wondered if he'd hit on who it was by random chance or logical deduction. If Jan could figure out who the killer was, I sure as hell should be able to.

More tears escaped down Brenda's cheeks. She said, "I wish we'd never gone to that basement. We never should have said anything to the police. It got Jan killed. I should have talked him out of it."

Lee said, "Brenda, Jan was a special kid. He wanted to make a difference. He tried his best. Everything he was will live in his friends' memories."

Lee and I spent some time comforting her.

When she was significantly calmer, I said, "I'd like to talk to some more of Jan's friends, especially anyone he may have spoken with today."

"I only know a few. You could maybe get the history from his computer."

"I'm not sure his parents would let me," I said. "I presume the police will do that. I'd like to talk to the kids, especially if they were gay. They might have a tough time talking to the cops."

She wrote down three of the names she remembered that Jan had mentioned. "Do you know all these kids?" I asked.

"Yeah, they use the clinic. They weren't here the night we heard Karek fighting."

"There's gotta be some reason he e-mailed them."

"Probably just to hear himself talk or shoot off his mouth. I'd give a great deal to listen to that for the next couple hours."

It was late. I was tired. Fortunately I had the next week off for spring break. Brenda called a friend who would keep her company.

Outside in the cool spring night after we'd left her, Lee tapped my arm and said, "The thing that bothers me the most about this is that it's hurt our relationship. I feel like I used you. I'm so sorry."

"It's not often we're accused of murder."

"I appreciate your faith in me."

Lee went home to Dustin.

I walked to my car.

26

I'd parked in the clinic lot. I heard a car alarm blaring. It was a sound never far away from you if you lived in the heart of the city. Usually it meant there was a malfunction, not a robbery. Dark alley. Trees casting shadows each more menacing than the last. Sound muffled. Sound ignored. I had my keys in my hand. As I neared my car, I saw someone sitting in the passenger seat. It was also clear that my car was letting off the annoying blasts. A little mystified, a lot apprehensive, and hugely pissed, I hurried forward. I pressed the button to unlock the door and stop the alarm. I was about ten feet from the car. In the silence I thought I heard footsteps rushing toward me. I spun around, pressed the panic alarm on the key chain. The alarm started blaring again. A fat lot of good the noise had done two minutes ago. Before my spin was complete, I caught a blur out of the corner of my eye. My spin had unbalanced me. A powerful shove hurtled me headfirst toward the car. My head bashed hard enough into the headlight to break it. I felt my attacker leaning over me. I thought I saw the flicker of a knife. I thrashed and kicked wildly. I managed to land a kick in my attacker's nuts. I heard an *oof.* He stumbled backward. I scrambled to my feet. My attacker was already hustling away. I tried to go after him. Dizziness and nausea swept over me. I leaned against my car and tried to get a fix on my attacker. I could tell nothing more than that he was a large person dressed in dark clothes. I felt my head where it had hit the car. I could feel a lump. I looked at my hand. Blood. I took out my cell phone. For a moment the numbers swam in and out of focus. I hit 9-1-1 and gasped out my call for help.

The damn car alarm was still blaring. Not a soul in sight to check it out. I pressed the button. Blessed silence. When my dizziness and nausea where under control, I approached the person sitting in the car.

I opened the passenger side door and looked inside. It was Billy Karek. The head of a screwdriver was sticking out of his right ear. He wouldn't be dodging any more microphones. Blood was smeared over his beige cashmere sweater, his jeans, the car seat, the headrest, the floor, and some black, leather-bound books scattered on the floor.

Even Todd was going to have to strain to make something humorous out of this one. This many people can't die and there still be a one-liner left to tell. I called and woke him up.

"I'll be there," was all he said. He didn't say that he thought Karek was really screwed up, but unfortunately, I thought it. At least Todd hadn't said it.

My eyes kept straying to the wreckage that was Karek. I felt worse than I had when I found the head. Then I thought about the books on the car floor. They weren't mine. They'd looked like ledger books. He must have been carrying them.

The police arrived.

The next few hours lacked peace and joy.

The most important thing that happened was that I didn't get a chance to call Scott and tell him that I loved him. We usually talk every night when he's on the road. If we don't, it's because of previously arranged plans that we both know about. He would wonder where I was, and he would worry. With my involvement in the murder, his concern would be heightened.

The second most important thing was that I didn't get arrested. Third was that the paramedics said I didn't need stitches. I resisted their suggestion about stopping at the hospital to get my head checked.

The police were not happy about a whole bunch of things. They asked me where I'd been after the questioning about Jan. When I mentioned Lee, I thought Abernathy might begin salivating. They'd be hounding Lee again.

They took the body away. The cops wouldn't let me have my car back. Near the end I asked, "Could I get something out of the car?" A cop watched me take the books from the floor and my briefcase from the back seat. The cops had examined all of them. They had evinced no interest in the books nor in the contents of the briefcase. I didn't think they'd want to grade freshman essays.

Todd drove me home about three. I called Scott. He'd been asleep. He didn't mind and I didn't either. We talked and I told him I loved him. He said the same. With my headache from the collision with the headlight, any other long-distance intimacy didn't seem appropriate.

27

The next morning I awoke dizzy and sore. Scott would be home by this time tomorrow. That cheered me up considerably. I ate plain toast and orange juice. My stomach seemed okay with that. Three dead bodies. I had trouble wrapping both my reason and my imagination around that.

I was convinced the attack on me was connected to the murders. How could it not be? Who was I a threat to? Did I know something that was a threat to someone? If I did, I sure wished I knew what that was.

I examined the books from the car floor. They were ledger books. From the clinic. A second set of ledger books? I was nowhere near enough of an accountant to know if I had a real or fake set of books or both. I was determined to get some answers. Pre the accumulation of dead bodies, I'd originally planned to do some laundry and work on requirements for a web project I planned to assign the kids after spring break. *Après* the mound of corpses, I began with phone calls. It was a little after nine. I wanted to talk to all the people who'd been looking into the financial dealings at the clinic. Better yet, I needed to get all of them into one room. I wanted them talking to each other. I was fed up with this secrecy crap. If finances were the basis for murder, then I wanted to shine a bright light on them. How Jan's murder worked into the financial mix, I had no idea. Karek with a set of books was more than enough to put him at the top of the suspect list. Him being dead also put a huge crimp in placing him anywhere on the suspect list. I could believe Jan saw something, or thought he saw something, that got himself killed. At least if the killer thought Jan knew something, it might cause the teen to be killed. By the time I'd made several rounds of phone calls and more than one threat to simply call the straight press and spill the beans, everyone connected with the clinic's finances agreed to meet at eleven. The people doing the investigating were eager to show up, the reporter for the gay papers presumably eager for a story. Others perhaps ready to blow the whistle on enemies in factions they hated. Or maybe just honest people as fed up with this crap as I was.

I intended to get the name of Larry's boyfriend out of Larry. That threat would be simple: no boyfriend's name, I call the police. I phoned him. I asked. He stalled. Under intense pressure from me, he agreed to get the guy to the Rainbow Café by three that afternoon.

I called the three kids whose names Brenda had given me who knew Jan and that she'd mentioned he'd talked to. Whether they were scared, or simply didn't know me, or didn't trust another adult, I got no help from them.

I called Abernathy to find out if she'd tell me the cause of Jan's death. She said, "Strangled with that feather boa, then strung up to make it look like suicide."

"You're sure."

"That's what the ME said. I can't imagine he'd lie."

"I didn't assume he was lying. It was murder."

"Yep."

"No suspects?"

"You'd make a good one."

"Could you give me the approximate time of death?"

She laughed.

I gave up on getting anything out of her that would help me.

It wasn't suicide. I felt better about that, but not much.

The day was oppressively humid and close for early April. A front was approaching and was scheduled to pass overnight with the possibility of violent weather.

I called Todd. I said, "Have you been in touch with Lee since I talked to him last night?"

"Yes."

"Did he give you the information that I suggested he give you?"

"You know I won't answer that question. Ask him." I called Lee and left a message on his machine.

When I talked to Walter Truby I asked him to bring Timothy Chong, the board's investigator. He wanted to know who gave me Chong's name. I said, "From a gossip columnist." That seemed to deflate him. I asked, "Can you get me an introduction to the other Fitch siblings?"

"I only know the two brothers."

"It might help if I could talk to them."

"I can try."

Tajeda called my cell phone about ten. "How are Abdel and Max doing?" I asked.

"I did find two gay guys who are active in the foster care system who would take them in."

"You'd think they'd be pretty well known for taking care of gay kids."

"They live in Rockford. It's not a unit we deal with often. It took a great deal of effort to find them, even more to get the two boys placed there. A placement out of the area is definitely an odd thing to do. Then again, none of our local agencies had someone willing to take two gay teens."

"But they're together?"

"For now. They want to talk to you."

"About what?"

"They wouldn't say."

"Do I go there or do they come here?"

"The foster parents have agreed to bring them to the Rainbow Café." I suggested four that afternoon.

In one of the café's upstairs rooms, I met late that morning with Ken Wells, the head of fundraising, Marty Bennet, one of his assistants and a fighter with Charley at a party, Irene Kang, the executive assistant, Walter Truby, the head of the board of Directors, Chong, the board's investigator, Susanna Fitch, Evan Smith, the investigative reporter, and Todd, my lawyer. At my request, Ken Wells had brought the clinic's books with him.

I said, "I gathered you all here because, one, some, or all of you were investigating this place's finances. One, some, or all of you were responsible for this place's finances. I think the time for this bullshit fiddling around with who knows what needs to be out in the open." Several of them glared at me. Few of them looked at each other. I sensed nervousness, defensiveness, and outright hostility.

"Why is this lawyer here?" Truby asked.

"He's protecting my interests," I said.

"Shouldn't we have the clinic's lawyer here?" Susanna asked.

"I don't know," I said.

Irene Kang said, "Is somebody making an accusation?"

"I will," Evan Smith said. "How come there was never as much money made from clinic fundraisers as the same type of fundraisers in other cities?"

"Talk to the people in charge," Kang said. "That had nothing to do with me. I just counted the money."

"But it's possible to overcount and undercount," Smith said.

"Is that an accusation?" Kang asked.

"Is it true?" Marty Bennet asked.

Kang said, "You're just an assistant around here. You have no standing to say anything, much less make accusations."

"Must we play territorial games?" Ken Wells asked.

"I'm not playing a game," Kang said. "This is serious business. I took pride in my work. I counted everything right. Charley always checked my work."

I said, "I heard he was going to fire you."

"Who told you that?"

"I did," Smith said.

"It's not true." She pointed at the reporter. "Who told you?"

"Fitch did."

Kang snorted. "And he's not here to tell us what a liar you are."

I wanted to get us back onto the finances. I asked, "Who actually handed you the money?"

"Charley or Ken usually did. Sometimes if it was less than a couple hundred, one of the volunteers. Maybe one of them was shorting the money. It didn't have to be me or Charley."

"I saw evidence of more than one set of books," Smith said.

"Where are they?" Kang demanded. She pointed to the pile of ledgers next to Wells. "There's only one set of books here."

Smith said, "Then somebody took the second set of books. I saw evidence they existed the night of the murder."

"Is that when you found them?" Bennet asked.

"Yes."

"You were searching," Kang said, "while we were meeting? You used a ruse to snoop and pry. How do we know you didn't hide out and commit the murder?"

"I have no reason to kill Charley Fitch."

"You would if he caught you," Kang said.

I was tired of this. I undid the snaps on my briefcase and dumped the second set of ledger books on the table. Rather than touch the now dried blood, I'd encased them in plastic.

"You took them!" Susanna exclaimed.

"Nope. I found them on my car floor after someone killed Billy Karek. I'm the one who gets to be shocked and outraged here. I'm the one finding dead bodies. I was attacked last night. You people have explaining to do. Do it." I'd made copies and given them to Todd before the meeting.

They all began to talk at once. A couple reached for the books and began to examine them.

After leafing through several pages, Kang said, "Maybe you fabricated these."

"I might be able to make up the ledgers, but the banks themselves will have records of clinic transactions. One of these sets of books will match their records."

Truby said, "We can't have a scandal. The clinic will go up in flames. All the good work for gay kids will be destroyed. Was what Charley did all that illegal?"

Susanna Fitch said, "We haven't established that he did anything illegal. Karek actually had the second set of books. It looks like he'd be the guilty party. The money for this place comes from our family. Most of it anyway."

"Half isn't most," Ken Wells said. "Five million came from the family, five million from fundraising."

"And how much money is missing?" Susanna asked.

No one knew.

"Isn't that the first thing we need to find out?" Susanna asked.

"One of many things," Ken Wells said.

Bennet asked, "Who's going to conduct an audit or an investigation? Does any one of us trust the others to do this?"

"There can't be a cover-up," Smith said. "The people who gave the five million in donations have a right to an accounting."

Truby said, "And all the kids this place serves. If it closes, where will they go?"

"Kids survived before this place," Susanna said. "There are other outlets."

"Not that many for gay kids," Truby said.

"You're just worried about covering your board of directors' ass," Wells said.

"No," Truby said. "Think what you want of me. I care about these kids. I didn't have this kind of thing growing up. This clinic fills a need."

"You can't fill a need by committing fraud," Smith said.

"Could the clinic stay open with just the family money?" I asked.

Susanna said, "With Charley gone, I'm not sure how interested the family would be in keeping that place in business."

"Then it's hopeless anyway," Truby said. "Maybe we should just call the police or give up and go home. This scandal will hit more than just Charley. Good people are going to be tarnished by this."

"I'd like to keep Charley's name clean," Susanna said. "If at all possible. He was a good man. He wasn't a crook. Maybe the discrepancies in the amount raised compared to other fundraisers can be explained."

Smith said, "I don't know how you're going to explain away a separate set of books."

"You self-righteous prig." Susanna looked ready to belt him one.

I said, "But this whole thing seems to be backwards. If Charley was stealing, why is he dead? Why wouldn't he be the one who tried to kill whoever was trying to expose him?"

"Maybe he did," Wells said. "Maybe he tried, failed, and the other person, in protecting himself or herself, landed a lucky blow."

"Then why chop him up?" I asked.

"Blackmailer turned sicko," Bennet said.

Wells said, "If the murders are connected, they'd have to

be explained in terms of all three of them. I've seen Jan do any number of wildly impulsive or stupid things. I don't know how Karek would fit into that."

"We're not going to be able to solve the murder," Truby said. "That's up to the police. We've got to take action about this scandal. I think the whole board should meet. This isn't a public company."

Smith said, "Public or private, embezzlement is still a crime. And I think it would be a very interesting question to find out why Karek had the second set of books."

"Mason actually had them," Susanna said. "He says Karek had them. His friend, Lee Weaver, was arrested. Maybe he'd do a great deal to get him off."

"But how would stealing Charley's books do that?" I asked. "And we have no connection between Lee and the books and fundraising."

She had no answer to that.

Wells said, "Weaver never had anything to do with helping to raise money. He used to sneer at it. I don't know why. It helped pay his salary. The guy could have been at least grateful at times. Never said thank you. It was like pulling teeth to get him to come to an event. What we have to do is examine both sets of books and find out if anybody else knew about this or was in it with him."

"Him who?" Susanna asked. "Charley or Karek or someone else?"

"Anybody connected with finances," Wells said. "I know I'd be one of the suspects. I suppose any of us who had anything to do with the money would be. We've got to get to the truth just to clear our own names. I was honest with turning over the money from the fundraisers. Kang and Charley were the ones who got it to the bank."

Kang said, "I resent the implication that I did something wrong. I'm not going to help convict myself."

"You won't be in trouble if you didn't do anything wrong," Truby said.

I said, "Karek told me one of his checks to the clinic came through one of Charley's private accounts. Maybe you could get those records as well as the clinic's."

Wells said, "That might help."

"I'm not sure I want to do that," Susanna said.

"Why not?" Wells asked. "Unless you think there's something to hide."

She leapt across the table. Wells's chair fell back as he dodged out of the way. It took several minutes before everyone was finally reseated and calm.

For the next half hour, I sat and listened to them fight and argue.

During a break, while some were getting coffee from downstairs, I pulled Marty Bennet aside. I said, "You had a fight with Charley at a party."

Bennet said, "I didn't kill him. I only care that I don't get smeared in this mess."

So much for help.

Walter Truby informed me that the rest of the Fitch menagerie would meet with me. After he filled me in on their background, I figured menagerie was the right word. He said, "Susanna won't tell them anything. They figure they might get something out of you."

I found out that Smith had done his snooping from around 6 to 6:30 and that Chong had been in Snarly's office around 7:30. Chong didn't have the combination to the safe.

I left them to their bickering so I could meet with Charley Fitch's relatives.

28

Charley Fitch's family members were an eccentric and gritty bunch in that frivolous way some of the rich can be. Three cousins sat on the opposite side of a large polished-wood table. One had had his ear bitten off by a grizzly bear when he was in college on an expedition to the Yukon where they only wore loincloths and could only carry implements used in the Stone Age. The grizzly'd had the same implements he'd always had. The cousin lost the argument with the bear. Another wore a pink beret and made comments that I guess he thought were funny. The third wore a T-shirt with a large bulls-eye on it that said YOU'RE NEXT. On my side of the table, next to me on my right, was Fitch's older brother. He wore a bright blue business suit, but no underwear. This was obvious from the excessively prominent bulge in his pants, which he spread his legs wide for all to see. Either that or he'd attached the largest dildo in history from his crotch to his knee. The one who seemed to have most of the grit was on my left. He was the younger brother. He wore crossed bandoliers over his naked chest. His upper torso and face, below his severely brush-cut hair, were painted with streaks of black greasepaint. Swaths of dirt artfully smeared parts of his anatomy. His tight black jeans encased a taut set of hips. His hair was dirty and matted. He'd either just spritzed himself from a spray bottle of water or had run up the fifty flights of stairs to this office in the John Hancock Center. The gritty one, Harley Fitch, said, "I want my part of this money and I want it now."

"You're never going to get any of it," the older brother, Barley Fitch, said. "We'll out-vote you. Nobody's going to spend the money on your second-amendment causes. No one cares." Harley? Barley? Charley? Their parents must have been nuts. No wonder they were such an odd bunch.

"I care," Harley said.

Barley Fitch said, "What can you tell us? Susanna is being hateful. She won't say a word."

I told them the parts that were not confidential.

When I finished, Barley said, "So nobody knows much of anything."

"Who would Charley's death benefit most directly?" I asked.

Harley said, "Susanna always voted with him. They managed to control the way this money was spent."

I asked, "Who had the controlling last one percent?"

Barley said, "A committee of bankers who controlled the trust. They would have had no benefit from Charley's death. They still collected their fees no matter what happened to us."

One of the cousins, Mabel Fitch, said, "Charley was a hateful, mean sow."

"You never said that when he was alive," Harley said.

"Not to you, maybe, but to others," Mabel said. "I knew he had to be sucked up to. I for one am glad he's dead. I can't wait to start voting without him."

"Susanna has to be here for any vote to be valid," Bethina, another cousin said.

"She does?" I asked.

Barley said, "It's in the by-laws of the trust. Either she or Charley has to be present."

"How come they got so much power and you others didn't?"

Harley said, "My father was a fucking moron. He claimed he was bisexual. He liked having a gay and a lesbian kid. He hated the rest of us normal kids."

I gazed around the table at what he was describing as 'normal.' Maybe for the Manson family.

Barley said, "According to my father, they were the most responsible of the kids. He should have just divided it up equally."

"How come the cousins were in on it?"

Harley said, "More bullshit. He wanted a series of checks and balances on everybody. Hell, we're only playing with the interest here. Only Barley has anything to do with the company and that doesn't happen that often. And he doesn't have access to the profits of the company or the principal of the trust. None of us does."

"What's your role with the company?" I asked Barley.

"Basically I'm to keep out of the way of the business managers. I'm just supposed to make sure they don't make off with the company the way the Enron and WorldCom executives did."

"Did they try?"

"Our company is sound."

"Did you all get along with Charley?"

"Hardly," said Barley.

"Barely," said Harley.

No smiles. They weren't trying to be funny.

The cousins reported doing various amounts of sucking up in order to get cash for themselves.

I asked, "Did the police question you about your whereabouts the night of the killing?"

Harley said, "The fascists attempted to corner me. I kept them at bay."

"What does that mean?" I asked.

Bethina said, "It means he was drunk out of his mind the way he is every night and didn't have the capacity to move out of whatever bar he was in."

None of them had an alibi for all three murders, but each of them claimed to be able to prove they were in someone else's presence during at least one of the murders. The police would have to be checking up on that.

"Did Charley and Susanna get along?"

"Better than all of us did with the two of them," Mabel said.

"Fights in Aruba," Harley said.

"Pardon?"

Harley said, "The yearly family meetings took place in Aruba. Generally for the last half of January. The two of them would fight from beginning to end."

"I was told they got along."

Barley said, "Outside of the family that was the front they put up. They fought like mad at the meetings."

"About what?"

"Money," Harley said, "and how to spend it."

"But they lived together."

Harley said, "It was my father's old place. Those two inherited it. We didn't. Those two loved the place. Neither one would let go."

"They voted together?" I asked.

"On the clinic. Not much else," Barley said.

"Would she kill him?" I asked.

Silence for several beats. Each reluctantly shook their head. "No," Harley said. "That would be going too far."

"Who inherits his money and his voting share?"

"Susanna," Barley said.

Harley added, "The bitch is going to bust us."

29

I met Larry and his boyfriend at the Rainbow Café just after three. Larry corralled me at the front door. He said, "What's happening with Mr. Weaver? Is he okay?"

"He's out on bail. I talked to him for a while last night. He's doing as well as can be expected."

"That's good. Real good."

"Where's your friend?"

"I used the same threats you did, about the police. He really doesn't want to be here. He's really embarrassed. He's really worried someone might see him."

"Why? Doesn't he go out to cafés with people?"

"Well, yeah, I guess. But people know you're gay."

"But you're meeting with me."

"Well, yeah, I guess. It's just so complicated."

I said, "Why don't the three of us sit down together and talk this over?"

"It feels weird, you checking up on me like this."

"I'd be remiss if I didn't check everything."

"Yeah, I guess."

Wayne Jenkins sat at a table in the obscure alcove the

kids had sat in when they talked to me on Saturday. Jenkins had immense shoulders, incredibly narrow hips, and legs that he could barely fit under the table. His arms were crossed over his chest. Larry introduced us. "Wayne's a wide receiver on the team."

When we shook hands, Jenkins allowed the contact for about a half a second. He had a very soft voice. The first thing he said was, "I'm not gay."

Not the most auspicious opening.

"You don't have to worry about him," Larry said. "You can trust him."

"I'm not gay," Jenkins repeated.

I thought I'd try to be reassuring. "I'm not concerned about your sexuality. I just need to check the times that everything happened Friday night."

"Nothing happened." He added a sullen look to his minimal response.

"Were you in the basement of the clinic?"

He glanced around the room several times and then leaned close and mumbled inaudibly.

I let the adult exasperation I was feeling into my voice. Not for me the saintly teenager who spouts wisdom. I've known few teenage saints and the amount of wisdom I'd heard from them wouldn't fill a cliché. I said, "Since there was a murder done that night, that makes what happened a bit more than nothing. Where you there at the same time as Larry?"

"Yeah." He added arms crossed over his chest and clenched fists to his sullen look.

Hostile teenagers. What could be better? My kingdom for a filing cabinet.

I said, "I don't understand why you're a hostile teenager."

"Larry forced me to come here. He said it was either talk to you or the police. I don't like to be threatened."

"Why not just come on your own?" I asked. "Did you kill him?"

"This is such shit. I didn't do anything, and you're asking me such bullshit."

"Would you rather it be the police?" I asked.

"I'd rather it be nobody."

"That's not an option," I said.

"Come on, Wayne," Larry pleaded. "Please, just help out, okay. We can leave and go talk as soon as you're done."

"You said I had to be here. I'm not gay. I don't want to go anywhere and talk."

"But you were with me. We made . . . did stuff. I did stuff with you that I never did before with a guy."

"I've got a girlfriend. You wanted to fool around, and I figured what the hell. I wasn't doing anything. I barely touched you. I was horny."

"Your dick was hard."

"I get turned on. So what? I get more turned on with my girlfriend."

I normally don't sit in on a lover's quarrel, or more accurately a closet-case maelstrom, but this was murder and these guys might know something.

Larry said, "I thought you were serious about wanting to be with me."

"I was just having a good time."

Larry looked like his heart was breaking. I could see tears gathering at the corners of his eyes.

"You did touch me. We kissed. When we were done, you said you wanted to see me again. You told me you loved me."

There's an oops.

Jenkins blushed. He looked around the café as if secret spies might be ready to swoop in and take him to hetero prison. He leaned forward and whispered, "Would you keep your voice down?" Nobody was sitting within six feet of us. I didn't think Larry was talking all that loud. The café wasn't crowded. We were between shelves of nineteenth-century

British novels, volumes filled with stories of tawdry love that never did go quite right.

Larry said, "Was that a lie? Huh? Why'd you tell me you loved me? I've never said that to anybody before. You said you didn't either. You said we'd always be together."

"Hey, come on," Jenkins said. "Okay. I said that stuff. Okay. Just, kind of, back off, okay? I'm . . . look, I can't be gay. Nobody can know any of this stuff. It felt okay being with you. I like you. You're a nice guy. I got my rocks off. I shouldn't have said a lot of that stuff."

"Did you mean any of it?"

"I . . . yes . . . no. Hey, why does this have to be so complicated?"

I'd heard enough of their pain. I didn't hold out the slightest hope for their relationship. Gay guys can be awfully rough on each other's emotions. Young gay guys often have little practice in dealing with interpersonal emotions. They've had no experience in relating to the simplest crushes that happen in the normal course of a heterosexual kid's life. The gay boy is terrified of revealing himself as gay. Then add the general repression males feel about expressing emotions in this society. Young gay guys are caught in a tough spot.

I said, "I'd like to help you two work this out, but for the moment, I need you to focus on that night. There was a murder. I'd like to get as much information as I can."

Jenkins shrugged. That teenage shrug. That mixture of hostility and indifference that they develop on their thirteenth birthday. All of us high-school teachers have seen that teenage shrug. We'd be rich beyond our wildest dreams if we got a buck for every shrug we've seen. Or if we all kept filing cabinets handy, they'd be full of severed teenage heads.

I said, "Wayne, what did you hear that night?"

"I wasn't paying much attention."

"So you were involved," Larry said. "It did mean something."

Jenkins exploded. "Okay. I kissed you. I put my tongue in your mouth. I touched your dick and sucked it. You sucked mine. We fucked." He pointed at me. "Is that what you want to know? Are you some kind of pervert?" No misty eyes bordering on tears here. He was pissed. Good for him. So was I.

I said, "No, to both questions. I'm just trying to find out about the murder and the sequence of events that night. You're the one who keeps talking about sex and relationships. I'm not the one with the hang-up here."

Jenkins refolded his arms over his chest.

I said, "Look, you're both possible witnesses in a murder case. Talking to me might be tough, but it's going to be easier than talking to the cops. Talking to me does not have to involve your parents. Talking to the police could very well involve them."

"Son of a bitch," Jenkins said.

"Mr. Weaver is a good person," I said. I think I still believed that. "But he's put you both in a very tough position. Larry's talked to the police and hasn't told them this information. Wayne, you're part of that now."

"I don't want to be," Jenkins said.

"Wants have nothing to do with it."

"Shit."

I said, "I'm going to try to help you guys. I don't want to bring harm to you. Gay kids have it tough enough. Larry, why don't you give me the sequence of events. Wayne, why don't you just confirm or correct them as the need arises."

He glared at me, but he didn't return the conversation to sex, and he didn't say no.

I said, "You guys got there about what time?"

"Eight," Larry said.

Barely a nod from Jenkins.

"First you heard . . ."

"A woman arguing with a man," Larry said. "From what I've been told that must have been Mr. Fitch with that woman counselor who's always so nice."

"Daisy Tajeda?"

"Yeah. Then it was quiet pretty much for a long time. Once in a while I thought I heard people talking. Then about ten thirty we heard male voices shouting. I recognized Mr. Weaver's voice. I heard him say 'Charley,' so I knew the other guy was Mr. Fitch."

"Is that who you heard?" I asked Jenkins.

"If that's who he says they were. I don't know any of these people."

"You were down there from eight to ten thirty?"

Both boys blushed and mumbled, "Yeah." Score points for youthful stamina.

"Did you hear them say their names, the same as Larry heard?"

"I heard the names. I'm not sure who was who. If they were talking about themselves or other people."

"Could you hear them plainly?"

"Yeah," Larry said. Jenkins nodded.

They gave me the same run-down on the conversation as Lee had. Their version was as close to Lee's as to be almost verbatim. These two might be in collusion, but I was reasonably certain they were not in collusion with Lee.

"You must have stopped to listen," I said.

Larry said, "All that yelling kind of destroyed the mood for a little while."

"Did you hear Mr. Weaver leave?"

"No," Larry said. "They got softer at times. I don't know if anybody left or not. Nobody screamed as if they were being attacked. It was kind of quiet, but then we got kind of busy again."

"You didn't see or hear anything as you walked down the alley as you left?"

Jenkins said, "You didn't mention Jan being just outside the café. He was doing that fucking Jack McFarland effeminate bullshit. I hate that. I'm not like that."

"Nor are you required to be," I said. I turned to Larry. "Did Jan see you?"

Larry shook his head no. Jenkins confirmed it. "And you heard no sounds in the basement itself?"

Both boys shook their heads. "Did you see Jan when you arrived?"

Both boys said no. Could Jan have seen them and crept back to watch?

I asked, "What time did you get home?

"About twelve," Jenkins said. Larry nodded. Which didn't mean either one of them couldn't have come back.

30

Max and Abdel showed up at four. The foster parents were in their fifties. Tajeda had given me a little background on them. One was a former steel worker with one glass eye and a huge gut. The other was a school teacher with two real eyes and a huge gut. They seemed pleasant enough. Max and Abdel seemed comfortable with them. The two adults left me to talk to the teens alone.

Late on this Monday afternoon the café was becoming crowded. The cold front had passed earlier with a lot of wind but without any storms or rain.

"How are things working out?" I asked.

"Okay for now," Max said. They held hands. "We had to talk to you."

"Yeah," Abdel said. "We think we know something about the murder."

"How's that?" I asked.

Abdel said, "That wasn't the first time my dad was at the clinic."

"How do you know this?"

"I talked to my sister. She's got her own cell phone. If I

called the house, nobody in my family would have told her I was on the phone. She's a year older than I am. She hates the repression she has to live with. She can't wait to leave. She's afraid that my brothers might do something to her."

"Like what?"

"Send her back to Saudi Arabia. She wants to be out on her own. She heard my brothers and my dad talking about me. She didn't have to sneak around to listen. They treat her like she wasn't there. My dad said he'd been to the clinic looking for me before."

"He said he only became suspicious on Saturday."

"That was a lie. He's been suspicious for a long time. He'd met Mr. Fitch, the guy who died. I guess they had this big argument."

"When was this?"

"A week ago."

"How'd he find out about the clinic?"

"My older brother is the one who started it. He's always been mean to the point of cruelty. He picks at me about not being tough enough. My brother started a long time ago trying to find out if I was gay. He searched my room before. He found the pamphlet for the clinic a few weeks ago. I'd borrowed Max's chemistry book. He accidentally left it in there. My brother told my dad."

"But why would he assume he would find you there?"

"My brother had called the clinic and even gone there once to visit."

"Maybe he's gay."

"Not likely. My brother followed us one of the other times we tried to see you. We didn't go on a Saturday the first time. We didn't know that's when you volunteered. He told my dad where we'd been."

"Why didn't either of them confront you before this?"

"My dad wanted to investigate. When my dad went, that Mr. Fitch wouldn't tell him if we'd been there or not. Fitch talked about confidentiality. My dad was waiting for me to be out of the house this Saturday. He suspected I was lying from the beginning."

"There've been two more killings," I said. "I think they're all connected. Did your dad know Jan Aiello or Billy Karek?"

"I never heard of them," Abdel said. "I don't see how my dad could have. Maybe he met them when he confronted Mr. Fitch."

Max said, "I don't know them."

I said, "It makes no sense for your dad to be killing these other two. Why would you think he'd kill Charley Fitch?"

"You don't know my dad," Abdel said. "If he thought a gay guy was insulting him, he might go crazy. He hates all this modern stuff. He hates that gay people have parades. He helped push a wall over on some gay guys in the Middle East."

This wasn't the first time I'd heard of that happening.

"My dad would like to be involved with that kind of thing," Max said. "He attacked you."

"Why would your dad kill anybody?"

"He wouldn't, I guess, but it would sure make sense for the two of them to have done it together."

"Make sense to whom?" I asked.

They both looked a little chagrined. I said, "You can't go around accusing people of murder without some kind of proof."

"My dad was at the clinic," Abdel said.

"A week ago. We have no proof he was out of your house at the time of the killing. He may have met Fitch, but other than Fitch being terminally rude, he had no cause to kill him and the other two. You guys are letting your imaginations run away with you."

"We were just trying to help," Max said.

"I appreciate that, but an excess of suspects is almost as bad as no suspects. Flights of illogic aren't going to help anything."

Abdel said, "I think you should talk to my older brother or for sure my dad. He knows more than he said."

"I don't know why either one would be willing to talk to me. I barely met your dad, and I doubt if he's happy with me."

"You could try," Abdel said.

I supposed I could. Teenagers. Eternally optimistic, when they weren't contemplating suicide or weeping on my shoulder.

31

At about 5:30 I met with Benton Fredricks, the cable show host. Fredricks had a mane of poofy hair with a bald spot mostly unhidden by the mass of tangles. He was in his forties. He wore jeans that were too tight two sizes ago. He wore a sport jacket with leather elbow patches over a T-shirt that proclaimed him a fan of TROGLODYTES FOREVER. I didn't know if this was a political philosophy or the name of an obscure modern rock group.

Fredericks had a lot of bounce in his manner. We met in his office at his studio. He looked like he enjoyed cleaning as much as I did. Mostly his clutter was CDs, DVDs, cassette tapes, and electronic equipment. I counted seven sets of headphones.

He began, "I'd love to get you and your lover on the show."

"I don't think it's the kind of venue we'd be interested in."

"Maybe I wouldn't be interested in giving you information if you weren't."

"Is that why you met with me? To make deals?"

"That's what makes the world go around. Deals."

"If the information you give me leads to the real murderer, I'll consider it. I can't speak for Scott."

He mulled this over then said, "I suppose that's as good as I'm going to get. You guys would be great. I could get some right-wing opponents and have a real debate."

"No."

"No?"

"We won't do shows for debate purposes. We don't think we should be debating our rights. You don't debate black or women's rights. We won't appear with any right-wing people."

"I guess the two of you would do."

"I've made no commitments. You've got to know something first and it's got to be significant."

Fredericks sighed. "I'm not sure I do."

"You had Karek and Fitch on your show."

"Many times. They were great. They hated each other."

"What actually happened the night of the show with the chair incident?"

"I sold that tape for a fortune. It couldn't have been better. They ran into each other in the lobby as they walked in. They were snapping at each other before we even went on the air. I think I should have offered to have them duel. That would have sold tickets."

"And boosted ratings."

"It's all about ratings."

"What started the fight?"

"Transgender rights. I guess it was this big sticking point. You know there was a big controversy just before the vote in New York on the gay rights bill? Two of the legislators wouldn't support the bill if it didn't include transgender rights. Fitch went crazy. Karek did, too. Karek said aligning gay rights with every fringe group was the road to madness. He said that Fitch never could see what was reality and what was crap. Fitch just lost it."

"Is that what they were fighting about earlier?"

"That was my understanding."

"How did it end?"

"Well, Karek was there cowering under the table. I think Fitch just came to his senses. Neither actually landed a blow. Karek put a big dent in the console with that chair. At the end Karek chased after him, and I guess there was a to-do in the parking lot, but I don't have tape of that."

"What was the to-do about?"

"I heard by that time it was personal. It wasn't about anybody's rights, it was about them being pissed at each other. That's what gets the best ratings for me, when people are pissed at each other."

"Did they have any other particular enemies?"

"You know about Marlex and Bergland?"

"Yes."

"That's about it. I didn't know these people personally. I didn't care about their politics. I only cared about my ratings. Will you and your lover consider being on the show?"

"I won't." I left.

I called Karek's lover, Reece. He said he'd been calling my answering service, trying to set up a meeting. If I spent much more time at the Rainbow Café, I could just move in.

32

Reece Coleman had his six-foot-six frame draped in the darkest corner of the café. He had a cup of hot chocolate in front of him. His hair was awry. His shirt and khaki pants looked like they'd been slept in.

He said, "Thanks for coming."

I got myself some hot chocolate. The night was cool with the mid-April temperature back to normal. The café was quiet at seven on a Monday.

He said, "I need to tell someone what I've found out. I can't go to the police."

I nodded. He looked worn and defeated.

He began, "I loved Billy with all my heart and soul." He sipped his chocolate and sighed.

"But you were worried."

"When we met Sunday, I didn't know anything specific and now he's dead. The guy who was investigating for him, Evan Smith, I know him. He called me. He told me you found the second set of books and that Billy had them." He drew a deep breath. "Billy was cheating with Charley Fitch to defraud the clinic."

"Billy said he'd asked for an investigation."

"He did." He rubbed his nose, scratched his neck. I noticed his large hands were red and raw. "Billy was playing a dangerous game. He figured he was safe. If it came out, it would be Charley's word against his. Charley wasn't a big detail guy. Billy kept the second set of books. He took care of all the figures. He had it worked so it looked like Fitch committed all the crimes. He was a liar and a thief. How could I have been so blind as to miss all that? How could I not see I was living with a criminal?"

I asked, "How did you find all this out?"

"He left records with his will. Records of all his deposits that he never told me about. I checked the dates and fundraising. I began to figure it out. Every time he met Charley Fitch on a talk show, he made a deposit within twenty-four hours in an account I knew nothing about. The talk shows were used as a cover-up for their embezzlement conspiracy. This is so sad and so sick. How could I have been so blind?"

"Who would want to kill him?" I asked.

"The police questioned me. I don't know. There's so much happening on the gay political scene, but I can't imagine gay politics would lead to murder. We were so committed to our cause. At least I was."

"You loved him," I said. "You've got grief that he's gone, and you're feeling betrayed at the same time."

"I feel like shit." He drank more chocolate. "How was it finding him?"

"Absolute hell."

He nodded.

I said, "I heard rumors that Fitch tried to sabotage some of the fundraisers. Do you know anything about that?"

"Billy's notes said it was another part of the plan. If things went wrong, they would try and shift the blame. Wells was an awfully smart guy and it was difficult. They floated some of the rumors of sabotage themselves."

"Did Wells ever find out?"

"Not from what Billy said in the notes."

And Wells hadn't said anything at any of our meetings.

I said, "The staff talked about getting a series of threatening calls recently."

Reece said, "That was part of the plan. They wanted uncertainty and suspicion. But Billy was double-crossing Fitch. He might have gotten away with it. If he could have substituted the second set of books, Fitch could have been in deep trouble."

I said, "But that fight at the television station sure looked real."

"The public stuff was supposedly an act. I guess Billy didn't believe in his politics. He was just out to cheat. They thought people might have been getting suspicious of them. You know how on some talk shows they shout at each other and then they're all laughing and buddies. They didn't want anyone to think they were cooperating."

I said, "But the kids said they heard the two of them fighting in Fitch's office about a week before the murder."

"Some of their fights were real. Billy hated Fitch. It's all over his notes. He was using him. He wrote about the arguments they had. They were making each other rich with their scheme, but they didn't like each other. It was more like they needed each other."

"Charley was rich. Why did he need your lover?"

"I guess Billy was sort of blackmailing him. Fitch could get money for his clinic from his family, but he had a harder time getting cash for himself. Supposedly Fitch's sister is a holy terror. They were in it together though. Since they were lovers. They'd been doing this for years. It was like they each had hold of the others balls and were squeezing hard. Each was afraid to let go."

"What was Billy doing with the set of books on him when they found him dead?"

"I don't know. He must have been trying to substitute one set for the other. I do know that the night of the killing they were making more plans. But Billy didn't kill him. I know he didn't." He paused. "I don't think he did. He made no mention of that in his notes."

So the financial scandal was hatched by two of those who were dead. Was someone they defrauded pissed off? And how would I find out? I couldn't imagine Jan fitting into Karek's and Fitch's conspiracy. Why involve a teenager who would be likely to blab? Whoever killed Karek must not have had a notion that the books were important. Did this mean the killer was not involved in any of the clinic finances? Seemed a logical conclusion.

Reece said, "I don't know if this helps you. I'm trying to do right. Doesn't seem to help much. My lover's gone." I said as many comforting words as I could muster. He left.

I phoned Susanna Fitch to get her perspective on the fights in Aruba, as reported by the rest of the Fitch clan. She said, "Those bastards are fucked up." And hung up on me.

I decided to pay a visit to Lee Weaver and his lover Dustin. I needed to ask Dustin a few questions.

They were in. They sat together on the couch. Not as close as first-time lovers. Not at the ends like two people feuding in a relationship beyond repair.

"I heard you were attacked," Lee said. "Are you all right?"

"Not as right as I wish I was."

"What's happening?" Lee asked.

I said, "I need to find out where Dustin was the night of the murder."

"What did you tell him?" Dustin demanded.

"You weren't here when I first came home."

"You made me a murder suspect?"

Lee reached out his hand and touched him. Dustin shook it off violently and stood up. He said, "I can't believe you'd do that."

Lee said, "You've always been so adamant in your feelings about Charley Fitch."

"And you think I'd kill him? You think I'm that kind of person?"

"You weren't home. You're not home a lot."

"And that's worth accusing me of murder?"

Lee was on his feet. "I wasn't accusing you. I didn't tell the police. I was worried."

"Maybe you were trying to divert suspicion from yourself."

Lee said, "If I wanted to divert suspicion, I would have told the cops. I told Tom, not them. I'm scared."

"Of what?" Dustin asked.

"Of losing you."

"Do you think I'm a killer?"

Lee held out a hand to him. "No. Never."

I said, "I'm going to leave and let you two sort this out, but I need to know before I leave, Dustin, where were you?"

"When I'm worried I prefer to be alone."

"What were you worried about?"

"Losing Lee. To his work, his job, those kids."

I left them to work out their lives.

33

Benjamin Awarjak, the gossip columnist, had set up a meeting for me with Roland Welp, an escort that Fitch had used recently. I was feeling woozy from being bashed into the car the night before, but I wanted to finish this. I was appalled by the carnage I'd seen, my mind nearly numb from trying to come to grips with the images that flashed through it at unbidden moments.

We meet in a hustler bar on Ashland Avenue near where it crossed Elston. The neighborhood was as gritty and seedy as the bar. Fat old guys with white beards sat at the bar eyeing every new person who walked in. Scott called it the Santa-Claus-is-horny effect. They reminded me of the way a starving great white shark must eye a swimmer a mile out in the ocean. No feeding frenzy occurred while Awarjak and I were there.

Roland wore aviator sunglasses, a black muscle T-shirt, and leather pants that fit well on his slender frame. His teeth were so white I assumed he must polish them on a regular basis or keep several tooth whitening companies in business. Not much eccentricity and definitely no grit. He spoke in a soft, deep voice. I bought him a beer. He said, "I can't stay long. I've got a customer in a little while."

Got to admire a guy with standards. I said, "Would you take your sunglasses off, please? I find it disconcerting talking to someone whose eyes I can't see."

He complied. His eyes were soft brown.

I said, "Benjamin says Charley Fitch hired you."

"You aren't the cops?"

"No."

Awarjak said, "You know Tom Mason. At least you've heard of his lover, Scott Carpenter."

"I guess. I don't read newspapers much."

Awarjak said, "The baseball player who's openly gay."

"Oh, yeah. I guess."

"I trust him," Awarjak said. "He needs help in solving a murder in the gay community."

"I'm not trying to bring trouble to you," I said. "I'm not with the police. I have no interest in getting you involved with them."

"I don't like cops. They hassle me."

I thought, Perhaps if you'd chosen a different profession, they wouldn't be terribly interested.

I said, "We'll keep the police out of it."

"Okay, I guess."

"How long had Charley been your client?"

"About six months."

"What can you tell me about him?"

"You mean sordid sex stuff?"

"I mean anything you can remember."

"It's one of the rules of the profession, we don't rat on clients."

"He won't care," I said. "He's dead."

"Oh, yeah. I guess."

I repeated my question. "What can you tell me?"

"Well, I met him through the service. He asked for college

guy types, but decently built, maybe a little rough around the edges. I can do that easily. He was actually pretty nice to me."

I said, "He had a reputation as being snarly and rude."

"Not with me. It was kind of funny that we always had to meet in that clinic. He'd like me to ride him like a horse. You know how dads have their three-year-olds ride them around. He'd beg to be ridden all through the clinic. I thought it was kinda nuts, but I'm not paid for my opinion. I'm paid for showing them a good time."

"Always at the office?"

"Yeah. We usually started before ten, never got going later than twelve."

"Playing horsy doesn't sound too violent."

"It wasn't, and that was about the only thing that was odd except at the end. He liked to suck me off while I was sitting in his chair with all my clothes on and just my pants unzipped. He was a pretty easy client. He came real fast, never quibbled about price, and gave decent tips."

"Were you the only call boy he hired?"

"I'd don't know," Roland said.

"I don't think so," Awarjak added.

"Were you there last Friday?"

"I met him every Friday. This week was a little before ten. He called my pager and gave me the go-ahead."

"Anything strange happen?"

"Nope. We played around and he came all in about half an hour and I left."

"Did you hear anything out of the ordinary?"

"Nope. He always had his stereo turned to a classical music CD. It wasn't real loud. I never heard any noises. I didn't last Friday. The phone never rang or anything."

"You never got caught being there?"

"Nah. I wouldn't have cared. He didn't seem any more or less paranoid than any other client."

This kid had been there on Friday. Certainly the police

would be unhappy if they knew I had withheld that bit of news. Did I trust this kid? I had no reason to. I had no reason not to. I said, “Did you ever use the clinic services when you were a kid?”

“I’m not from here. I grew up in Newton, Iowa.” His pager went off. He glanced at it. “I gotta go,” he said. He stood up. “We done here?”

I said, “I guess.”

He left.

Awarjak said, “Roland is a good kid. He’s not violent. He’s always eager to please. I know. He wouldn’t kill anybody.”

“Wouldn’t be the first time a hustler got violent with a client.”

“He’s a good kid.”

At the moment I had no way to prove otherwise. Awarjak and I agreed to keep in touch.

34

I tried to call Larry to confirm the bits Roland the escort had told me. His dad answered the phone. Larry was out. "You've been such a help," his dad said. "He really appreciates all you've done. I've had problems with him. That Mr. Weaver has been great for him, too. It's good that he's got another adult to talk to."

I said, "I'm just checking times and information from Friday night."

"All I know is Larry got home around two."

"You let him come in that late?"

"He's a senior. It's spring break. He's an athlete. They can take care of themselves."

He gave me Larry's cell-phone number. I called. Busy.

I tried Jenkins' number. He sounded as sullen and annoyed as he had that afternoon.

"I wish you wouldn't call me," he said.

"There's no choice," I said. "Did you say you wanted to talk to the cops instead?"

"No." A little nasty sullen in his tone. I didn't give a rat's ass.

I said, "I talked to the hustler who was with Charley Fitch the night you were in the basement."

"Which night?"

"You were there more than once?"

"Yeah."

"When?"

"About six months ago."

"You didn't mention this."

"You didn't ask."

"Larry said it was his first time doing anything."

"It wasn't my first."

"Who were you there with?"

"Jan Aiello."

Oh. "I thought you said you didn't like effeminate guys."

"I don't. He wasn't effeminate during what we did."

"Did you talk to him any time between when you saw Larry Friday and when you talked to me?"

"He called. He asked if I knew anything. I said no."

"Did you tell him you were down there Friday night?"

"Yeah."

"With Larry?"

"Yeah."

"Jan must have talked with Larry."

"He could have."

"Who drove Friday night?"

"Larry and I had separate cars."

"What time did you get home?"

"About twelve."

"You must live farther out than Larry."

"I'm in Palatine. He's in Arlington Heights."

Larry lived closer to the city, but he got in later. I wanted an explanation. Again, I called Larry's cell phone. He answered. I told him we needed to meet. He was mystified but agreed. Then he told me he was in the basement of the clinic.

"Are you all right?" I asked.

"No." I heard him gulp or gurgle.

I said, "I need to meet you at the café. You need to get out of that basement." The phone clicked off. I tried calling again. No answer. I drove to the clinic.

I wasn't about to meet him in the clinic basement. That was nuts. I had no physical evidence that he was the killer, but I had an anomaly and a suspicion. I called the café and asked for Gordon Jackson, the owner. He agreed to keep a lookout for Larry and to stick close in case anything seemed wrong. If Larry was a killer of three people, I wasn't about to give him an unprotected chance at me.

I had very mixed feelings about Larry. As a troubled gay kid, he had all my sympathy. As a possible killer, I was completely on guard. I wanted to talk to him before involving the police. If he wasn't the killer, it was not right for me to bring grief to him. A small part of me was afraid I would find his lifeless body in the basement instead of waiting for me in the café.

As I walked to the clinic I listened to the city night noises. I wished they were more comforting. A light rain was falling. As I entered, Gordon hurried toward me. He said, "Kid's in the Shakespeare room." I thanked him.

Larry sat with his head down. He glanced up briefly when I joined him.

I said, "The time you got back the night of the first murder doesn't check out. Jenkins says one thing. Your dad another. You live closer to the city. You should have been home earlier than Wayne."

"I wasn't checking the time."

"You can't lie about timing when you're a suspect in a murder. You talked to Jan. He knew you were down there the night of the killing. He knew Jenkins. Jan must have been suspicious of you. Why?"

I thought he might try to lie. Big tears began to flow. They weren't going to work. He blubbered for a while. I waited. Finally, when he got himself under enough control, he said, "Jan was an asshole. He saw Wayne and me go into the basement. He came and watched. That was sick. When we were about to leave, he managed to get out without us noticing him. When he called me, he described what we did. Then he bragged that he'd had sex with Wayne. I thought I was Wayne's first. That pissed me off."

"You got home late. Where were you?"

"I didn't mean for anything to happen."

"What did you do that night?"

"I wanted to relax for a few minutes. I wanted to enjoy how happy I was. This was my first time with a guy. I knew I'd always remember it. It was so perfect. Hard to believe I felt so good in a dump like that. Wayne was real gentle. Two willing guys. He was so masculine."

"What went wrong?"

"Fitch caught me down there."

"How?"

"It was stupid. I lit up a joint. He smelled smoke. He came down. He started yelling at me. Just like my dad does. Fitch is such a fanatic about dope and keeping things clean. We hadn't cleaned up. There was a used condom on the floor. He was just crazy. He told me I was banned from the clinic. I followed him upstairs begging and pleading. He said if I didn't stay out, he'd call the police. If the cops were called, my name could be in the paper. He was mean. Brutal. I didn't want to stay away. This place is perfect for me. Then I could picture everybody finding out about me, about losing my chance at playing ball in college. With each plea he got meaner and nastier. He wouldn't listen. I just went nuts. I saw the ax in Mr. Weaver's office. I thought I'd threaten him with it. He laughed at me. Just like my dad does. I held the ax high over my head. He laughed even harder. He turned to walk away from me. I brought it down on the back of his head."

"How'd you get your fingerprints off but leave Lee's on?"

"I wiped it where I touched it. I didn't clean the rest of it. I didn't care about the blood."

"How could you do that? Keep chopping?"

"I was crazy. I had to do something. I had to try and make the killing go away."

"Why use the basement?"

"I must have been thinking on some level. I took him down there so I wouldn't be caught."

"But then you distributed the body parts."

"I guess I thought it would make the police more confused. I don't know what the hell I was doing."

"But you dropped very little blood around the clinic as you moved the parts around."

"I put two garbage bags together. There's all kinds of garbage in that basement. I threw them away in a dumpster by a mall near my house."

"You wiped up after yourself. You were doing some kind of planning."

"No matter what my dad says, I'm not stupid. I was scared, and excited, and confused, and out of control, but everything was like I was going in slow motion."

"Why did you kill Jan?"

"He was figuring it out."

"Did he see you kill Fitch?"

"I don't think so. The next day he just called me and called me and got all smarmy. He kept implying that he knew stuff about the murder. He wouldn't tell me what unless we agreed to meet."

"He told me he'd been down there with a boyfriend."

"Bullshit. He didn't have a boyfriend. He was a pathetic loser. When Jan asked me about times I did stuff that night, about when I got home, I began to get worried. He knew what time Wayne got home. He pressed me and pressed me. He could be so obnoxious. I got him there with the promise of sex. When we got there, I told him I'd let him blow me but that was all. He got all bent out of shape about that. I think it was partly just to stop him from talking that I took that fucking feather boa and half strangled him with it. At least he finally shut up."

"I was told Jan was pretty strong."

"I took him by surprise. I was sort of fooling with the feather boa." He rubbed his hands together. "He fought as best he could, but I'm pretty big. After he passed out, then I strung him up."

"Why didn't you kill Wayne?"

"He only knew about us being down there. He didn't know about my return."

"Why did you even tell me about you and Wayne?"

"Because of what you said. You knew that everybody would find out about us hearing Karek and Mr. Fitch. You said that kind of thing always comes out. I figured I could tell part of the truth and that might keep you from getting suspicious of me. And I figured maybe I could cast suspicion on Mr. Weaver as the killer."

Not that long ago I had sympathized with his plight. That evaporated in the knowledge that he was a killer. It was becoming clearer with each word how calculating and odious he was.

"Why did Karek have to die?"

"After I finished with Jan, I turned around and there he was. I have no idea what he was doing there. I didn't care. I tackled him. I grabbed the first thing I could get my hands on, that screwdriver. I wanted to carry him away from the clinic."

"Why?"

"I couldn't explain two bodies down there. Jan claimed he

was keeping our meeting a secret. He believed in all that bullshit intrigue. Telling you I found Jan made sense."

"You took a risk carrying the body down the alley."

"I had to do something. It's awfully dark. Nobody saw me. I figured if I put him in your car, then you'd be more of a suspect. I'm sorry. You helped me, but I was desperate. Yours was the only car in the lot."

"You waited all that time last night to try and kill me?"

"You were learning too much. I couldn't take a chance."

"How'd you get back to attack me?"

"My dad and I had a big fight. When he talks to adults about me, he's all reasonable. When we got away from the cops and you that night, we had another fight. I always start to cry. That drives him nuts. Does me too. I'd come in my own car. He told me not to come home. I sat in my car and waited for you. I'll never get the sound of your car alarm out of my head. I saw you down the alley. I don't know what I was doing. I was so angry. I was so scared and screwed up."

"Why not just try to kill me now?"

"I can't. I'm tired. I just want this to end. And I can't sneak up on you. You're pretty strong." He stood up. I did, too. "I'm not going to try anything."

I said, "I need to call the police. I'll call my lawyer for you. Do you want to call your dad?"

How my innate sense of helping kids took over at this point, I have no idea. Larry Mullen was a killer, but I understood too well his frustrations and fear.

He shook his head. He began walking toward the door. I said, "Hey, wait."

He was big and he kept moving. Gordon noticed us and caught up with me as I pushed the door open. Larry stood at the corner of Monclair and Addison. I wasn't going to let him go. It was nearly eleven. Traffic was fairly light. I saw a bus barreling down from the east. I waited to make my calls until after its noise had passed. The DON'T WALK light was flashing. Larry started across the street. I reached for his arm and pulled him back to the curb.

The light turned orange. The bus was speeding up toward the intersection to beat the light. "Let me go." Larry jerked his arm from my grasp. He teetered slightly. Larry looked at the bus, then back at me. He said, "Thanks for trying to help me." He turned and dashed away. I grabbed for him. Missed.

I lunged after him. The next second I remember bright headlights, a rumbling engine, squealing brakes, and being yanked off my feet backwards.

There was an awful thud. I saw a blur of body and blood flung fifty feet. I looked behind me. Gordon had hold of my shirt and the waist of my jeans.

When I got to Larry, there was nothing to be done. Finding the head was bad. This was worse. It was hard to hold his lifeless and crushed corpse. All I kept thinking about was that not more than a minute before, I'd touched a living person and now all that he was, was gone forever. Five minutes before, I'd watched sad tormented eyes. I'd been disgusted by a gay killer, someone who'd been willing to kill me. The disgust now was mixed with pity. For a wasted life. For the moments of anger in a clinic designed to help.

I knew I hadn't pushed him physically. I didn't think I had. He just pulled away. His leap for the bus took numerous steps. If he'd been falling from the contact with me, he would have landed near the curb, not out in traffic. He'd made a choice, but one that I would have to live with.

I also knew that if Gordon hadn't pulled my back, I might have been dead as well. He stood next to me as I cradled what was once a life. After the paramedics arrived, I loosened my grip on Larry. I became aware of backed-up traffic and gawking spectators. I began to tremble. Gordon led me to a quiet spot in the café, sat next to me, and kept an arm around me.

My lawyer and the police showed up. I called Scott. His plane was flying over Southern California. He told me he loved me. I was too exhausted for tears.

35

The cop stuff that followed was a blur. Neither detective seemed willing to believe my explanations. I didn't much care. They had a corpse to deal with. Gordon had been a few steps behind me. He'd seen what happened. He tried to comfort me. I was glad he was there. I kept mumbling my thanks to him for saving my life. He offered to stay with me or find someone to stay with me until I felt better. Todd did the same. Scott would be home in a matter of hours. That would be enough, I hoped.

I kept going over what I could have done differently. Called the cops before going to talk to him? Hell, called a team of social workers to meet with him and me? Called Lee? He'd have come. Called Larry's dad? I didn't know what would have helped.

Then again, Larry had made the choice to kill people, then kill himself. Nevertheless, I was part of what had gone wrong with his life. And that didn't feel good. I didn't feel responsible. I didn't feel guiltless.

• • •

Scott returned from his road trip that morning about six. The all-night flights from the Coast were always a pain in the ass. He'd pitched, so he would be exhausted as well.

I was sitting in a chair in the penthouse living room watching the sun rise over the lake when he walked in.

He sat next to me on the couch. He gave me a hug. He said, "You look awful."

"I haven't slept."

He took my hand.

I don't know how long I talked. I know we'd spoken on the phone during his flight. He'd known the basics. Now he knew all the details.

When I was done he said, "I wish I'd been here."

I said, "It wouldn't have made a lot of difference. The same people would have died."

"Yeah, but I'd have been with you through it all."

"I thought I was doing good and right things. Instead I was used. I was stupid and oblivious. How could I miss that Larry was a killer? How could I not know he was using me?"

"The before-the-event insight? Had you but known?"

"No. It's more like, why didn't I know. Maybe I could have done or said something to make things come out differently."

It's hard to escape the assumption that if we'd have just said the right thing events would have turned out differently. This is what I call the magic-power-after-the-fact-but-said-before-the-fact syndrome. If the post-tragedy insight had happened prior to an awful event, somehow it would have led to the exact right words to prevent the tragedy. You'd think someone would have noticed what those exact right after-the-fact words are and written a million-selling self-help book. The truth is, of course, that there is no such thing, and the just-after-the-nick-of-time insight is unlikely to eliminate the tendency of the universe to act in random, cruel, and tragic ways.

In this case I kept reminding myself that Larry Mullen had

committed his first murder before I knew him. That thought mixed with flashes of the bus smashing into his body. But two other people had also died. The flashpoints had been a rude old queen and Larry's fear of being found out as gay. Sad and tragic and pretty fucked up.

Scott said, "You have more insight than most people. You are not expected to have magic powers of instant insight. Nobody can expect that. You know it, too. You were trying to help." I nodded, grateful for his words. "And he was willing to kill you," Scott pointed out.

"I know. That's not the part I'm sympathizing with. I think some of my own feelings of growing up gay got in the way of seeing Larry in an accurate light. Same with Lee. I felt sorry for both of them. I didn't think Lee would ever tell me that big of a lie."

"Feeling sorry for someone is not a criminal act. Maybe there was no way to see either Larry or Lee in an accurate light. Friends and lovers have flaws. Sometimes we can't see our own. The murders are a tragedy for which you are not responsible. You weren't in the basement. You are not snarly and rude. You tried to do some good. It wasn't enough. Sometimes it isn't. It's the trying that makes a difference."

"I want to believe that."

Something else was bothering me. I sat with him. He still held my hand. Our legs touched. I could smell his aftershave.

I said, "A few seconds the other way, and it could have been me."

"You were trying to save him."

"No. I mean, he might have shoved me instead of killing himself. I wasn't prepared."

Scott said, "No amount of preparation could have prevented what happened." He held me close. "You're here. You're safe. I love you."

• • •

In the next few days the police found enough forensic evidence to convince them that Larry had definitely been the killer. The timing of his movements was suspicious in itself. A partial print on the screwdriver that he'd used to kill Billy Karek finally tipped the scales. It might not have held up in court—partial prints can be dicey proof—but it was enough to help close the investigation. Larry had grabbed one of the tools lying around the clinic basement from the incomplete renovation. They'd found traces of Larry's DNA at each scene. Explainable at the clinic, not so at my car. Prior to the killing, he'd never been in it or near it.

I'd talked to Lee, who said the financial scandal was going to be hushed up. He confirmed that the books that I'd found in my car were a second set of clinic ledgers. Karek had gone to substitute the fake ones that night. So, he had gone back to implicate Fitch. The board of directors didn't want to bring any further scandal to an already reeling community. The two people who had profited from it were dead. There was no one to prosecute. Lee told me the preliminary report said they'd skimmed several million dollars off over the years. In order to minimize any scandal and stop things from becoming public, Susanna Fitch had agreed to fund the clinic with the family's money for as long as it took to replace what was stolen. The clinic would be safe for a while. Lee would also get his job back.

I asked him how he and Dustin were doing.

He said, "We're determined to work things out. I'm going to try my best." He paused. "The same with you and me. Our relationship may never be the same, but I will do what I can to stay your friend."

I said, "I may be wary for a while. We'll let time pass. My goal is that things between us be as close as they once were."

• • •

The night before the end of spring break, Scott and I were in bed talking. I was looking forward to getting back to the classroom. Teaching would break up my brooding about what could have been. Teenagers, no matter what tragedy you were in the middle of, had their needs and were seldom put off simply because the proximate adult was having problems.

The lights were out. All week Scott had been his usual tremendous comfort. I'd also eaten lots of chocolate and worked out for hours every day.

I said, "We can't let any more gay kids die by their own hand."

"You're not God and neither am I. We can't save all of them."

"I know."

He said, "After the Fitch family money runs out, we could fund the clinic."

"Yeah?"

"For a while. Until they secure some new revenue sources."

I said, "Gay kids still need help."

"I know. I'm sorry this happened to you."

I rolled into his arms. I said, "I'm glad you happened to me."